FINDING PEACE

BAYTOWN BOYS

MARYANN JORDAN

Finding Peace (Baytown Boys Series)
Copyright 2017 Maryann Jordan

All rights reserved. No part of this book may be reproduced or transmitted in any form or by any means, electronic or mechanical, including photocopying, recording, or by any information storage and retrieval system without the written permission of the author, except where permitted by law.

If you are reading this book and did not purchase it, then you are reading an illegal pirated copy. Make sure that you are only reading a copy that has been officially released by the author.

This book is a work of fiction. Names, characters, places, and incidents either are products of the author's imagination or are used fictitiously. Any resemblance to actual persons, living or dead, events, or locales is entirely coincidental.

Cover Design by: Graphics by Stacy
Cover and model Photographer: Eric McKinney
ISBN ebook: 978-1-947214-02-6
ISBN print: 978-1-947214-03-3

DEDICATION

There are times in our lives when our paths cross someone else's and we have no idea at the time how much that person will come to mean to us. For me, I have been so lucky to have met many people like that. But one, in particular, is my photographer, Eric McKinney.

Some authors use stock photographs but run the risk of similar, if not the same, covers. Many authors choose a picture for their cover, then contact the photographer to purchase the picture.

When I found the photograph for my book, Tony, I also discovered the photographer. Perhaps, it was that we both come from the hills of Tennessee. Perhaps, it was because he was so easy to work with. Maybe, it was because he took an interest in my books and helping to find just the right model for the character. Whatever the reason...a friendship began... one that I cherish. Eric has now provided almost all the cover photographs for my books and I know our collaborations will continue.

So, Eric...for everything you have become in my life...thank you!

Author's Note

I have lived in numerous states as well as overseas, but for the last twenty years have called Virginia my home. All my stories take place in this wonderful commonwealth, but I choose to use fictional city names with some geographical accuracies.

These fictionally named cities allow me to use my creativity and not feel constricted by attempting to accurately portray the areas.

It is my hope that my readers will allow me this creative license and understand my fictional world.

I also do quite a bit of research on my books and try to write on subjects with accuracy. There will always be points where creative license will be used to create scenes or plots.

Four years ago, my husband and I discovered the Eastern Shore of Virginia and fell in love with the area. The mostly rural strip of land forming the peninsula originating from Maryland, has managed to stay non-commercialized. The quiet, private area full of quaint towns captured our hearts and we rushed to buy a little place there.

It has become our retreat when we need to leave the hustle and bustle of our lives. I gather ideas, create characters, and spend time writing when not walking on the beach collecting sea glass.

1

The full moon cast a long strip of illumination dancing on the surface of the bay as the slight waves crashed against the sand. Pounding footsteps were barely heard over the heavy breathing of the man as he ran along the familiar stretch of beach. Pumping his arms as he ran on the packed sand close to the surf, he kept his eyes on the nearby waves tossing seafoam and seaweed in his path. Sweat poured off his large, muscular body, soaking his t-shirt and shorts. Not caring to wipe his brow, he let the sweat drops fall into his eyes, blinking against the sting.

Brogan MacFarlane had jarred awake in the wee hours, like so many nights, his chest tight and breathing ragged. He remembered the first time this occurred as though it were only a few hours ago instead of a few years ago. Wondering if he was having a heart attack, he had lay in his military bunk on the other side of the world, hoping he would live long enough to see his family again.

It was not a heart attack, but it would only be after he left the Marines that he would hear the term panic attack. A fuckin' panic attack. *Like I could tell anyone that I was in a panic.* Marines did not panic. So, he kept his nightmares to himself and learned to run as hard as he could to outpace the memories.

Growing up in Baytown, he had been glad to escape the tiny town…then glad to return. But nothing ever stays the same and returning to his hometown had exemplified that. He and his friends left after high school to join the various branches of the military, sure they had the answer to the world's problems, only to return later as hardened men, sure that the fucked-up world was no place to live.

His feet continued their steady beat on the sand as the moon slipped lower into the horizon, allowing the slightest hues of pink and blue to appear. He glanced toward the water, a heron taking flight from its water buffet, a small fish in its mouth. Slowing as he approached the dunes near the town, he bent over at the waist, gasping for breath.

He ran his hand over his head, the newly short hair feeling unfamiliar…or maybe more familiar if he thought back to his jarhead days. He told everyone it was easier to take care of. Snorting, he shook his head, knowing ease had nothing to do with his decision, but rather hoping *she* noticed. Standing, he looked over the bay, wishing the surf would wash away the tangle of thoughts going through his head.

Nothing really worked, when he awoke in the middle of the night, the memories slamming into him like a gunshot straight through the heart. Running, he had found, would come the closest to keeping the horror at bay. Heaving, he slowly began again, turning around so that he was heading toward his home.

Passing by the dunes near town, he missed the sharp eyes of the woman who was sitting alone at the top, near the tall seagrass, taking in the scenery.

Brogan continued to jog until his small house came into view. Actually, it was more of a tiny beach bungalow. He bought the run-down property when he returned to Baytown, only able to afford it because of its dilapidated state. The old man who previously owned it had no children and when he needed to go into a nursing home, he sold it to Brogan, preferring it to go into the hands of someone who valued the beach for its beauty and not the value of the land.

Brogan and a few friends had rebuilt it, not making it fancy, but just livable enough for his needs. Good roof to keep the rain out, new windows, and new siding to withstand the wind from the bay. The yard was sand, the only grass being tall seagrass, and he kept the picket fence that circled the property. A lean-to shed was built onto the side of the bungalow, housing his canoe, kayaks, fishing poles, and a few tools.

The inside consisted of one large, all purpose room in the front, with a sofa, chair, and TV stand on one end. The kitchen counter divided the space with a couple of barstools giving him a place to eat if he was not camped out on his sofa or out on the deck. He had never gotten around to buying a table, but figured he might one day if the need arose. And he hoped the need would arise.

The back of the dwelling held one bedroom, a king-sized bed taking up most of the space. When they rebuilt the bungalow, he enlarged the bedroom to accommodate a bed for his stature. At six feet, two inches he needed a big bed—his one luxury after sleeping on the ground or on a bunk. Other than a chest of drawers and a nightstand, the room had a small closet. Across the hall was a bathroom, also enlarged when rebuilt. A shower stall large enough to accommodate him comfortably was also a necessity.

As he approached his home, his pace slowed, seeing his grandfather sitting on his front step. Concerned, he hurried over. "You okay, Pops?"

Finn MacFarlane stared at his oldest grandchild—no longer a child—and grinned. "You run before the sun comes up, son?"

Stepping closer, he sat down next to Finn and replied, "Sometimes."

"Does it help?"

"Sometimes." Brogan did not need to look at his grandfather to know the expression on his face. Finn had the wizened appearance of a man who lived by the sea and spent a lot of time in its elements. His dark hair was now almost snowy white and the crinkles by his Irish blue eyes were from laughs, as well as time in the sun. And, right now, he knew those eyes were filled with concern.

"I remember when you boys would get up early to run before the coach could ride your ass in practice."

Chuckling, Brogan nodded, "Yeah."

"Good boys, every one of you. If you saw one of you youngsters in town, you saw the whole gang."

Brogan smiled at the memories of growing up in Baytown, his childhood playmates becoming teammates as they grew older. They had earned the nickname Baytown Boys and it stuck, even now. "We thought we needed to escape this little town, Pops."

"Everyone thinks that when they're growing up, son. I did. Your dad did. Some grow up, leave, and never return. Others leave and realize what they need in life is still back here in this little corner of the world."

"Most of us did come back," Brogan mused. He thought of his brother, Aiden, who returned to run Finn's Pub with him. Mitch Evans and Grant Wilder both returned from their time in the military to work for the Baytown Police Department. Zac Hamilton was now the Fire Chief and Callan Ward was still in the Coast Guard, but stationed at Baytown. Their numbers had grown as they had all invited fellow military friends, with no place to call home, to come live in Baytown.

"Yeah, but most 'a you all came back with scars deeper than the skin."

Brogan knew his grandfather was right, but had no response.

"So, you run in the wee hours…"

Sighing, Brogan added, "The physical release is good, Pops. I need the exercise."

"Might be true, but then it appears to me that you 'bout run yourself into the ground. You come staggering back here, looking like a man who's got the devil after him."

Nodding, Brogan said nothing. What was there to say? Pops was right. Sighing, he shoulder-bumped the older man slightly, asking, "So, did you come by here at the ass crack of dawn just to ride me about my nocturnal running?"

Finn chuckled as he placed his hand on Brogan's broad shoulder to give him leverage to push himself to a standing position. Grimacing, he cursed, "Damn knees. My body's wearing out before my mind is ready to let it go."

Standing quickly, Brogan peered at his beloved grandfather, seeing age where before he had only seen strength. "Pops, are you sure you're okay?"

"Hell, boy, it's just a little rheumatism. It's so early in the morning, my legs haven't gotten un-stiff yet."

"So…uh…why did you come by?"

Finn turned his gaze on his grandson and shook his head. "I guess you and me are more alike than I figured." He allowed his eyes to roam over the beachy yard, the seagrass sprouting up at all angles and the rickety picket fence separating the house from the dune. "You run when you can't sleep, to forget. I walk when I can't sleep, to remember."

"Remember?"

Smiling, Finn replied, "Your grandmother, son."

"I'm sorry, Pops." Brogan's heart squeezed, remembering his grandmother. Petite in size but a hellion when someone hurt her family—and her family included all the kids in the neighborhood.

"I had over fifty years with the most beautiful Irish girl I've ever laid eyes on. And when I can't sleep, I do some walking and the quiet morning allows me to remember all the good times we had."

Brogan steadied Finn as his grandfather took a step down the path. As Finn made it to the crooked gate, he turned and said, "I know you got demons, son. I know you can't find your peace. But I also know that life's passing you by. Make sure you find that special someone so you can make the memories that one day you'll cherish."

Brogan watched Finn as he meandered down the dirt road leading to his house. Sucking in a deep breath, he whispered into the sea breeze, "Already have found her, Pops. Already have." He headed inside to shower, stopping to pet the silky cat swirling about his legs. He wondered if the woman of his dreams would ever know the depths of his feelings. Or would ever reciprocate them.

Ginny Spencer had watched as Brogan ran by from her seat on the dune above. Unable to sleep, she had run to the beach from her house in the center of town and had not stopped until she collapsed on the north side of Baytown. As her feet rhythmically hit the sand, she had willed her mind to stop the images in her head and her stomach to cease churning. Finally slowing, she had climbed a dune and lay, looking up at the stars dimming as the sun chased them away.

As her breathing slowed, she heard someone's heavy footsteps coming closer and she sat up, observing Brogan churning up the sand as he hauled ass past her. He stopped further down the beach from where she sat and bent over, his breathing ragged. As it evened out, he continued his run toward his house outside of town. Snorting, she thought, *two peas in a pod*. Whatever haunted his nights had him out trying to run them off just as she did.

Now, half an hour later, she stepped into her shower, washing off the sweat and letting the water sluice away her stress. Standing underneath the hot spray, she squinted her eyes tightly, her face scrunched in a grimace. Leaning forward, she planted her palms flat on the shower wall. *Control. I am in control.* Most days she found her mantra to work, but then…other times the memories assaulted in a barrage of images that threatened to overtake her.

Breathe in. Breathe out. She knew the drill and finally the tightness in her chest eased. Shampooing her hair, she allowed her thoughts to move to the man she had watched running on the beach this morning. Brogan. Brogan MacFarlane.

As thoughts of the large, tatted man filled her mind, she slid her soapy hands over her body—*ring*.

Startled, she jerked her hands away at the sound of her phone ringing, while also jerking her eyes open. Turning, she yelped when the sting of water hit her face. By the time she shut the water off and stepped out of the shower, her phone was no longer ringing. Picking it up, she checked missed calls.

Calling back, she said, "Mildred, sorry, I was in the shower."

Baytown Police receptionist/dispatcher Mildred Score, efficient as always, said, "Good morning. Chief

Evans wanted to let you know the morning meeting would be half an hour earlier today."

Quickly looking at her watch, Ginny replied, "No problem. I'll be there in twenty minutes."

"I'll have coffee and breakfast sandwiches from the diner."

Grinning, she thanked Mildred before disconnecting. Wiping the steam from the mirror, Ginny stared at herself. Her shoulder length, dark hair was slicked back from her face. At five foot, six inches, she neither felt petite nor tall. Athletic figure, neither willowy nor lush. Average. Totally average.

Forcing her thoughts to step back from the trail they had wandered down, she quickly applied the minimum of make-up before blow-drying her hair. Pulling it up in her usual tight bun, she stepped into her bedroom. Khaki pants and a navy polo with the BPD logo over the breast pocket completed her outfit.

Sliding her socked feet into her shiny, steel-toed boots, she hooked her badge and gun belt on before grabbing her purse, just as her doorbell rang. Throwing open the door, she smiled at the handsome man standing on her front porch.

With a slight nod, she acknowledged, "Grant."

"Morning, sunshine," he joked.

Shaking her head, she chuckled. "Yeah, that nickname never really fit, did it?"

Stepping out onto the porch with her fellow officer, she locked her front door. Following him toward the police SUV, she asked, "How's Jillian?"

Grant Wilder's upcoming marriage to his high school girlfriend had the town's attention. It was not every day that one of Baytown's original golden boys married the town's prom queen. If both were not so genuinely nice, Ginny would have rolled her eyes. As it were, she was happy for them and even, if she admitted to herself, a little envious.

Grinning, Grant said, "She and the girls are busy planning the wedding. We want to keep it simple, but our parents are probably going to go overboard." Climbing into the SUV, he kept his eyes forward while saying, "I know Jillian would love to have you join the others in their planning sessions."

He peeked her way and, trying to ignore his stare, Ginny shook her head slightly. "Not really my scene, Grant."

"The planning sessions are really just a chance for the girls to get together and have some fun at one of their houses. Usually copious amounts of wine is involved and us guys go pick them up afterwards."

Keeping her eyes forward as he pulled onto the street heading toward the station, she replied, "I like them well enough, Grant. But hanging with a bunch of women, drinking wine, and talking about weddings is just not my idea of a fun night." *What the hell would I find to talk about?*

Nodding his acknowledgment, Grant dropped the subject and they continued to drive in silence the few blocks to the station. For a moment, Ginny closed her eyes trying to imagine sitting around with girlfriends, drinking wine, but, inwardly groaning, she realized her life was so different from the Baytown girls…maybe too different. *I'm fine. I like my life just the way it is.* Accepting that thought might be wishful thinking, she sighed.

2

Within a minute, Grant pulled into the parking lot of the Baytown Police Station. The police department consisted of Chief Mitch Evans, another original Baytown Boy, who had left for the military, came home to begin a career with the FBI, and then returned to the sleepy little town when his father, the former police chief, had a heart attack. The town welcomed the returning hometown hero with open arms and he managed to step gracefully into the much different role than what he played when with the FBI.

Four officers, plus Mildred, made up the rest of the department, although the new budget allowed for the soon hiring of another receptionist, affording Mildred more time for reporting as well as dispatch.

Moving into the cool interior, her boots clicking on the shiny floor, Ginny and Grant greeted Mildred as they headed into the workroom. The older woman's curly, grey hair with a slight purple hue bobbed at them as they walked by. Mitch was already there, tall and slender, his head bent over the files open on the table, but he looked up and nodded as they walked into the room. Sam Stubbis, the oldest member of the force, was also already seated, his eye on the pastries on the counter, but she noted he had not snatched one yet.

Burt Tobber, a young officer, married with two children came rushing in. "Sorry, trouble getting the kids ready today."

He received smiles as the five settled around the table and Mitch began to speak. "You'll be glad to know that we've got a new receptionist starting next month. She'll be shadowing Mildred and then will start taking over reception. Mildred will move back here with us, working in records."

"Who'd you hire?" Ginny asked.

Just then Mildred walked into the room, her smile wide with her arm around a woman so similar in looks to Mildred they had to be sisters. The new woman was slightly shorter, rounder, and her grey locks had a light bluish tint.

"Everyone, meet my sister, Mable. She's moved here with her husband."

"Welcomes" and "nice to have you" rang out and she smiled in return. "Well, just so you don't think I got this job because of my sister," Mable said, "I've been a 9-1-1 operator for almost fifteen years and recently was a dispatcher for the Virginia Beach Police Department."

Whistles of approval met her announcement and Mildred preened. "She'll officially start in a week, but has volunteered to start shadowing me occasionally."

As the two women walked out, Mitch continued his meeting agenda. "Ginny, I need you and Burt to drive over to Helen Collins' house as soon as we're finished. Mildred took a call from her saying that she was sure she saw a man peeping in her neighbor's window last evening—"

"And she just called it in this morning?"

Nodding, Mitch continued, "She said her neighbor's house is a rental and no one is occupying it this week."

"And she knows this how?"

"Seems she's the one who holds the spare key and is the point of contact for the renters. Said since no one was home, it didn't seem like a big deal."

Rubbing her hand over her face, Ginny nodded. "Got it. We'll talk to her and check out the neighbor's rental."

"I've got the next month's rotation assignments ready. Renters will be coming in droves and we need to stay diligent in our beach patrols. With one of the few public beaches on the Eastern Shore, it's gonna get crowded and harder to keep the glass, dogs, and trash off the beach."

Looking down at his list, Mitch added, "Finn's Pub just applied for a block-party license for the latter part of this month. They'd like to have a band play outside and to block off part of Fig Street. The plan is to have food trucks and they'll have the alcohol to sell. Proceeds are to be divided between the American Legion and the Fire Station."

Eyebrows raised at the mention of Brogan's family's pub and restaurant, and Ginny tilted her head as she frowned. "And the mayor agreed to this?" Knowing Corwin Banks' proclivity for law and order, she wondered how he felt about a block party hosted by the pub.

Mitch chuckled. "Well, in this instance, it appears the town manager thinks it's a good idea for bringing in visitors and money." Shrugging, he added, "Of course, Silas also thinks that if law and order isn't maintained, he'll come gunning for my badge."

Rolling her eyes, Ginny pursed her lips at the thought of the weasly town manager and the buffoonish mayor. Mitch ended the meeting, and she nodded at Burt as they headed out to start the day.

Ginny perched on the edge of the narrow sofa in Helen Collins' living room, the space mostly filled with cats. One curled up on the pillow next to her as another weaved figure-eights between her legs. Glancing over at Burt, she almost laughed as another cat circled his lap, its claws perilously close to his crotch, before sitting down. Burt's eyebrows were raised, hands held out to the side, unable to figure out what to do. A few more cats wandered in and out of the room as Helen settled into the chair nearest the fireplace. The older woman's grey hair was cut short and her print housedress flowed about her ankles as she sat.

Helen pushed her glasses up on her nose and said, "I try to keep an eye out on the Finley's place next door. Now, I ain't the person they call if there's a problem, you see. They got a rental company for that. But I do keep a spare key in case someone gets locked out or in case a repairman needs to be let in. If renters gotta come to me, the Finley's pay me ten dollars." Laughing, she said, "I know that's a lot of money to walk across the driveway and let someone in the house, but I figure if the Finley's want to pay, then I can use the money for cat food."

Eyeing the number of cats in the room, Ginny could well imagine every little bit of money for food would help. Nodding, she said, "I understand. Now, can you tell us about last night?"

Warming to her story, Helen leaned forward and explained, "I always like to watch a little TV at night before going to bed. I was already in bed, you see, with my lights off, but had the TV going."

"What time was this?" Burt asked, his notepad out but held to the side, away from the sleeping cat, as he scribbled down the information.

Wrinkling her nose in thought, she replied, "Well, now let's see. I was watching that nice show with the handsome man. He's kind of political, but he's awfully funny, so I like to watch him anyway."

"Uh…do you know what time that show was on?" Ginny asked, inwardly groaning at Helen's vague description.

"It comes on right after that cop show that I like so much."

"Was it on regular TV or a special channel?" Burt queried.

"Oh, I don't have any of those fancy channels. They want so much money just to be able to watch people take their clothes off. I don't hold with any of that," the older woman exclaimed. "Now, a good murder mystery is just fine with me, but I expect them people to keep their clothes on."

Ginny shot Burt a look as they attempted to pin Helen down more. Ginny pulled up her phone and quickly looked up the television shows that had been on the night before. At ten o'clock there were two mysteries, an early news show, a comedy, and a few movies. "Could it have been one of these?" she asked, holding her phone toward Helen.

Peering over her glasses at the screen, Helen exclaimed, "Oh, yes, it was that one. Mackintosh is the main character's name and he is so handsome. And he has a cat...well, I suppose I should say his character has a cat. A big, yellow cat with huge eyes. So pretty."

Nodding, Ginny tried to get her back on track, prompting, "This particular show goes off at eleven, then you were probably watching Nighttime with Newman?"

Clapping her hands together, startling the cat on her lap, Helen said with glee, "Oh, you are so smart. Yes, that's it. Now, let's see, the show was about half over when I shut it down, so that'd be about eleven thirty."

Burt's pen hovered over his pad and Ginny tried to hide her grin as the cat in his lap, now awake, tried to bat at it. Sucking in a deep breath, she said, "Well, please just tell us what you saw."

Helen leaned forward and said, "You can thank Percy that I have anything to tell at all."

Eyes wide, Ginny's brows dipped down in confusion. "Uh...Percy?"

Just then a large tabby strolled into the room. "Well, here's the man of the hour," Helen said. "He always sleeps with me, but last night he jumped up off my bed and onto the window seat, staring outside. I called to him, but he kept staring as though he was watching a bird or a bunny-rabbit. Which would make sense if it was during the day, but at night, I had no idea what he was looking at. Of course, cats have excellent night vision, but nonetheless I was determined that whatever he saw was unusual."

Ginny watched as Burt's lips twitched, finally snagging a moment of the cat's distraction to write on his pad. "Go on," she encouraged, wondering if they were going to be finished with the interview before lunchtime.

"I couldn't image what on earth he was staring at but, I trusted that he was definitely seeing something. I got out of bed and walked over to the window and peeked through the blinds. At first, I couldn't see anything," Helen stated, her face reflecting her frustration from the previous evening. "But I kept staring and finally saw movement."

She plopped her hands in her lap and smiled, appearing to have completed her tale. Ginny prodded, "And what did you see?"

"Oh, yes, well that would be helpful, wouldn't it?"

"Yes, ma'am," Ginny added, covering up the exasperated sigh from Burt. The cat in his lap, tired of batting at Burt's now inactive pen, began gnawing on the end of it as her partner feebly attempted to move the playful animal away.

"It was a man peeking in the lower window of the Finley's house. Now, you see, that particular room is where the second bedroom is. The master bedroom is on the other side of the house along with a hall bathroom."

"And can you describe him?"

Blinking, Helen said, "Well, it was dark, although there was a full moon last night."

"Yes, ma'am, but you must have seen something or why would you think it was a man?"

Eyes wide, Helen exclaimed, "Oh, aren't you clever! I never thought of that. Well..." tapping her chin, she added, "His hair was covered in a dark cap. Like a ball cap, but dark in color. Um...he was wearing pants—"

Burt snorted, then quickly recovered, shooting Ginny an apologetic look. "Please, go on."

"His clothes were also all dark, so I can't give you much detail. Let's see, I couldn't see his arms so he must have been wearing long sleeves."

"This is good," Ginny encouraged. "What else? Could you tell his race, height, body type?"

"I don't know how tall that window is from the ground, but I can tell you that when he peeked in, his head came to the first pane."

"Did he keep looking in that window or move to others? Could you see if he tried to get in or open the window?"

Sucking in her lips, Helen shook her head slowly. "No, no. I didn't see him try to get into the window. He just put his hands up like this," she lifted her hands to her face, cupping them around her eyes, "and pressed his face up to the window."

"How long was he there?"

"I was just pondering what to do when he left, jogging around the corner of the house. So, considering that Percy had been watching for about a minute and then I watched about a minute, I'd say he was there less than five minutes."

Burt's pen scratched across his pad as Ginny managed to pull out the last drop of information from Helen. No, she had never seen this before. No, she did not think to call the police at night. No, she was not worried. She simply thought she should report the incident as a *good citizen of Baytown.*

Thanking her, the two officers walked out of the house and toward the Finley's property. Ginny held up her hand toward Burt, cutting him off before he could begin, "Don't start. Just don't start."

"Hey," Burt said in defense, "the cat you had stayed at your side. I ended up with the one who wanted to attach himself to my crotch and then wouldn't let me write. And Mrs. Collins? I'm not sure her eyesight is as good as her story-telling."

"You don't believe her?" Ginny asked.

Shaking his head, Burt replied, "I don't know. She's never called anything in before so I wouldn't say she was attention seeking. But…maybe lonely."

Nodding, Ginny had to agree as they carefully watched where they stepped, looking for evidence. Within a moment, she called, "Burt? Look."

Moving next to her, he stared at the ground, noticing the flattened grass next to the window indicated. Examining the area, they found no evidence of forced entry at the window and Ginny measured the ground to first pane to be at approximately five and a half feet. "If he was looking into the first pane, he would be about five feet, eleven inches tall."

"Yes, but he could have had boots on. He might have stooped and she didn't notice. Or hell, he could have stood on his toes."

Nodding, Ginny bent to peer closely at the grass underneath the window. "No dirt for a print...just flattened grass."

Standing again, she looked up at the window, but was too short to look in. Looking to Burt, she asked, "What can you see? And while you're looking, I'll go get the fingerprint kit. Maybe we'll get lucky with a print on the window frame or glass."

A moment later she returned and handed him the kit. As he dusted for prints, he said, "There's a small bedroom inside. The bed is clearly visible from the window, but it was made up with a bedspread that looks as though it was not disturbed."

"That goes along with Helen's claim that the house is empty this week."

Finishing their examination, the two packed up and, after examining the rest of the outside of the house, they made their way back to the SUV.

"Drive by the beach on our way back," Ginny suggested. "Might as well get a beach patrol in this morning."

Only ten o'clock and Ginny felt the pull of fatigue on her body. *I need more sleep...or maybe less restless nights!*

3

"Aiden! Where the hell are you?"

Brogan's deep voice called out from behind the bar at Finn's, serving beers to the lunch crowd.

"What the hell are you yelling for?" Aiden asked, as he made his way from the back. "I told you there was a delivery today." Unlike Brogan, Aiden still sported the long hair from their post-Marine days, pulling it back in a sloppy ponytail as he walked. Leaning his forearms on the bar, he grinned at his brother. Of the two, only one year apart and so similar in looks they were often mistaken for twins, Aiden had definitely inherited the fun-loving gene from Pops.

Shaking his head, Brogan grumbled, "Why the fuck can't the beer truck get here in the morning and not right at the time we're getting slammed."

"With the Seafood Shack now open for the season, just be glad we're full."

"You don't gotta tell me about the other restaurants in town," he growled, slapping his towel down on the bar, aiming at Aiden's hands, barely missing them as Aiden jerked them back, holding them over his head.

"Missed!" Aiden's laugh rang out.

"Well, I see things are all normal around here," a feminine voice interrupted. "God, how old are you? Five?"

The two brothers looked up, smiles on their faces as their sister walked in. Brogan cherished finally seeing the spark in his sister's eyes after so many years of sadness. Having lost her fiancé to the war, she finally gave in to love with one of the newest members of the American Legion and businessmen in town, Gareth Harrison. She also found her perfect career with him, the two now working together in his private investigations firm.

"You here for lunch?" Brogan asked, nodding toward one of the servers to come over. "You and Gareth want your usual?"

"Not for him, he's out on a case, so I thought I'd come have lunch here and, when you have a free minute, we can talk about the block party." Looking around, she added, "But it looks like y'all are slammed."

Finn MacFarlane had left his pub to his son and it was now owned and managed by his three grandchildren. Katelyn continued to do their books and purchase orders, but left the day to day running to Brogan and Aiden. The pub retained the original look and appeal of days gone by. Never changing, the entrance held a dartboard to the right and an old fireplace and sofa on the left. The original building had been one of the early brick structures in the town. While renovated, it retained much of the original brickwork walls and floor. The bar ran the length of the right side with tall, mismatched, padded bar chairs up against the counter. The left contained tables already full of patrons and the kitchens were in the back.

The harbor now had a casual seafood restaurant that closed during the winter months, making the pub's crowds swell. But with the other restaurant open, they had been concerned about tourists deciding to walk to the harbor instead of partaking of the pub. Grateful that was not the case, Brogan nodded toward his sister and said, "We'll find a minute."

He watched as Katelyn settled onto a bar stool, smiling as she accepted the plate of fish and chips from the server. As she readily dove into the food, his normal, surly expression softened at the knowledge his sister had finally found happiness.

Looking up, he saw Mildred Score walk in and his eyes darted behind her to see if there were any other members of the police department behind her. His face met hers with a scowl when he saw she was alone, then blushed as she greeted him.

"Nice to see you too, Brogan. If I didn't know better I would think you were hoping to see someone else."

"Sorry, Mrs. Score. Just trying to keep an eye on the crowd," he lied.

"Uh huh. Well, I'm here to grab some to-go sandwich platters for the officers. They're in a meeting with the mayor and by the time the ol' windbag leaves, they'll have missed their lunch."

Unable to hide his slight grin at her accurate description of the town's mayor, he simply nodded as he turned away. "I'll get those lunches for you, Mrs. Score."

"How's Coach?" Aiden asked.

She grinned at him, and said, "He's loving his retirement and goes fishing every chance he gets. Give him a heads up on one of your days off and he'd love to take some of his old players fishing."

Aiden flashed a huge smile as he nodded. "Brogan and I'd love to go out with him. I'll give him a ring."

Back in the kitchen with her handwritten order, Brogan perused the one for Ginny. Half of a Finn's club, easy on the mayo. As the chef handed him the bags, he waited before turning back to the serving counter. Filling a container with homemade chips with the pub's special dipping sauce, he added it, along with a slice of cake, to the bag labeled **Ginny**. Turning, he saw a smirk on the line cook's face, so he mumbled, "She's too skinny. Needs to eat if she's gonna keep these streets safe."

Bursting out with laughter, the cook said, "Whatever you say, boss."

Brogan walked back to Mildred, grumbling under his breath. "Here you go, Mrs. Score."

With a nod, she left and he stood for a moment, wishing the lovely Officer Spencer had come in for lunch herself.

Shifting his eyes over the lunch crowd, seeing it had thinned, he nodded to Katelyn to follow. Whistling to Aiden, he jerked his head toward the back and headed to the office. Entering, he was glad Katelyn kept the office neat. The small space only held one desk, but they managed to fit two other chairs inside, as well as filing cabinets against one wall. The room had a tall, narrow window overlooking the alley behind. Not visually pleasing, it nonetheless allowed in light, and anyone inside to keep an eye on deliveries. The tiny window was not large enough for anyone to pass through, so it added a level a security for their important paperwork

Settling behind the desk, he pulled up the paperwork on the block party, signed by the town manager. Once Katelyn and Aiden were seated, they began to plan. Agreeing to food trucks who had applied to participate and looking over the contracts for the alcohol that they could serve from eight p.m. to midnight, they were pleased with their accomplishments.

Aiden reported on two local bands and another one from Virginia Beach that had agreed to come play. "The two smaller bands will play at eight and nine, and then I've got the Hummers coming at ten."

"Oh, Pops will love that," Katelyn grinned, knowing her grandfather's penchant for any band playing Irish music.

Nodding, Aiden said, "That's what I thought."

Katelyn twirled a long strand of hair, cutting her eyes over to Brogan. "So...uh...are you bringing anyone special to the block party?"

Glaring, he said, "Figure I'll be working. Kinda hard to have a date when you're pulling beers all night."

Katelyn's shoulder's slumped at her brother's reply.

Aiden, his eyes moving between the two of them, said, "Ain't no reason we can't hire some extra help that night—"

"No need," Brogan interrupted. Not wanting to

share his thoughts, he nonetheless figured Ginny would be working as a cop that evening, and she sure as hell was the only person he wanted to spend time with. Moving the conversation along, he glared at the two expectantly, "Y'all gonna be working that night?"

Scowling, Katelyn retorted, "I'm not an idiot, Brogan. Of course. And Gareth will probably work for us as well, just to give us an extra pair of hands."

"Sorry," mumbled Brogan, missing the eye-rolling between his siblings.

The trio spent the next hour planning the menu and alcohol orders for the party, before Katelyn's phone rang. Checking her texts, her smile turned dreamy as she stood.

"Guess that's lover-boy," Aiden teased.

Ignoring him, Katelyn looked at Brogan, "We good here?"

Nodding, he confirmed, "Yeah, we're good."

As soon as Mildred stepped into the reception area with the lunch bags, Ginny hustled by, grabbing hers and tossing out her thanks. "Sorry, I'm heading to do town patrol. Sam got stung by a bee at the beach and he's allergic. Didn't have his EpiPen with him, so Grant took him to the doctor's office." Seeing Mildred's concerned face, she quickly added, "He's fine. Just pissed at himself and knows his wife'll give him hell for forgetting his meds."

Mildred was still clucking in concern as Ginny jogged through the door. Once in the patrol SUV, she began the drive though the small town, the streets familiar to her. Having never heard of Baytown, she had answered the call when she saw an advertisement placed on the state's website for openings in police departments. Shunning the large cities, she had searched for something small. A place where no one knew her...no one had expectations. A place where she could start over. And Baytown had delivered. When she interviewed with Mitch's dad, then Police Chief, he sold her on the town's residents watching out for each other. Not to mention, the first time she had stared at the sunset over the Chesapeake Bay, she felt the pull.

The oldest part of Baytown was built on a square grid, with Main Street on one side, closer to the small harbor. Another side faced the bay where the public beach enticed townspeople and visitors, and a park sat in the middle of town. About fifteen years prior, a developer built a golf course community on a large farm and it was annexed into the city as well. On the north side, another developer built large vacation rental homes as well as a marina and a seafood restaurant.

Formerly plantations, the land was purchased in the late 1800s by a man intent on running the Pennsylvania Railroad down to the end of the Eastern Shore of Virginia where a harbor would allow goods and passengers to travel by water to Virginia Beach or Norfolk. By 1885, Baytown was already bustling with commercial and residential buildings. As Ginny drove past the main business section, she knew most of the buildings were the original structures from the late 1800's.

Ginny had studied her new hometown and knew this epicenter of North Heron County took a nose dive during World War II, when trucks and highways took over much of the carrying of goods after the Bay Bridge and Tunnels were built. Now, Baytown resembled more of a sleepy village until the warm weather vacationers came through. But for her…it was perfect.

Driving along the roads, she carefully observed the children riding bicycles and families walking toward the beach. Making a pass along one of the side streets she saw Katelyn standing outside the private investigation business she worked for. Katelyn waved and Ginny parked in front. Swinging out of the SUV, she smiled at the pretty brunette with the same blue eyes as her brothers.

"Are you locked out?" Ginny asked, wondering why Katelyn was standing outside.

Laughing, Katelyn said, "No, I'm waiting for the glass cleaners to come. I need to let them in and then I can go—oh, here they are."

Ginny turned and watched an older man pull into the parking space next to hers, viewing **Hudgins Glass and Window Cleaning Service** on the side of his truck.

"Saul, I'm so glad you're here. Gareth called and needs me to meet him," Katelyn said, shaking his hand.

Ginny smiled as Saul Hudgins shook Katelyn's hand before turning to her. "Officer Spencer," he greeted, his wizened face grinning at her.

"Nice to see you, Saul." Turning to look at the large plate glass window in the front of Harrison Investigations, she said, "I hear Katelyn's putting you to work."

He laughed and said, "I been doing these windows for so long, it's fun to see new businesses going into the old buildings."

A younger man came from the back of the truck, his hands full of equipment. "Where do you want me to start, Saul?"

Saul smiled at the young man and said, "Got me some new help and he's a hard worker." Looking at Katelyn, he said, "You head on out, missy, and we'll get started on your windows."

Nodding toward Saul and waving at Katelyn, Ginny climbed back in her SUV to continue her patrol. Focusing on the streets in front of her, the scent of lunch wafted through the cab of the SUV and she finally gave in to temptation. Parking along the road leading to the marina, she opened the bag and peeked in. It seemed fuller than just her half-sandwich and she found a full turkey club along with chips and dip and, at the bottom, a large piece of carrot-cake, carefully wrapped.

Scrunching her brow, she held the bag up, clearly seeing her name written on the side. Mildred never made mistakes, but she wondered how she ended up with so much food. Pulling out the napkins, she noticed writing on one.

You need to eat. B.

Sucking in her lips, she tried to still the smile that threatened to appear. Brogan. Shaking her head, she dove in, not stopping until she was stuffed. Unable to finish, she carefully placed the leftovers in the container, knowing she now had a ready-made dinner for the evening.

Brogan had caught her attention the first time she visited Finn's Pub, but the stoic bartender always seemed to avoid looking her. She had wondered if he had an aversion to her being a police officer. But over the past year she began to realize that he seemed to notice her as well. He never made a move. Never asked her out. But at the last beach bonfire, he finally sat next to her. No talking. Just sat. But she liked him sitting next to her. His large, solid presence gave her a sense of peace.

The bonfire had been roaring, already casting shadows and light over the faces of those sitting around its warmth. Ginny had observed the changing group. Katelyn, with Gareth's arms around her, Grant leaning against a large log, Jillian tucked in close to his side. Callan, Jason, and some guys from the Coast Guard had played volleyball on the beach. Jade and Belle had shared a blanket on the sand. Ginny had sat in a beach chair, her legs stretched out in front of her.

Mitch and Tori had walked from the deck with trays of snacks in their hands, as Aiden and Brogan followed them with a beer-filled cooler.

Brogan had walked by and offered a beer to Ginny, startling her, but taking it, she had nodded her thanks. Her gaze had continued to follow him as he made his way around the gathering, but when he looked over his shoulder, she jerked her head toward the sunset. He had eventually come back over, sitting on the sand next to her. The move had surprised her, and she had tried to be nonchalant, but it had been hard. Just having him so close muddled her head.

But that was okay…she liked the quiet man of strength. Turned off by flirts, loud men full of themselves, or men whose expectations exceeded hers, she liked sitting next to him. Now, as she leaned back in the seat of the police SUV, her stomach full, she dropped the napkins into the bag and began to crumple it up. Halting, she dug out the napkin with the note and placed it on her lap before wadding up the refuse. Looking down, she smoothed out the napkin, the simple words filling her with warmth.

4

The dew hung heavy on the grass at the ball field for the early morning game. The old field had been in a state of decline for years, until the American Legion had cleared the tall grass and re-established the game field. The metal stands were filled with parents and townspeople, all enjoying a Saturday morning watching the children play. Ginny yelled for the girl rounding third base as Katelyn screamed for the batter to make it to second. A run was scored and Ginny grinned as the crowd cheered from the stands.

The American Legion had spent the past six months coaching the youth in the area and the fruits of their labor were shining through. The teams were made up of anyone who wanted to play at no cost to the parents. Offering the disadvantaged children in the area a chance to play a sport without fear of not being able to afford the uniforms or even snacks, had now gained the support of the whole community and game days were a town event.

The girls finished their game and jogged off the field as the boys ran out to warm up, wanting to get their game over with before the heat of the day made it miserable for participants as well as observers. Passing near third base, Ginny saw Brogan stalking toward her. Eyes wide, she said, "I heard you got your hair cut…it looks really good."

Rubbing his hand over his head, he felt the heat of blush rising to his cheeks. "Thanks." Always tongue-tied around her, he commented, "Good game. Good coaching."

"Thanks," she said, smiling in return. It was hard to keep her eyes on his, when all she wanted to do was drink him in. Tall. Muscular. A tight, green, American Legion t-shirt with *AL Baseball* imprinted across the chest dragged her eyes downward. Brogan was big. No one would call him overweight, but there were muscles on top of muscles over his entire body. His jeans fit perfectly and she knew he probably just jumped into his clothes without any preamble. Looking good came naturally to him. Blinking, she jerked her eyes back to his face and now the blush was spreading over her cheeks from being caught drooling over him.

"Well, uh…" she stammered, "I'll…uh…I'll see you later." She turned to walk toward the stands, but he called out her name. Turning back, she watched as he ran his hand over his head once more.

"Are you going to go to Finn's afterwards? After the kids go home?"

"I hadn't planned on it, but uh…"

"Oh, okay," he said, disappointment on his face. "I'll see you around." Walking away, he sighed heavily, wishing he had the courage to ask her out. *She's a pretty cop with a college degree and I'm a bartender from a little hick town. Why the hell would she want to have anything to do with a fucked-up me?* With a glance backward, he watched a young man approached her as she was leaving he field. Narrow eyed, he turned fully around, his hands on his hips, staring.

"Ginny," James Smithson called out.

Recognizing one of the teachers from the high school, she stopped and waited as he jogged over. "James," she said in greeting.

"Hey, your girls were good out there today."

Smiling her appreciation, she said, "Thanks, but they're not *my* girls. We have several coaches."

"Yeah, but you're the prettiest," he said, his confident smile wide and eager eyes focused on her.

Blinking, she was not sure how to respond. *Is he flirting with me?* He was tall, handsome in a surfer way, and she had no doubt the teenage girls loved having him for a gym teacher, but as her gaze jumped over his shoulder, she was caught by the dark, mountainous stature of Brogan, whose blazing eyes were aimed right at her.

Jerking as James spoke again, she said, "Sorry?"

"I asked if you'd like to have some lunch after the boys finish playing their game. I know a great place."

Offering a small smile, she shook her head, saying, "Thank you, but I've got plans. Uh…maybe some other time."

He grinned as he reached out and touched her shoulder. "Absolutely. You can count on it."

Watching him walk away, her gaze followed James as

she mentally kicked herself. *Maybe some other time? God, why couldn't I have just said 'no'? Ugh!* Sucking in a deep breath, she looked around, seeing Brogan still staring at her, his face unreadable, before he turned and headed over to the game.

Standing rooted to the ground, she watched him walk away, her heart pounding with the desire to spend more time with Brogan and the desire to protect her heart at the same time. Scrubbing her hand over her face, she silently screamed in frustration. Dropping her chin to her chest, she startled when Katelyn came up beside her.

"Hey, the girls did good today," Katelyn enthused.

Grinning in return, Ginny agreed.

"So, um…are you going to stay for the boys' game?" Katelyn asked, her smile wide.

"Yeah—"

"Good," Katelyn beamed, linking her arm with Ginny's as she began to walk toward the bleachers.

"Uh, I usually just sit on the side to watch—"

"Oh, there's no need to be down there. You can see so much better from the stands."

Glancing sideways, Ginny eyed the pretty, dark-haired sister of Brogan and Aiden. Even after a hot morning of coaching, Katelyn's lush beauty shined through. Wondering what her motive was, Ginny quickly understood as soon as she saw the stadium seats she was being led to. Mitch's wife, Tori, as well as Grant's fiancé, Jillian, were sitting there smiling at the approaching women. *Great…a welcoming committee of the town's original Baytown Girls.* Tori, with her red hair, always appeared put-together, her clothes and makeup just right. Jillian's long blonde hair, tied back, showcased her heart-shaped face. Right behind them sat several more of the women that seemed to always be together. She recognized Jade, a pretty schoolteacher, and Belle, a nurse at the local nursing home, both in cute sundresses. The women all appeared natural beauties and Ginny felt hot and sweaty next to them.

Plastering a smile on her face, she allowed Katelyn to lead her directly into the middle of the women as they all scooted to make room. Sitting on the already warm bleacher seats, she accepted the winning game congratulations from the townspeople and parents sitting nearby.

Looking at Katelyn, she had to acknowledge that the girls they coached had really improved and all seemed to enjoy playing. It was satisfying to see the self-conscious ones build more confidence as they were each able to play to their skill level, all team members contributing.

Jillian smiled at Ginny and handed her a water bottle from a small cooler. "Here, I thought you could use this. I can't believe how hot it is already."

Drinking gratefully, she took several long gulps, the cool liquid quenching her thirst. Before she had a chance to cheer for the boys' team, Katelyn leaned over and asked, "So, what do you think of Baytown? I know we coach together and hang out at some of the same events, but we've never really had a chance to talk."

Choking on her last swallow, Ginny sputtered, "Baytown? Um…it's a nice little town…I suppose. Uh…"

Tori, pushing her hair from her face before twisting it up in a ponytail, nodded. "I agree. I used to spend my summers here with my grandmother. I grew up in Virginia Beach but prefer this little coastal town instead of the big city."

"Grant was a police officer in Virginia Beach before coming back home," Jillian commented. "He liked it there, but said that Baytown would always be home to him."

Ginny, aware that the other women's eyes were on her, felt she needed to enter the small-talk conversation, but never knew what to say, so she just nodded.

"Where did you come from?" Katelyn prodded.

"All over, really. My family moved a lot."

"Oh, that must have been interesting," Belle gushed, sighing slightly. "I've only ever lived in Baytown, so seeing different places must have been fun."

Ginny tried to keep her expression neutral, relying on her cop-face. Moving around from one military base to another throughout her entire childhood was hardly what she would have called fun. "It was fine. It was all I was accustomed to," she offered, attempting a smile that she knew barely hid her true feelings.

"Being in the military yourself must have been interesting as well," Jade added, her green eyes shaded from the bright sun by her hand on her forehead.

"Here," Katelyn said, handing an extra ball cap to Jade. "You've got to be prepared out here."

Ginny noticed the small things these women did for each other—offering water, sunshade, and even friendship—things she was not used to. Blinking, she suddenly found her eyes stinging at the loneliness that sometimes attempted to drown her. *How can I feel so lonely in the middle of a crowd?*

"You're different from other women—"

"Katelyn!" Jillian exclaimed, in an obvious attempt to hush her friend.

Katelyn rolled her eyes. "Oh, Ginny, I didn't mean that badly. I know you're one of a few women in the American Legion, so you get to know the guys, who went to war like you did. I just meant that it gives you a perspective that we don't have."

Glancing at the other women, Ginny saw sincerity in their eyes. "I know I'm different…I was in the Army, but not with a lot of other women. I now work with mostly men, unless you count Mildred—" at that the others snickered, imagining the indomitable Mildred Score as just one of the girls. "And being part of the American Legion and also the Legionnaires gives me a kind of double uniqueness. I belong to the former military and to the family of military." Shrugging, she added, "And as a police officer, I don't seem to cozy up to people very easily."

"I think you're wonderful," a soft voice from behind spoke.

Turning, Ginny peered at Jade and smiled. "You only say that because I come to the elementary school and talk to your kids."

"True, but," Jade agreed, waving her hand toward the ball field, "look at what you do for these girls. I saw James talking to you. You're gonna have most of the teen girls jealous 'cause they all think he's so cute."

Rolling her eyes, Ginny said, "I assure you I have no interest in James. And I hope he's careful in his dealings with the teenagers. Rumors that get started are ugly things."

Nodding, Jade agreed. "I can image, but I haven't heard any rumors. He's never alone with any of them and he's very polite to the staff." Winking, she added, "I think he'd make a great boyfriend."

"Uh...not interested," Ginny stammered.

"Not interested in James or in a boyfriend?" Katelyn asked, her voice more pointed than before.

"Um...well...uh, I guess him, I suppose," Ginny answered, hating the feeling that she was under a microscope and every word was being analyzed. It did not escape her notice that Katelyn smiled widely, seeming to relax her shoulders, as though Ginny has passed a test.

Jillian grinned, saying, "I've got a wedding planning meeting coming up soon and you're welcome to join us."

Ginny ducked her head, a small smile on her face. "Uh...I've been told about these meetings. You all drink and dance in one of your houses and then someone has to come pick you up—"

"That snake!" Jillian complained. "Grant's been telling tales!"

The conversation halted as the cheers from the crowd drowned out the others and Ginny was glad for the reprieve. It felt nice to be in the stands cheering alongside the other townswomen, but the scrutiny was exhausting. As the others' conversations flowed from one topic to another, her gaze landed on Brogan, standing nearby, coaching third base for the boys. Suddenly he turned and his eyes seemed to search her out.

Time stood still as a silent thread of need tightened

between them. Neither looked away, tied to each other, bound together until a boy running toward third interrupted their moment. Blinking rapidly, Ginny wondered if she imagined the connection.

Turning, she saw Katelyn staring at her, a slight smile on her face. "Ginny, we're all going to Finn's after the game. I think you definitely need to join us."

Denial hung on Ginny's lips, but at the last second, she swallowed it back. "Thank you," she agreed, "I think I will."

The crowd was already loud by the time she got there. Ginny had driven several of the girls and boys home after the games were complete, taking a minute to talk to their parents. She stopped by the trailer park on the north side of town last, taking one of her favorite children to her home.

The young girl had not started playing ball until recently but seemed to greatly enjoy the activity. Driving through the trailer park, Ginny's observant eyes continually scoped out the area and she was pleased to see how the new owner had cleaned up the place. Each trailer appeared neat and tidy, with trash cans set to the side and flowers planted in most yards.

As they wound their way toward the back, the trailers began to appear more unkempt and ragged with weed-infested, unmown yards.

Brittany's shoulder's slumped as they neared a trailer in the back. "I know it don't look good. Mama's been kinda sick lately and hasn't kept things up."

Ginny smiled and said, "I'll check into getting some help here. I know the park owner is working slowly on making things better. I'm sure he's getting to this section."

Brittany shrugged and said, "I don't know. He don't come around here much."

Determined to check into the situation, Ginny just smiled at the young girl as she pulled up to the overflowing trash cans outside the trailer. "I'll just pop in and say 'hi' to your mom."

"Oh, no. You best not," Brittany said, her voice rushed and strident. "Mama don't like company, especially when she don't feel good."

"That might be, but I—"

"No, please, Miss Ginny," Brittany implored, placing her hand on Ginny's arm, stilling her in her seat. "When Mama's not happy, she can get real...uh...extra not happy."

Ginny listened as Brittany stammered and knew what the girl was telling her. *If I attempt to go in, her mother is going to make things harder for Brittany.* Plastering on a smile, she said, "Sure, honey. You go on in and I'll see you at the next practice."

Now, twenty minutes later, she walked into Finns' Pub and made her way to the bar, her gaze searching for Brogan. Irish music blared from the speakers and as she pushed her way forward, she noted there were no empty barstools. In the back, she saw a group of her co-workers and fellow American Legion members.

Mitch stood with Tori tucked underneath his arm, smiling at the group in the booths. The other men known as the Baytown Boys, plus the new additions, filled the space as well. Aiden, with his easy laugh, served drinks, but Brogan was nowhere to be seen. Grant, in the corner of the booth, had Jillian leaning against his arm and Ginny recognized the smitten expression on his face. She remembered, when she first came to work at Baytown, Grant had managed to juggle quite a few women at one time, but his eye had always been on his former girlfriend. Mentally shaking her head, Ginny wondered how some men could be so stupid at times, but at least Grant got his head out of his ass and snagged the love of his life in the end.

Zac, the local Fire Chief, and Callan, still active duty with the Coast Guard station at the town's harbor, sat at the other end of the bar, surrounded with some of the older men from the American Legion as well as a few of the CG, sharing war stories. Jason, a newcomer to town who ran the only garage and was also starting a tattoo business, was standing at the bar with a few of the locals eager to see his shop open. Jade and Belle sat to the side, laughing and talking with a few others around.

Ginny had noted some of the tattoos on Jason's arms in the past, war memories engraved into the young man's skin, wearing his pain. *If I had my memories tatted onto my skin, I'd hate to think what they'd be.* Sighing, she glanced up, seeing Gareth and Katelyn approaching from the back, both carrying platters of nachos and fish tacos, setting them down on the table in front of their friends. Everyone already seemed settled—*why do I still feel like an outsider looking in?*

Suddenly too tired and uncertain to interject herself into the group, she turned to leave, slamming into a brick wall. Staggering backward, she felt steel bands clamp her upper arms as she jerked her head up, seeing Brogan holding onto her. Blushing at her awkward position, she stammered, "Sorry!"

"No worries. I shouldn't have walked up behind you," Brogan said. He loosened his grip on her arms, self-conscious, but immediately missed the feel of her warmth. "You leaving? You just got here."

Not giving into the temptation to consider how, with the busy crowd, he knew she had just arrived, she nodded. "Uh, yeah. Seems busy…which is good for your business, but…uh…" Shrugging, she knew the heat from her face must be evident, but she forced herself to keep her eyes on his.

"Don't go," he said. "I was hoping you'd come… alone. I saved a seat for you."

Wrinkling her brow, she cast her gaze about. Not seeing an empty table, she allowed herself to be led to a narrow, spiral staircase near the back of the pub.

5

How have I never seen this before?

As Brogan undid the chain across the bottom of the stairs, Ginny eyed the structure dubiously. His massive body ambled up the spiral and, halfway up, he turned and lifted his eyebrow in silent question as he held his hand out toward her. Self-conscious in her baseball jersey and old jeans, she wiped her sweaty palms on her thighs.

Without thinking, she reached up, sliding her hand in his much larger one, allowing him to gently guide her upward. The feel of his hand holding tightly onto hers was unfamiliar and yet comforting. The thought that she would love to hold his hand more often, relishing the feel of his skin touching hers, washed over her. Curling around to the top, she was delighted to see a small loft that overlooked the pub. Even though they were no longer on the stairs, he continued to hold her hand as he led her to a table.

"We usually have live bands play up here on the

weekends and keep it closed the rest of the time. It's too hard for our servers to get drinks and food up here."

There were two small tables with chairs but the rest of the space would easily fit a small band. Looking around, Ginny was unable to hide the smile from her face. "I really like it."

Nodding, Brogan said, "I kinda figured you might be more comfortable away from the crowd, but I wasn't sure you were coming alone."

She peered at him, watching his normal grimace now paired with a specter of doubt in his blue eyes. "I had no one else I wanted to be with," she confessed, surprised that the words left her mouth. The sense of vulnerability usually had her keep her mouth shut, but seeing the uncertainty in his eyes made her want to reach out. She watched in fascination as his shoulders relaxed slightly.

Brogan glanced down at their group of friends, some smiling up at him and others trying to hide their smiles. Sighing, he added, "Always a crowd, isn't there? Anyway, you got stuck in the bleachers with my sister and her gaggle."

"Gaggle?" she repeated with her lips quirking, sitting in the chair he indicated.

"Yeah," he shrugged. "You know? They're all good and stuff…but sometimes, they like to get into everyone's business."

Fiddling with the napkin on the table, she shrugged. "They're fine…actually, they're great. It's just a little weird…you know. Being an outsider and all." Immediately wishing she had not given away that tidbit, she rushed on, "But, it's all good. They're…uh…good."

Erupting in a chuckle, Brogan said, "You gonna keep trying to convince me or yourself about that?"

Ginny's eyes jumped to his, realizing she had never heard him laugh before. The sound was deep and reverberated through her even with the Irish music playing in the background. Her gaze dropped to his mouth, surrounded by dark, scruffy beard and her mind emptied of all thoughts other than those perfect lips. Hearing him clear his throat, she blinked. "Oh, sorry. I lost my train of thought for a second."

"Yeah, I kinda got that."

Shaking her head ruefully, she tried to get back on track. "No, really. Your sister is nice and I like coaching with her. I'm getting to know the others through the AL Auxiliary, but," shrugging again, "my job doesn't allow a lot of socializing time."

Nodding, he commiserated. "Yeah, same here. Always something to do."

Looking down at the busy crowd, she asked, "Is it hard…uh…running a family business?" His eyes pierced hers, his attention never wavering, but he said nothing. "God, I'm sorry," she rushed. "That must have sounded bad. It's just that your family seems so close, but I wondered if working together made you closer."

Nodding in understanding, he said, "It's good. Pops…that's my grandfather, ran the business until he gave it to our dad. Then he passed it on to me, Aiden, and Katelyn so he and Mom could have an early retirement." He rubbed his whiskers for a moment before adding, "I reckon they wanted us to have something to come home to."

It was on the tip of Ginny's tongue to ask more

about him, but a call up from Mitch interrupted their conversation.

"Ginny! Got a call."

Jumping up, she blushed as though she had been caught out late by her father. "I've got to go."

Brogan stood as well, his body towering over hers, his eyes stormy, full of regret. "You didn't get a chance to eat. You gotta be hungry."

Offering a small smile, she said, "I'll just grab something later. But…uh…thanks for sitting with me."

"Maybe we can do it again sometime?"

She looked up into his eyes and smiled, her breath catching in her throat. "That'd be nice." Hearing Mitch call out again, she lifted her shoulder as she turned and said, "See you around."

Brogan watched her descend the spiral staircase, thinking of her job and wondering what kind of call she was being sent to investigate. Sighing, he wanted to know more—actually everything—about the pretty woman that filled his thoughts. Standing, he watched as she headed out the front door of the pub and whispered, "Be safe."

"Mrs. Collins, we meet again," Ginny greeted, as the older woman answered her door, a cat in her arms. "I apologize for my appearance. I came from a ball game."

"Come in, come in, Officer Spencer. Please, call me Helen. And you look fine, dear."

Ginny followed her in, once more walking around several cats, all of whom appeared to be fascinated with her legs. Sitting on the sofa, she took out her pad, while shooing another cat from trying to play with her pen.

"So, I understand you saw something else last night? Helen, I have to say that it would be helpful if you would call suspicious activity in right away so that we can come out and possibly catch whoever you see."

"I didn't want to get anyone out of bed unless I knew it was a crime," Helen protested, fluffing another flowered housedress around her ankles. "And bein' it's a Saturday morning, I figured the police might be sleeping late."

"Ma'am, there's a direct line that feeds into an all-night dispatcher for the town and the county of North Heron. You can call anytime."

Settling back against the chair cushions, Helen smiled as she absentmindedly rubbed a cat. "Well, that's nice, isn't it?"

"So…last night?" Ginny prompted.

"Oh, yes," Helen exclaimed. "Well, you see, this time I was awoken about one a.m."

"Did you hear a noise?"

"Oh, no. I had to go tinkle."

Pen poised over her pad, Ginny halted as she looked up, eyebrows raised.

Disturbing a cat in her lap as she giggled, Helen said, "You know, my dear, at my age, I have to get up to use the bathroom several times during the night. Older women have a hard time holding on to their pee."

Nodding, as she once more slapped the official cop-face on, Ginny said, "Go on, please."

"Well," Helen said, leaning forward, her eyes bright, "my bathroom faces the back of the house and so the little window there looks to the backyard of my back neighbor. There were some clouds so we didn't have as much moonlight, but they have a small light outside their back door. I knew no one was home—"

"Are they rentals also?"

"Oh, no. That's the Masterson's home. They live there, but left town two days ago. Their daughter is having a baby and they're spending a few days in Norfolk. Their daughter is married to some military type man and I think he might be gone right now, so the Masterson's wanted to be with her. It is so hard when the husband isn't around for the birth. I, myself, never married, but I have quite a few nieces and nephews that I stay in contact with, and a couple of them have married men in the Navy. I suppose that makes sense with the Naval base in Norfolk—"

"Last night, Helen," Ginny prodded.

"Yes, yes. I saw a little movement and when I looked out my window, I could see a man standing just in the shadow of their back porch, peeking in the window. And what bothered me, was they have added on to the back of their house and made a first-floor master bedroom, since Jim had his back surgery a few years ago. And that was just where the man was peeking!"

Leaning back as though exhausted from her tale, Helen smiled at Ginny, who tried to hide her sigh. "Okay, can you describe the man? What made you think he was a man? How was he dressed? You know, like you did the other day."

"Hmm, well, he was once again dressed in all black. Long sleeved shirt and pants. Um..." she tapped her chin, "he was standing on the porch so his head was much taller at the window. He was looking into the upper part of the windowpane. And his hands were cupped together around his face again."

"How long did he stay?"

"Well, from the time I saw him, I'd say he was there about another minute before he took off between the houses at the side and I couldn't see him anymore."

"Helen, you must call the police if you see suspicious activity in the future. We have a better chance of catching him if we are called right away."

Frowning, Helen's shoulders slumped. Rubbing another cat, she sighed. "I know…it's hard living alone, you know."

Ginny cocked her head to the side, waiting for Helen to continue.

"You see, I get along with my neighbors, but when you live alone…and with so many pets, I know people can get an idea that I might be a little…uh…batty."

Laying her pen down, Ginny smiled at the older woman. "Oh, Mrs. Collins, I don't think you're batty at all."

Helen's grey eyes brightened as she looked up at Ginny. "Thank you, my dear. I know what I saw, but once he ran off I began to doubt myself. Was I dreaming? Are my eyes deceiving me? Will anyone believe me?" Sighing once more, she said, "Both times, I had to convince myself that it was the right thing to do to call the police."

Standing, Ginny agreed, "Ma'am, if you see anything suspicious, I want you to call the police immediately. You're a good neighbor and we want to keep Baytown safe."

Accepting a hug from the older woman, Ginny walked between the houses to the back of the Masterson's residence, wondering if there would be any evidence to collect.

By the time Brogan descended the spiral stairs to the ground floor, he found his group of friends to be quietly staring at him, all with smiles on their faces. With narrow eyes, he groused, "What the hell y'all looking at?"

Katelyn walked over, sliding her arm around his waist. "Just nice to see you smiling...well, before you immediately turned back into a sour-puss."

Glaring at her, he looked at Aiden's huge grin and said, "Shouldn't you be working? We got people to feed around here."

Aiden walked past Brogan, shoulder bumping him on his way back to the bar. "Ease up, Bro. Everyone here has your back."

Hating to be the object of his friends' attention, he glanced at the group, seeing Mitch and Grant still sitting with Tori and Jillian. Turning to Mitch, he asked, "Who'd you send Ginny out with? Sam or Burt?"

Mitch shook his head. "Neither. Sam's off and Burt's got the evening shift."

Planting his beefy hands on his hips, Brogan pierced his old friend with his stare. "So, Ginny's out answering a call by herself?"

The others looked on in wide-eyed shock as Mitch squared off with Brogan. "I know how to run my department, Brogan. If she needs assistance, she calls for it. She may be a woman, but she's still an officer, with the same duties and responsibilities that the rest of us have."

Brogan took a breath, his anger becoming palpable as his face reddened. "Well, Chief Evans—"

"Brogan!" Katelyn called out, now pulling on his arm. "Let's not say something we'll regret!"

"Seriously, Katelyn? This ain't no *we* thing…this is a *me* thing!"

"You know what I mean. Ginny's fine and you need to get behind the bar with Aiden before he gives away too many drinks to some of the women in here."

With one last glare, Brogan stalked away from the others, leaving them staring in awe in his wake.

"Damn," Zac said. "I've never seen him like this."

Grant squeezed Jillian's waist and said, "It's 'bout time he finally makes the approach. He's been eying Ginny ever since she's been in town."

Belle, standing to the side, said softly, "I don't think it's easy for either of them." The group turned her way and she blushed as she added, "Sometimes the love we seek gets stuck on our past."

6

Ginny stepped into the hot summer sun, crossing through Helen's yard into the Masterson's. She focused on the ground, but with the grass recently cut and the summer heat burning the green to brown, there was no evidence of footprints. As she approached the wooden back porch, she stood, staring at the back of the house. The porch ran three-quarters of the length, from the sliding glass door of the family room to the end of what Helen indicated was the master bedroom. Studying the porch, she saw no dusty footprints either.

Sighing, she carefully walked over to the sliding glass door, looking for clues that someone might have tried to break in. Leaning down, she studied the wooden doorframe, but noticed nothing. No marks in the wood. No attempted entry.

Stepping back, with her hands on her hips, she slid her gaze over the entire back of the house. Walking along the deck, she moved to the window Helen indicated the man had peered into. No footprints on the porch below. No evidence of attempted entry. Pulling out the fingerprint kit, she dusted the window. Nothing.

Helen had not been able to see clearly enough to say whether the man wore gloves, but with no other evidence, Ginny assumed he probably did.

Peeking through the window, she viewed the master bedroom, noting there were blinds on the window, but they were angled so that light shone through—and eyes would be able to see in. Ten feet further, at the end of the porch, was a higher window. Unable to see into it, she stood on her tiptoes enough to tell that it was probably the bathroom. Stepping back again, she shook her head, trying to see anything out of the ordinary.

"Officer, is something wrong?"

Startled, Ginny whirled around, seeing a middle-aged man standing in the next-door backyard, a hoe in his hand. "Hello," she called out, walking toward him. Stopping a few feet from the fence border, she smiled at him. "I'm Officer Spencer and I'm checking out the Masterson's home since they are out of town. Have you seen anyone back here that made you suspicious?"

"No, ma'am. I'm Jeffrey Teestor and if I saw someone back here besides the Mastersons, I'd have called the police."

Chuckling, she nodded, and said, "That would be the right response. But one of your neighbors reported seeing a man on the back porch here last night, looking into the window. So, I'm just checking the house to see if I can find any evidence of a problem."

His eyes jumped to his neighbor's house before returning to Ginny's face. "Did you find anything? Was there someone there?"

"No, sir, but I want to make sure. Have you seen anyone at the rental property behind your house…next to Mrs. Collins' house?"

His eyes narrowed as he nodded slowly. "Mrs. Collins. Is she the one who reported seeing someone? Let me tell you, she's a nice lady but, Officer, she lives alone with all those cats and I gotta tell you, I think she'd be the type who might need some attention, if you know what I mean."

Not acknowledging his opinion of Helen, she continued, "So, you haven't seen anyone suspicious?"

"This whole town has a bunch of rentals this time of year. There're a lot visitors, so no way would I necessarily pay attention to someone I didn't know. And, as I said before, if I did see someone suspicious, I'd sure as hell call the police."

Thanking him, Ginny walked through the yard to the other neighbors and began knocking on doors. She found the same answers as Mr. Teestor's—and several with the same opinion of Helen Collins.

Driving back to the station, she pondered the possibilities. *Was Helen mistaken? If a man was not breaking and entering, was he scoping the area for future break-ins? Or just looking in bedrooms?* And, if so, a probable motive snaked through her.

"So, is Mrs. Collins just an attention seeker?" Burt asked, looking across the table at Ginny. "I don't like to doubt people, but so far, she's the only one who saw anyone."

Ginny realized Burt, Mitch, Sam, and Grant's eyes were all focused on her. Sighing heavily, she shook her head slowly. "This sucks because I really want to believe her. Yes, she's lonely. Yes, she's kind of a stereotypical cat lady. But to completely ignore her could possibly lead to someone actually breaking into a home."

"Or we could be just encouraging someone who takes up our services to have someone to talk to."

"Just because we have no proof now doesn't mean her concerns need to be dismissed!" Ginny argued, her frustration close to the surface.

Mitch nodded and said, "I agree. We need to be more vigilant. When on night patrol, keep your eyes and ears open. We don't want to scare the townspeople but we need to make sure we don't have someone scoping out places to break into." Looking over at Ginny, he said, "Good work."

"Just doing my job, Chief," she replied, but a small smile curved the corners of her mouth.

"Next on the agenda," Mitch continued, "is the block party hosted by Finn's Pub. It's in three weeks and we'll need all hands on deck. It'll bring in townspeople, people from the county, and visitors. I've got Sheriff Hudson and Chief Freeman coming as well."

The others approved of the fellow law enforcement officers from the surrounding county and nearby town offering their assistance.

"Alcohol will be flowing," Grant commented, "and that can add to people's idiotic behavior."

"Speaking from experience?" Sam joked.

Having the grace to blush, Grant nodded. "Oh,

harsh, Sam, but yeah…I made plenty of mistakes in my younger days when drinking too much."

They all chuckled before getting back to the reports. Mitch added, "The mayor, town council, and town manager have all signed off on the party, but make no mistake—one problem and they'll be on us like white on rice."

Sam reached over and started to take a donut, then hesitated before pulling his hand back empty. Seeing the lifted eyebrows all focused on him, he ducked his head, saying, "Wife's got me watching my diet again. Cholesterol and blood pressure a bit high." Rubbing his chin, he said, "Don't worry, though. I'm not ready to retire yet."

"Good to hear," Mitch said.

As they finished their briefing, Grant called out, "Don't forget the American Legion meeting tomorrow."

Ginny nodded before stepping out into the parking lot. Her shift over, she relished her walk home on the tree-lined streets. Suddenly, she halted, the sight before her causing her to stumble.

Brogan was leaning against one of the patrol cars, one booted, jean-clad leg crossed over the other. His arms were crossed as well, straining his shirt sleeves. His eyes were covered with reflective sunglasses, but she felt the warmth of his stare nonetheless. As she approached, he slowly released his arms and slid his glasses from his face. She was right—his stare was sending more warmth her way than the sun. Sucking in a quick breath, her legs continued to move forward of their own accord. The closer she got, the farther her head had to lean back. Sucking in her lips, she cocked her head to the side in silent question.

"Hey," he said, his voice rough and yet soothing.

"Hey, yourself," she smiled. "What are you doing here?"

"I thought I might walk you home from your shift."

She watched as his cheeks reddened slightly and she smiled. "How do you know I walk home?"

Shrugging, he replied, "It's a small town. Not hard to pick up on people's habits. Sometimes you drive, but not usually."

"Oh, you know all the work habits of the residents?" she joked.

Standing to his full height, he stepped closer, peering down at her. "No...just the ones that matter."

"Oh..." Ginny blinked, a ribbon of pleasure unfurling about her.

"Is that okay?"

Stammering, she said, "Uh, is what okay?"

Brogan grinned, "That I walk you home."

Nodding, she smiled. "I am a police officer, you know. I'm pretty sure I'm safe."

"I'm sure you are, but I'd still like to walk with you."

They held each other's gazes for a moment, no words spoken, but with a longing that threatened to overtake them. Swallowing deeply, Ginny nodded. "Yes, you may walk me home."

Dropping his chin to his chest, Brogan let out the breath he had been holding. Lifting his gaze to pierce her, his blue eyes locked on her hazel ones. With a grin, he replied, "Well, all right then."

The town's sidewalks were old and often cracked

but Ginny felt as though she were floating along on a cloud. Staring straight ahead, she wondered what was happening. *I'm a cop, not some teenager.* Slanting her eyes, she looked over at Brogan, his normally taciturn expression softened. Unable to keep a chuckle from slipping out, she noted he jerked his gaze down to her.

"I'm sorry," she said. "It's just that I seemed to be unable to think of what to talk about."

"Yeah, me too," he admitted. They continued down the shaded sidewalk toward her house. "You could tell me about what's going on in the police world of our big city," he joked.

Laughing, she said, "Well, with our huge crime rate in this metropolis, it's hard to know what's going on at all times." Noting Brogan shortened his gait so that he stayed beside her, she continued, "Let's see. Nell Holstead called because her neighbor's crabapple tree is dropping apples in her yard and she's afraid the raccoons will come spread diseases to her dogs." Seeing Brogan's eyebrow raise, she continued. "We had to issue three citations today to beach visitors. One for letting his dog poop on the beach and two for glass alcohol bottles. We also had to issue two speeding tickets. One to a visitor and one to old man Simmons for driving his golf cart erratically."

"No way!" Brogan exclaimed.

"Hey, at least we didn't have to deal with Paula Thompkins trying to run over her neighbor's kids with her motorized wheelchair."

His large shoulders moved up and down as he laughed. "Anything else?"

She nodded. "Well, we've had a possible sighting of a man peeking into windows in the middle of the night."

Immediately sobering, Brogan halted his steps, placing his hand on her shoulder, stopping her as well. "Wait, is that what you were investigating this afternoon? I don't like the idea that you have to—"

"Brogan," she interrupted, "this is my job."

Sucking in a deep breath, he let it out slowly, for once trying to think of the right thing to say. "I know, Ginny. It just...well, I guess I just worry about you."

Realizing they were standing on the sidewalk in front of her little house she looked up, seeing uncertainty on his face. Placing her hand on his arm, the steel of his muscles underneath her fingertips almost knocked all other thoughts from her mind. For a long minute, they simply stood and held each other's eyes. A car honking down the street jerked them both back to the present.

"I'm here," she said, unnecessarily, nodding toward her house.

"I know," he said softly.

"You know where I live?" she asked, leaning her head to the side.

"Small town, remember?"

Her lips curved into a smile as she chuckled. "Yeah, I remember. So...I'll see you tomorrow night at the meeting?"

"Yeah, see you there." Unable to think of anything else to say, Brogan watched as she turned and walked up the path to her front door. He lifted his hand in response to her wave just before she stepped inside.

Awakening in a sweat, Brogan cursed. He had actually hoped that Ginny's gentle touch might take away the inability to make it through a night without the war slipping through. "Sorry, MB," he said to the cat whose sleep he disturbed. Sighing, he rose from his bed, careful not to toss the covers on the silky black cat, and made his way to the bathroom to change into his running clothes. Once more, he headed out to the beach, hoping the pounding surf and sand would drown out the memories.

7

Ginny looked up as she placed more folding chairs in rows in the meeting hall of the American Legion building. The former church had sat empty for several years and when the new AL chapter needed their own hall, the owner gladly sold the building to them for a very reasonable price. The large meeting room was the former sanctuary, tall windows standing guard on both sides. The dais at the front served as their platform stage where Grant was currently checking out the microphone, making sure it worked properly. Unable to afford new equipment, the members made do with what they had.

Feeling the back of her neck prickle, Ginny turned around to see Grant staring at her. Lifting her eyebrow, she waited to see what was on his mind.

Plopping down on the edge of the dais, his long legs swinging over the side, he said, "I wanted to thank you…for what you talked about several months ago.

You know…about pushing counseling for the AL members."

"It really helped you, didn't it?" she asked, a small smile playing about her lips, remembering his tumultuous relationship in the early days with Jillian.

Ducking his head, he grinned. "Yeah, thank God." Looking back up at her, he said, "I know it's a personal question, but I was wondering if you'd ever taken your own advice?"

Pinching her lips together, she considered not answering, but knew that was a chicken-shit response. Sucking in a deep breath, she let it out slowly. "A bit…in the past…kind of forced on me when I was getting out of the Army." She let the implication that she needed it at the time hang between them. "Since I've been here, I've seen a counselor a couple of times."

"Helping?"

Nodding, she said, "For the most part. Haven't seen them recently. What about you?"

"Oh, hell yeah. I wouldn't have been able to have a healthy relationship with Jillian if I hadn't taken your advice. PTSD is a fucker, for sure."

Bending to set up another chair, she nodded again. "Yeah, and it takes all forms. When trust is gone, it's…well…"

Standing she noticed Grant looking over her shoulder. Twisting her head, she saw Brogan's large body filling the doorway, hands in his pockets, eyes unreadable.

Mitch, Commander of the local chapter of the American Legion, rapped the gavel on the podium. Brogan, the Sergeant at Arms, closed the doors of the meeting room of their new space. With another three raps of the gavel, the members stood as Mitch called out, "The Color Bearer will advance the Colors." Jason, standing in the back with Brogan, marched forward, the American flagpole in his hands, and set it in the floor stand.

"The Chaplain will offer prayer." The Methodist minister, a member of the American Legion, stood and prayed as the group bowed their heads in unison.

The POW/MIA Empty Chair Ceremony followed. The chair was designated as a symbol of the thousands of American POW/MIAs still unaccounted for from all wars and conflicts involving the United States of America. The POW/MIA flag was placed on the Empty Chair.

The eclectic assembly included men, plus a few women, ages running from about twenty-five to almost ninety. At the moment, there was unity as all faces turned toward the Empty Chair, a haunted expression on many of them.

After the Pledge of Allegiance and the Preamble to the American Legion Constitution were spoken in unison, the gavel was rapped once more to indicate that everyone could take a seat.

Aiden, the post adjunct, read the minutes from the last meeting and checked to see if there were any changes or additions that needed to be made. Brogan grinned as his normally jovial brother sat down next to him, amazed—and proud—with Aiden's decorum.

The finance officer, Zac, read the treasurer's report

and a short discussion ensued about the upcoming fundraisers. "I'm going to ask Brogan MacFarlane to come up and talk about the block party."

Brogan, hating the spotlight on him, stood and made his way toward the podium, stepping over Ginny's legs as he exited his row of chairs. As their legs touched briefly, he was shocked by the warmth that traveled from her body to his. Glancing down, he was unable to hide the slight smile that always seemed to appear when she was looking up at him.

"As most of you know, the pub got permission to hold a block party next month. We'll block off the street next to Finn's and invite townspeople to listen to music, dance, and have some good food. We're charging a premium rate for the food trucks to come in and have several local bands who will cut the costs of their appearances. All the proceeds will be donated to the Baytown American Legion and the Baytown Fire and Rescue Services."

At that, applause erupted and Brogan blushed, shaking his head. With a head jerk toward Mitch, he walked back to his seat, this time making sure his leg touched Ginny's knee as he passed by.

Gareth reported on the statistics of the youth baseball teams they had created. "We have almost fifty children, ranging in age from five to seventeen, who come out almost every weekend. We now have the support of the community and the parents. Many of the parents cannot afford to give financial assistance, but they offer what they can and have participated in some fundraising. Our community assistance drive is in full swing and we now have sponsorships from Baytown Furniture, Sunset Marina, Sam's Golf Carts, the Baytown Hotel, and the Dunes Pro Golf Shop. This means we can get uniforms at no cost to us or the kids."

Another round of applause ensued and the officers grinned. Initial announcements over, a member in his early fifties came forward and approached the podium, nodding toward the group. Ginny leaned forward, curious as to his story.

"I was an F-15 pilot in Desert Storm and we were successful in our missions to damage Saddam's vaunted Republican Guard. I was proud of what we did. Proud of who I served with. I left the Air Force ten years later and had a career as a pilot with a large airline company. Always looked back with pride." He rubbed his hand over the back of his neck and said, "It wasn't until years later that I started having trouble sleeping. Nightmares. Disturbing thoughts during the day. I would watch the news and see bombed buildings in different battles and locations and my mind would take a dark path. With the encouragement of my wife, I began counseling about five years ago, before we retired to Baytown. It helped a lot because what I had never realized was that while I wasn't on the ground fighting, I was…no pun intended…above it all. I never knew that a lot of pilots suffer from PTSD, just like any other soldier. My nightmares would be about who all might have died in my raids that were innocents. Children. Women. I can't say that my dark thoughts have all gone, but it helps to have a counselor that understands all forms of PTSD and to have the support of a good woman that keeps me balanced. And, of course, this group here. I can't go back and, to be honest, I served and by that service, I performed the missions assigned, so going back wouldn't change anything. But by the activities that this AL organization is involved in, I am able to do something productive and giving."

The group applauded and Ginny was glad that Mitch had instituted a time during each meeting where a member could share their experience. It helped to bridge the age and war gap, plus gave the members a chance to know they were not alone in their feelings.

Ginny looked around at the group, happy for the work the AL was doing for the small community. Jason, Grant, Zac, and Brogan sat on one side of her while Lance, quiet as ever, sat stoically on the other side next to Aiden, his ever-present smile firmly in place, completing the row. She knew all of them, but had to admit Lance was the mystery. A friend of Mitch's, he had relocated to the Eastern Shore after being discharged from the Army, but somewhat of a recluse, he kept to himself.

Behind her sat Callan, one of the original Baytown Boys, and his CG buddies, all of who had joined the American Legion.

Bringing her attention back to the meeting, Mitch was discussing the American Legion Auxiliary. "Ginny Spencer, would you come up and discuss what is going on with the Auxiliary?"

Feeling Brogan's eyes on her as she stepped up on the dais, she tried to focus on the entire assembly and not just the man sitting next to the chair she just vacated. "I'm in a unique position of being a member of the American Legion and the Auxiliary since I served, as well as come from a military family. They've done great work so far and their fundraisers are going well. The Cavalcade of Memories is ongoing and if you did not look at it in the foyer as you came in, please do so on your way out. Any articles for display can be given to Katelyn MacFarlane."

As she started to leave the podium, Mitch called her to speak as the Post Service Officer. Giving a short nod, she moved back to the microphone. "This is just a reminder that many of you have taken up the offer of counseling from the Eastern Shore Mental Health Group. This is an ongoing and very important outreach that they perform and we know that those who have served have a…variety…of…uh…" For a few seconds, Ginny looked out onto the crowd and felt the room sway. Instead of the expressions of warm acceptance from the gathering, all she could see was faces from the past of censure, disbelief, and anger. Her breath became labored, but just as the room began to darken, she felt a touch on her arm and her name being called softly.

"Ginny? Ginny?" Mitch said, placing his hand on her arm.

Jerking, she blinked rapidly. "Fuck," she whispered. Looking out on the concerned and confused faces, she rushed, "Oh, sorry. Wow, I probably shouldn't have skipped supper." The members gently laughed as she shook her head to clear out the fog. "But anyway, just remember that they are there if you need them." With a mumbled apology toward Mitch, she stepped away from the podium, but instead of making her way back to her seat, she slipped out the side door into the cool night air. Not wanting to be seen, she ran to the back of the building and through the alley, her house only being four blocks away. Her chest heaved as she unlocked her door and rushed in, slamming it shut behind her.

Sliding down the door, she landed on her rump, willing her breathing to slow, taking long, deep breaths.

A knock on the door behind her caused her to jump. "Ginny." The deep, recognizable voice reverberated through her body as she squeezed her eyes tightly shut for a few seconds.

"I know you're in there. I was right behind you," Brogan said. His voice softened as he continued, "Come on, Ginny, let me in."

Unable to come up with a plausible excuse, Ginny stood and swiped her hand over her face. Sucking in a deep breath, she threw open the door, plastering on a smile. "Hey, Brogan. Sorry to worry you. I was just feeling a little light-headed so I thought I'd head home so I could eat something and get some sleep."

He stood on the porch, his gaze piercing hers, trying to judge her honesty. Running his hands over his head in frustration, he said, "I was worried."

Swallowing audibly, she shook her head. "You shouldn't be."

"But I am. And I do."

Unable to think of what to say, she stood rooted to the floor as she pinched her lips together. Finally, she whispered, "Did I look like a fool? You know…up there, in front of everybody."

Brogan knew how hard those words were for her to say. To admit that she might have appeared vulnerable when her persona was so strong. His fingers itched to reach out, pull her close, and tell her he would always be there for her. Always take care of her. Chase away whatever haunted her. Fisting his large hands at his hips, he simply replied, "No. No one noticed. They were finishing the meeting. No one paid attention to you leaving."

She lifted her eyes up to his, her voice shaky. "But you did."

Nodding, he said, "I notice everything about you, Ginny."

The two stood a few feet apart on her stoop, neither aware of anything but each other. After several, long, silent minutes, Ginny said, "Thank you for…well, just thank you."

Brogan, his gaze still assessing, nodded. "My pleasure." Turning, he ambled down the steps toward the road before swinging back around. "If you ever want to go out with me some time…to talk or eat or…uh, anything, let me know." Even to his ears, it was the worse date-asking in the world. Red-faced, he began to walk back down her front path.

"Yes."

The one word had him turn back to her, his eyes narrowed in confusion.

Ginny's hesitant smile hid her pounding heart, and she repeated, "Yes. I'd like to go out with you sometime."

The smile crossing Brogan's face was unlike anything she had ever seen. He smiled with his whole being and the light from his eyes pierced her coldness. "Well, all right," he said. With a wave, he headed back down the road, leaving her standing in her doorway, heartbeat still pounding but with a lightness she had not felt in years.

"You want to tell me what happened last night?"

Brogan looked over at Aiden, standing at the bar with a dishtowel slung over his shoulder. "What do you mean?"

"Ginny," Aiden replied, rolling his eyes. "Who else?" Still staring, he added, "And I saw you high-tail it after her when she left suddenly."

"She wasn't feeling well, so I wanted to make sure she got home okay." Brogan lifted a heavy crate of alcohol and moved it to the bar, where he opened it and began to sort the liquor. Not hearing anything from Aiden, he dared to glance up, not surprised to see his inquisitive brother still staring. "You got something to say?" he growled.

"Yeah, I do," Aiden said, tossing the rag down onto the bar with a slap. "You never were Mr. Talkative, so I don't expect that. But after you got outta the Marines, you sure as shit came home different." Jerking his hand up, he said, "I know. I know. We all came back changed, some just older and wiser. But you…you're different, Bro. It's like you've dug a hole, buried yourself, and have been content to stay there."

Grimacing, Brogan remained silent, wanting to refute Aiden's description but not willing to lie.

"At least until recently."

At those words from Aiden, Brogan looked up, his brow knitted in question. "Recently?" he asked.

Nodding, Aiden placed his forearms on the bar as he leaned forward. "Yeah. The first couple of years we were back, we threw ourselves into taking over Finn's. You worked harder than anybody, but we all just figured you needed the work to keep focused—"

"We?"

Aiden rolled his eyes. "Are you shittin' me, Brogan? Of course, we. Hell, you think in this family, anything is hidden from Pops, Mom, Dad? Sure-as-shit not Katelyn."

Silence acknowledged Aiden's words, so he kept going. "You grew your hair...so did I. Mom hated it but we both had that *finally out of the military* rebellion thing going on." Seeing Brogan about to speak, he added, "Okay, that's what I had. What you had going on was an *I don't give a fuck what I look like*."

Brogan's lips twitched, knowing Aiden hit the nail on the head. He really had not given a fuck what anyone thought since getting out.

"Then suddenly Ms. Spencer shows up in town as the new cop, and a pretty one at that, and we all see you're interested. Oh, I know you tried to hide it, but hell, Brogan, you'd have to be dead not to get a walking hard-on when she's around."

At that, Brogan growled, stepping forward, his fist at the ready. Laughing, Aiden danced back from the bar, now safely out of reach.

"Sorry, Bro. I just had to get that in there to see what your reaction would be."

"You fuckin' prick," Brogan bit out, his eyes narrowed, irritated that Aiden got a rise out of him. "You keep your eyes to yourself when she's around."

Still laughing, Aiden nodded. "Honestly, I think of her like a sister." Seeing Brogan's dubious expression, he admitted, "Okay, a really pretty sister that I think is perfect for your ugly, old, grumpy ass." Staring at Brogan for a moment, catching a slight change in his expression, Aiden remarked, "Wait. You don't think you're good enough for her. Man, that's fucked."

Brogan said nothing, his hands now resting on the bar, his head hanging. Aiden was right—that was exactly what he thought. Sighing, he lifted his head, pinning his brother with his stare. "She's college educated…I'm just a former jarhead, bartender. She's gorgeous…I'm a big lug, known for my brawn, sure as hell not my sparkling personality. Hell, I cut my hair, thinking that it might make me more presentable to a cop, but now I look in the mirror and feel stupid seeing my whole face."

"Look, man, all I know is that you're a good brother, good Marine, good friend, good businessman, and a helluva man. You are good enough for anyone you want, but especially that nice cop you're sweet on. You've got issues you need to work on, but she'd be a lucky woman to have you around."

Shaking his head, not believing Aiden's words, he said, "Don't know about any of that, but I did ask her out. Last night."

Aiden blew out his breath in a rush, as though hit in the gut. "Oh, man. I'm sorry. I can't believe she turned you down."

At that, Brogan's gaze jumped back to Aiden's. "You've got it wrong. She said *yes*."

Aiden stared at him for a moment, his smile growing wider by the second until Brogan was sure his brother's face was going to split. Unable to keep his lips from curling at the same time, the two brothers simply stared, both feeling the weight of the moment.

Slapping his hand on the bar once more, Aiden said, "Well, all right. Then let's get back to work, asshole."

Walking past, Brogan cuffed Aiden on the back of the head. "No cussing in the bar. We're gonna have fuckin' customers soon."

8

The call came in as Ginny was on night patrol. 10-14. Possible prowler.

Hearing the address, Ginny knew she was not dealing with Helen Collins this time. Only a few blocks away, she hurried to the scene, acknowledging her location when she arrived. Her sharp gaze searched the area, observing no movement in the neighborhood but knowing the darkness of night offered many hidden locations where someone could be watching.

Seeing the lights on at the residence, she quickly moved to the front porch. She looked back as headlights turned onto the street and a car stopped behind her SUV. Grant stepped from the driver's seat and headed her way. As the officer on call for the evening, he would be her backup.

Nodding to him, he had just arrived at the door when it opened. Celia Ring. The mayor's secretary. Smiling, Ginny introduced herself and Grant as they stepped inside.

"I know who you are," Celia said, wrapping her silky robe tighter around her body, tying the belt about her waist. Her eyes darted around and she urged, "Shut the door! He might still be out there."

Grant complied and motioned, "Let's have a seat and you can tell us what you saw." Ginny led the way as Celia stood in the hallway, seemingly unable to move. Finally following, the three sat in the living room, the blinds closed to the outside world.

Ginny watched Celia's behavior closely, uncertain what to expect. Celia had a reputation in town—an oversexed flirt, a woman on the prowl, and she had even been rumored to not care if a man was married. Ginny immediately stifled a flinch, knowing she needed to maintain professionalism.

"Ms. Ring, can you tell us what you saw?"

Swallowing, Celia licked her lips before sucking them in. "I had been out...uh...on a date this...uh, last evening." Bringing her shaky hand up to her face, she wiped her brow. "Shit, I can't seem to get it straight."

"Ma'am," Grant said, "why don't you just start at the beginning. Sometimes that helps."

Nodding in jerks, Celia said, "Sure. Yes." Clearing her throat, she began again, "I had a date last night. We went out for drinks and then, uh...drove around some." Her pale face was suddenly painted with bright blush stains on her cheeks, as she looked down at her hands. "I got back home sometime after midnight and went upstairs to get ready for bed. I showered, put on my gown, and then came back downstairs. I always double check my locks before turning in for the night."

"Yes, ma'am," Ginny prodded for Celia to continue.

"That's when I saw him," Celia stated, voice quivering. "Right there," she pointed to the living room window at the side of the house.

"Him?"

"A face…at the corner of the window. It was partially covered with his hands as he peeked in. But he was staring straight at me."

"What did you do?"

"Do?" Celia's voice raised. "I screamed and ran toward the kitchen to get away from his face!"

"Okay, okay," Ginny said gently as she nodded encouragingly. "You did the right thing by getting to a safe place and calling us."

Celia's breath left her lungs in a long sigh. "Thank you," she whispered.

"Did you drive back by yourself or did your date bring you home?" Grant asked.

"Myself," Celia replied quickly.

"And who were you out with?" Ginny asked.

Celia blinked, her pale face reddening. "Uh…that's private. It's not pertinent, I assure you."

"It would help to corroborate the time you were home—"

"No," she refused vehemently. "I'm sure it was around midnight,"

"Okay…can you describe the person you saw at the window?" Grant asked. "You said *he*. What did you see exactly?"

Her brow drawn down, Celia said, "Uh…it was so fast. It was…I don't know…a face!"

"Pale or dark? Glasses? Mustache?" Ginny prompted.

"Oh…uh…no glasses. No beard. Caucasian. Um…"

her eyes turned imploringly toward Ginny. "That's it. That's all I remember."

"You're doing great, Ms. Ring," she said. "I'm going to have Officer Grant go outside and check the window area. You and I will go into the kitchen for a few minutes and I'll make some tea."

Leading Celia out of the room, she and Grant passed a knowing look between them. Watching Grant go out the front door, she turned back to the shaken woman.

Rubbing her tired eyes, Ginny gratefully accepted the cup of coffee from Mildred. The others soon filed into the room and Mitch eyed her carefully.

"You okay?"

Unsure if he meant about her surreptitiously leaving the AL meeting the night before, dealing with Celia Ring, or sitting at a meeting after pulling an all-night shift, she decided to go with the simplest answer. "I'm fine."

He stared for a moment and just as she was about to retort, he sat down and opened the report she had written along with the evidence from Grant.

"You've all had a chance to check out what Ginny and Grant were dealing with last night. Ginny, impressions to go along with your facts?"

"Celia was shaken. Her description was articulate, once prodded, although we aren't sure about the time. I checked her doors and windows—all were locked. She normally leaves her downstairs blinds up but said they will be down in the future."

Sam leaned back and peered at her over his glasses. "Do you think someone like her is believable?"

Jerking her head around, Ginny tilted her head. "Excuse me?"

"Did you find her believable? Let's face it, Celia's got a reputation in town."

"Reputation?" Ginny's voice rose. She knew the rumors, but could not believe her fellow officer's line of inquiry.

"She's an attention-seeking, man-hunting, doesn't care who she steps on kind of woman. Hell, Mayor Banks' wife keeps him on a short leash since he hired her," Sam said.

Seeing red, Ginny leaned forward in her chair. "I can't believe you said that." Her voice calm, but cold, she continued, "Her reputation is irrelevant here."

Mitch stepped in, his hands raised. "Ginny's right, but we do have to look at the evidence. Grant found no indication of someone's boots, but he did say the ground was disturbed and that could have been from someone covering their tracks. There were no finger or palm prints on the window, but Celia reported his hands were dark, which would indicate gloves."

Ginny sat in her chair, her body strung tight as a bow.

Sam and Burt exchanged a look, before Sam apologized. "Ginny, I'm sorry. That came out all wrong. I've got a wife and a daughter and the thought of someone peeking in at them makes my blood boil." Sighing, he added, "But I know Celia Ring can seek attention if she doesn't think she's getting any…I just wondered, that's all."

Forcing her breathing to slow, Ginny nodded. "Apology accepted." Sucking in a deep breath, she clarified, "I know her reputation. I know her refusal to tell us who she was out with last night is a possible indication that he was married and she doesn't want us to know. But..." she pinned them all with her hard stare, "she is still a victim who reported a crime and deserves our utmost service."

"Abso-fuckin-lutely right," Grant said, earning a slight smile from Ginny.

Mitch nodded and they continued with the evidence gathered. A few minutes later, the sound of Mildred's voice carried through to the workroom.

"I'll announce you and Chief Evans can see you when—"

"I'll be seen right now!"

The officers shared a grimace at the sound of the mayor's voice. Within a few seconds, he came blustering into their room.

"I get a call from my secretary at the ass-crack of dawn this morning and let me tell you, my wife does not like that. So, I've got a hysterical secretary and a pissed-off wife. Neither of which makes my life any easier!"

"Mayor—" Mitch began.

"Don't give me any excuses. Celia tells me we got a peeping tom in town and I want him gone! I can't have any reason for our vacation visitors to pull outta here. So find him and find him now!"

With that, Corwin stalked out of the police station, leaving Mitch and his officers shaking their heads.

After another few minutes of discussion, Mitch said,

"Sam, I want you on patrol and keeping an eye out for anything out of the ordinary…more than usual. Grant, you and Burt go back to Celia's house and search for more evidence in the light of day. Ginny, go home, get some sleep, and report back tomorrow."

Stepping out into the sunshine, Ginny walked to her car. Placing her hand on the doorframe, she hung her head in fatigue for a moment, allowing the warmth of the sun to settle onto her back.

Hearing her name, she looked up at Grant walking toward her.

The two stood silently observing each other for a moment before he finally spoke. "Look, it doesn't take a rocket scientist to see that something happened to you. Something not good. And something you need to deal with, 'cause you're carrying it around inside."

Opening her mouth to speak, she closed it quickly, no words coming. Not even the ready denial.

"All I'm saying," he continued, "is that you tell the rest of us to get help with our problems, whether from the war or something else. I'm telling you, that you need to take your own advice, and not just occasionally."

With a curt nod, she turned to open her car door, but his next words stopped her in her tracks.

"Without sounding like we're in fuckin' middle school, I can tell Brogan likes you and you like him. I know he's got some demons and hell, girl, so do you. But for anything to work in a relationship, you need to work on yours. At least think about it."

Climbing into her car, Ginny drove the short distance home, Grant's words ringing in her ears. *I do like Brogan. But how do I trust…*

Once inside, she kicked off her boots before walking into her kitchen and making a cup of herbal tea. As it steeped, she looked at the Eastern Shore Mental Health card stuck to her refrigerator. Pulling out her phone, she placed a call.

Date night. *When was the last time I went on a date?*

Ginny hung her head as she stood in her bathroom, staring at her underwear clad body in the mirror. Plain-Jane panties and a plain, white bra. No lace. No satin. Comfortable cotton. *Fuck it...he's not going to see the underwear anyway!*

Taking the green, wrap-dress from the hangar, she slipped on the jersey material, tying the sash around her waist. With a dab of blush and swipe of mascara as her only make-up, she stood back again, perusing her appearance. For once, her hair was down, the ends swinging just below her shoulders. After a sweep of her body, her gaze landed back on her eyes in the reflection. *Maybe a little more for the eyes.*

Adding some soft eyeshadow and liner, she assessed her face again. Satisfied, she squared her shoulders, and said, "You got this." As she turned to walk back into her bedroom, she hoped the words were true.

Brogan stood on Ginny's front porch, his heart racing and palms sweating. Fighting the urge to run back down the walk, the desire to see her outweighed any of his inhibitions. Before he had a chance to ponder what he was doing any more, the door swung open.

Holy shit. He stared a second, his jaw tight with nerves, before his gaze caressed her appearance.

Her dark hair, normally in a regulation bun, was flowing just over her shoulders. Her fresh face sported a hint more makeup than usual, making her hazel eyes appear larger and even more expressive. A slash of color on her lips made him want to taste them, but licking his own was all he managed to do.

Wearing a deep green dress that wrapped around her waist, showcased her athletic figure to perfection, including the legs that he rarely got to see. And on her feet, she wore heels, still only bringing her eyes to his chin.

As he was staring, Ginny drank him in. His hair still neatly shorn matched his neatly trimmed beard. His blue eyes, always somewhat stormy, were now bright. His lips, moist where he licked them, beckoned her and she forced her feet to stay in place or she knew she would have leaned in to taste him.

His broad shoulders pulled tightly at the light-blue dress shirt he wore. Tucked into dark pants, he looked every bit the successful businessman he was. And yet, she noted the uncomfortable way he tugged at his collar.

"Ready?" he asked, cocking his elbow out for her to take.

Smiling, she locked her door and placed her hand in the crook of his arm. "Where are we going?" she asked.

"Hungry?"

"Oh, yeah. I worked a night shift and have been fitfully sleeping today. So, I'm ready to eat."

Nodding in approval, he moved to the door of his

old truck, wincing at the creak as it opened. Wishing he had a better mode of transportation, he was glad he had at least cleaned the inside. Assisting her up into the cab of his truck, he attempted not to stare at her legs as her dress slid up her thighs. Sucking in a deep breath to keep his blood from leaving his brain and rushing to his cock, he slammed the door harder than he meant.

Ginny watched Brogan warily as he stomped around the front of his truck, his jaw hard and his eyes narrow. Wondering if she upset him, she smoothed her hands over the skirt of her dress, hoping to still her nerves.

Watching out of the corner of her eye as he swung himself into the driver's side, he still appeared irritated. Driving the short distance to the Sunset Restaurant near the Sunset Marina, she was surprised by his choice. The classy eatery was a very nice place for a date but did not seem to fit Brogan.

Seeing the very full parking lot, Brogan inwardly groaned. The restaurant was a popular place for sunset weddings and from the look of the crowd, that was what they had entered. The upstairs was always open for regular guests, but the chance to spend a quiet evening with Ginny just went up in flames.

"They seem kind of crowded, don't they?" she asked, leaning forward as she peered out the windshield.

"I'll bet it's a wedding," he explained, hoping to salvage the date. "But the upstairs is always open."

Assisting her down from the cab, he smiled as her light touch stayed on his arm. Opening the door, he ushered her in proudly then immediately stiffened as her back bounced against his chest. "What the he—"

The crowd just inside the door kept Ginny from

advancing, causing her to be pushed backward against Brogan's hard body. Surprised, she quickly righted herself. She heard him growl and felt it reverberate through her body.

Brogan realized the waiting list would be too long, especially since Ginny had said she was hungry. Closing his eyes for a second, he grimaced as he watched his perfectly planned dinner date go up in smoke.

9

Knowing the date was over before it began, Brogan inwardly cursed. A light touch on his arm jolted him out of his misery and he opened his eyes, seeing Ginny's beautiful face turned up toward his.

"Can we get out of here?" she asked.

"Sure. I guess the date is kind of a failure," he tried to joke. "I can take you home."

"Home? You're taking me home?"

"Uh…I thought that was what you meant?" he said, his brow lowered in confusion.

"No," she laughed. "But I'd like to be somewhere less noisy…somewhere we can have a conversation…and less stuffy."

Relief flooded through him as he heaved a sigh. Tucking her hand underneath his arm, he escorted her back to his truck, trying to come up with a backup plan. The Seafood Shack was good, but it would also be crowded and they would run into a lot of people they knew. Finn's was out of the question. Other places would be perfect but take a while to get to. As he jumped into the driver's side again, he observed her on her phone, her fingers flying over the keypad.

She smiled as she looked up and directed, "Swing by Bill's Takeout. I've placed an order."

"Okay," he said, both glad she took charge of dinner and confused by her request. A few minutes later, he pulled into a parking place outside the small shop just off Main Street. Seeing her hand on the door, he said, "Oh, hell no, Ginny. You may have ordered it, but I'm paying. Call me old fashioned, but that's how it's gonna be."

Nodding, she said, "Okay. Just tell him to add extra napkins and I'll return the cooler tomorrow."

With those instructions, Brogan climbed out and walked inside the takeout place. A few minutes later, he returned carrying a large chest. Placing it in the back of his truck, he climbed inside before turning to her and asking, "So, where to?"

"How about the beach," she replied. "In fact, park near the pier." She watched as his head tilted toward her and she shrugged. "I've never had a picnic on the pier but I've always wanted to. I figure I might as well do it with someone I really like."

With that explanation exploding in his chest, Brogan smiled and backed out of the parking space.

Ten minutes later, they walked to the end of the town pier and set the chest down. Opening it, Ginny pulled out a small tablecloth, that she spread on the wooden planks, and sat on one corner, tucking her legs to the side. She reached inside again and pulled out paper plates, plastic cutlery, an abundance of napkins, and several plastic containers. Grinning up at Brogan, still standing with his hands on his hips, she said, "You just gonna stand there or are you gonna join me?"

Chuckling, he settled his large frame on the opposite corner of the cloth and watched in awe as she popped the top off one of the containers. The smell of Old Bay seasoning mixed with butter hit his nostrils as he peered inside, seeing steamed shrimp. Another container opened revealing two large crabcakes and a bag of seasoned fries complemented the meal. His eyes opened wide as she pulled out a bag of buttered corn of the cob. Near the bottom was a plastic container and as she popped the top off, he viewed chocolate cannoli. And the last thing she pulled out were two large iced teas.

Looking at the bounty, he realized this was the first time a woman had gone to so much trouble for him. And he could not remember the last time he had a picnic on the pier…*not since I was a kid.* Lifting his eyes to her, he shook his head.

"Is this okay?" she asked, doubt seeping in.

Unable to stop himself, he leaned over and placed his hand on the back of her head pulling her gently forward until his lips settled on hers. His kiss was light…soft…and oh, so sweet.

Letting go reluctantly, he blushed. "Sorry. I—"

Laughing, Ginny said, "Don't you dare apologize, Brogan MacFarlane! I've been wanting to do that for a long time."

Her confession surprised him, lightening his heart. A rare grin split his face. "Then I'm glad I took the chance."

"Oh, yeah," she agreed, her face softening with a gentle smile. "So, you ready to eat?"

Chuckling, Brogan nodded and the two piled their plates full. Looking at the iced teas, he asked, "You didn't want beer with your seafood?"

Holding his gaze, she shook her head. "I notice you don't drink. I figure you have your reasons and tonight is about getting to know each other."

Stunned and touched...Brogan simply stared, unable to believe Ginny Spencer wanted to know more about him.

Timeless. The ever-present surf undulated beneath the wooden planks of the pier, creating a soothing background noise as Brogan and Ginny finished their dinner. Digging into the basket, she pulled out the wet-wipes Bill's Takeout had provided and handed several to Brogan. He accepted them gratefully, his fingers messy from the peel-and-eat shrimp. He stood, picking up the refuse and walked the few feet to a trash can.

Ginny leaned back against the pier railing, her eyes planted on his ass. His body was a piece of work and she had admired it from afar for a while, but seeing him up close and being able to gawk without anyone noticing had her sighing in appreciation. His arms were large, but she knew it was from hefting heavy cartons and crates at the pub. His legs were firm, but from running on the beach. She could not imagine him in a gym, preening as he ran on a treadmill. No, he had the easy grace of a man comfortable with his body and not giving a damn what anyone else thought.

As Brogan turned, he caught Ginny's eyes lifting to his and he grinned, realizing she had been checking him out. Chuckling as he walked back, he planted his fists on his hips and said, "Like anything?"

Red-faced at being caught, she shrugged nonchalantly. "You're alright, I guess," she joked.

"If I was interested in a huge, muscular, well-built man with gorgeous blue eyes and interesting tattoos."

Plopping down beside her, his back against the same railing, he propped his forearms on his bent knees. "Guess it's a good thing you find my tattoos interesting."

Grinning, she said, "I do. But, then, I find all of you interesting."

At that, his smile dropped as he turned to stare into her face, finding nothing but sincerity. Shaking his head, he said, "Can't imagine why. I'm just me."

Twisting so she could hold his gaze, she placed her hand on his arm, feeling the tension in his muscles underneath her fingertips. "Brogan…you're unique. And I like that. I like you…just the way you are."

Cocking his head to the side, he watched as she pursed her lips for a moment before she continued.

"I like that there's no bullshit with you. What you see is what you get. Quiet strength. Character. A good soul."

"You see all that?" he asked, lifting one eyebrow.

Nodding slowly, she said, "Yeah."

They sat, side by side, shoulders touching, as the sun sunk lower in the sky over the water. Where his shoulder contacted hers burned warm, the tingling moving all the way down his arm. "Don't know anyone's ever seen me...not like that," he said softly, his voice carried away in the breeze.

"It's hard when you have to be tough," she said. "You're the eldest in your family...the one others rely on. I'm a cop, with a certain persona I need to portray."

Nodding, Brogan agreed. "You're right. That makes it hard sometimes. Hard to let someone in. Hard to just let your guard down."

"Hard to trust," added Ginny.

He cut his eyes over while keeping his face forward, seeing her blink as though tearful. As the sun continued to create a colorful panorama in front of them he said softly, "You can trust me, Ginny."

She swallowed deeply as she nodded, but no other words came.

Nervous, terrified of making the wrong move, he lifted his arm and settled it across her shoulders, allowing her to lean her head against his chest. The scent of her floral shampoo wafted by and he inhaled just to hold on to her fragrance.

As the sun finally settled into the horizon, a slight chill swept by and Ginny shivered. Brogan curved his arm, pulling her in closer while rubbing his hand up and down her arm. He knew the chivalrous action was to suggest they leave, but his heart screamed for them to stay. Stay connected, touching, holding.

"Ginny, I wanted to ask you something," he said, finally, gathering his courage. "I was wondering if you'd give me a suggestion for a counselor to talk to at the Mental Health group." He noticed as her breathing changed and plunged ahead before he lost his courage. "I'd like to...uh...I guess talk to someone."

Ginny nodded, not trusting her voice.

He continued, "I figure it's time I got some help with…well, some of the shit I came back with."

Swallowing deeply, she leaned forward so she could twist around to face him, her eyes full of understanding. "I'd be happy to," she smiled.

Brogan watched her shiver once more. "I hate like hell to leave, but you're chilly." Standing, he gently pulled her up, not letting go of her hand until she was inside his truck.

At her front door, she turned, her eyes imploring. "Do you want to come in?"

Lifting his face, searching the heavens for the right answer, he dropped his chin and pierced her with his intense blue eyes. "The answer is yes. I want to come in. But I'm not going to." Seeing her about to protest, he added, "I want to see you again…soon."

Tilting her head, she said, "How soon?"

"Is tomorrow too soon?"

Laughing, she said, "No. Tomorrow is perfect." Digging in her purse, she pulled out a card for the Eastern Shore Mental Health Clinic. "Here. I hope they help. I…well, I'm seeing them too. I see a woman named June, but if you prefer a man, I know one there named Charles who is supposed to be really good as well." Holding his gaze as she smiled up into his face, she added, "Maybe there's hope for both of us."

Leaning down, he kissed her lightly. Just a taste…just enough to remind him this was real and not a dream.

10

Brogan lifted the heavy crate of bottles from the storeroom, carrying them with ease toward the bar. His heart as light as his mind, he performed the mundane tasks to get ready for the day. He still felt the sensation of Ginny's lips on his, soft and gentle, smooth and silky. With just the hint of chocolate from their dessert.

"What the hell is that noise?" Aiden yelled from the front door.

Brogan looked up suddenly, his eyes narrowed as he spied Aiden and Katelyn walking toward him. Katelyn's smile spread across her pretty face and Aiden's shit-eatin' grin almost matched hers. "What? What noise?"

"Brother dear," Katelyn purred, "I do believe I heard whistling when I came into the pub."

"Sounded more like a fuckin' cat howling, if you ask me," Aiden quipped, walking behind the bar.

Cuffing Aiden on the back of the head, Brogan groused, "No one asked you, asshole."

Rolling her eyes at both of them, Katelyn hopped up

on a barstool and said, "So tell me about your date last night with Ginny."

"How'd you know about a date?"

Throwing her head back in laughter, Katelyn's blue eyes danced. "Seriously? Grant found out because Ginny said she wouldn't be available last night unless it was an emergency and that was unusual for her nights off. So, he pressed and she confessed she had a date, which he then told Jillian. Jillian was looking for me, but found Gareth instead, so she told him to tell me to call her. But he was curious, so she told him first... which kind of pisses me off, that he knew before I did. But anyway, he told me last night."

Brogan's hard stare pierced her, but she was unshakeable. Instead, she just perched on her stool, a wide-eyed, expectant look on her face. Dropping his head, he said, "What the hell's wrong with this town? Ain't nobody got nothin' better to do than get all up in people's business?"

"Nope," Aiden and Katelyn said in unison.

Rubbing his hand over his head, Brogan lifted his head, but his retort died on his lips as Katelyn's hand snaked across the bar and gently squeezed his. Sighing, he said, "Not much to tell. The Sunset Restaurant was having some kinda shindig and was too crowded, so I figured the date was over before it got started. But she ordered some food from Bill's Takeout and we went to the pier."

Katelyn's mouth fell open, but no words came out and, as Brogan glanced at Aiden, he caught his brother smiling. Shrugging, he added, "It was nice."

Expecting Aiden to make a brash comment, he was

stunned when he just walked by, slapped him on the back, and said, "Good job, Bro. Sounds like it was perfect."

Brogan watched as Aiden picked up the now-empty crate and walked toward the back. Feeling the squeeze on his hand again, he turned and looked at Katelyn.

"Aiden's right, you know. It does sound perfect."

Nodding slowly, he said, "Yeah. She's special. What the hell she sees in me, I don't know, but I'm just glad she does."

"Do you remember how you said that when you came back from the war, I was different? After Philip died, I seemed to die as well?" Seeing Brogan's surprised nod, she continued, "You were different too. You were always the serious brother, but when you came back, you were positively somber. You didn't smile. You didn't joke. You didn't drink. You were…well, different."

Saying nothing, Brogan listened, knowing every word she said was true.

"We were all worried, but you came back, worked hard here to continue to make the pub a success, and we all got used to the new Brogan." She slid from the stool and walked over to him. Lifting on her toes, she kissed his cheek. "I love you, but want you to be happy…not just to exist. And I think Ginny can make you very happy. In fact, I think you can make her happy too." With that, she headed out the door.

Ginny walked into Mitch's office and got right to the point. "Got a smudge print on Celia Ring's window."

Mitch's eyes jumped to the report she laid on his desk as she continued to speak. "It's not identifiable, but it does corroborate her story of someone looking in. She has a lawn care service, so it could have come from them, so I know it's not conclusive, but it still lets us know someone was at the window. We know that peeping toms can escalate. It's not just harmless pranks, but is behavior that can lead to more invasive and intrusive actions."

Holding up his hand, Mitch halted her explanations. "I know and I agree."

Letting out a breath she had not realized she had been holding, she nodded. "Thanks, Chief."

Continuing to pin her with his gaze, he said, "It's none of my business, but you seem particularly… moved…by the subject."

Blinking, she sat up straighter, swallowing deeply. She opened her mouth in denial, but clamped it shut quickly. Looking past his shoulder, focusing on a spot on the wall, she said, "No one has a right to invade someone's privacy and…well…no one."

Mitch nodded and changed the subject. "Keep up the good work, Ginny, and let us know what you find."

Grateful for the reprieve, she stepped out of his office. Leaning her back against the cool wall, she closed her eyes for a moment, willing her heart to slow its pounding. After a moment, she sucked in a cleansing breath and walked out of the station.

That afternoon, Ginny walked into the high school with

Grant, making their way to the office. After greeting the principal, he took them into a conference room where five young, teenage boys sat. Their expressions ranged from frightened to cocky and Ginny narrowed her attention on the cocky ones. The principal explained that it had come to their attention that the boys were passing around cell phone pictures of a girl from a neighboring school.

Ginny took the proffered phone and skimmed through the photographs before turning back to the boys. Fighting the urge to smack the smirk off the face of one of them, she leaned down and said, "Do you realize this is illegal? Do you realize that you not only face expulsion, but also arrest?"

Two of the boys grew wide-eyed and, for an instant, she thought one of them might throw up. Turning her attention to the one still smirking, she got in his face. "You think this is funny? You have no idea how much trouble you're in."

"Oh, yeah, well that slut sent me those pictures," he argued, holding her stare.

"Really? For your information, it's illegal to share those, send those, and have those on your phone." Seeing the first glimmer of doubt in his eyes, she continued, her voice raising with each word, "And, furthermore, a couple of those pictures were not taken by the person in them—especially the one in the locker room, so after the principal calls your parents, I suggest they call a lawyer, 'cause I'm confiscating the phones as evidence and we'll be obtaining a search warrant for other sites you may have uploaded these pictures to."

By now, four of the boys were staring wide eyed,

their gazes shooting between Grant and Ginny. As the principal took the boys to his office, the last one turned and smiled at her, his eyes roaming from the top of her head to her boots and back up again, lingering on her breasts.

Seeing red, she stepped forward, her body tense with adrenaline. Grant put his hand on her shoulder, his fingers squeezing slightly, causing her body to halt. Silence enveloped the two of them as they stood in the now empty room. Blinking several times as she breathed deeply, she jerked her head in a short nod before they left the room.

Once inside their SUV, Grant called it in before pulling out onto the road. No words had been spoken, but as he opened his mouth, she jumped in, "I know. I'm working on it."

Nodding slowly, he replied, "If you ever need someone else to talk to—"

Snorting, she interrupted, "You volunteering to be my counselor now?"

"Hell, no." After a moment, he said, "But, I'm glad you're seeing one."

Ginny peered out the window at the scenery flying by, but her thoughts were across the world in Afghanistan. Grimacing as she attempted to block out the images, she whispered, "Yeah."

"You're doing really well," the counselor encouraged, peering at her over her glasses.

Ginny nodded toward June, her chest tight from

reliving the anger, but she knew she was on the road to finally gaining some peace. "Thank you. It's not easy."

"Counseling isn't always easy," June commented. "While the end goal is to find a way to deal with things that have happened, the process can be very painful." After a moment of silence, she asked, "How are you doing with the coping mechanisms?"

"Mostly…I run."

June stared at her for a moment, but when no other reply came, she asked, "Have you found anyone in town that you feel would understand your burden? I know that you did not find that with your family, but since you've moved here, any friends you can talk to?"

Shrugging, Ginny replied, "I'm trying." Since June remained silent, she continued, "It's not easy. I'm a cop."

"So, tell me how that affects you."

"I've got a duty to the community…I want to be friendly, but it's sometimes hard to make friends. I've only been in town for two years and it's taken me a while to fit in. And, hell, being the only female cop around isn't easy. I've got to be just as tough, just as dedicated, just as committed as my fellow officers and yet, not seen as some hard-nosed bitch. My time in the military police gave me the balls to do the job, but in the civilian world, in a little town, it's a hard line to walk."

"And your relationships?"

"I'm good with the guys, which might surprise you considering what I'm dealing with. But I trust the men I work with. And the American Legion and the Auxiliary that we've started have given me a sense of fellowship. Coaching gives me a chance to work with some young girls and maybe help make some of them stronger."

Snorting, she added, "And it seems that I'm being *inducted* into the *Katelyn, Jillian, and Tori club*."

June laughed, "Oh, lordy! I remember those girls from when I worked at the high school. If they're including you, you'll have lots of friends to talk to." Sobering, she said, "Do you plan on talking to them about what happened to you when you were in the service?"

Ginny looked down at her lap, pondering June's question. "I don't know," she finally admitted. "My family certainly didn't take it well when they found out."

A soft look on her face, June replied, "Our families are sometimes our biggest critics when they should be our biggest supporters."

As Ginny walked out into the sunshine, she slid her sunglasses on her face and thought of June's words. *Yes, they are.*

Sitting in the bleachers, Ginny cheered on the AL boys, watching one round third as he headed toward home plate. Her gaze stopped on third base, lingering on Brogan as he coached. The normally stoic man was animated on the field—cheering and encouraging every player. A smile slipped across her lips as she remembered the touch of his mouth on hers. She had not seen him yesterday, as she had hoped, with work interfering. But he had sent her a text last night and asked her to come to Finn's for lunch after the games. Still smiling, she realized the bleachers around her were silent.

Blinking out of her reverie, she observed Tori, Jillian, Katelyn, Jade, and Belle all staring…and smiling. "What?" she asked, her voice more strident than she intended.

Laughter all around had her blushing, as Katelyn shoulder bumped her. "Nothing. We're just glad to see that smile on your face, that's all."

"Humph," Ginny groused, embarrassed to have been caught with a teenage, dreamy expression on her face.

Before she had a chance to deny the cause of her smile, the boys' game was over and the bleachers began to empty. As she stepped off the last step, James approached, his jaw tight, his normally easy-going expression buried behind a scowl.

"Ginny, can I have a word?"

His surfer, blond looks no longer held her attention now that her eyes were filled with Brogan. Curious, she nodded and followed him to the side of the bleachers. "What can I do for you?"

He smiled but she immediately noticed it did not reach his eyes. "Well, look honey, here's the thing—"

Her hand moved upward as she halted his words. "Honey?"

Reddening, he said, "No, don't take that wrong. It's just a saying…you know, just a greeting."

"James, I would prefer if you do not call me *honey*."

His smile dropped as he took a step forward. "Okay, Officer Spencer…is that better?

She stared at him for a moment until he squirmed slightly before replying, "If this is official, then yes, Officer Spencer is correct. If this is just a friendly conversation, then Ginny is appropriate."

He rubbed his hand over the back of his neck. "I seem to be stepping in it this morning."

"James, how can I help you?" Wanting to get to Brogan before he left to take some of the kids home, she hoped James would begin talking.

"Okay, here's the thing. It seems some of my wrestlers got into a little bit of trouble and I was wondering if you could help them out."

A snake of nerves crawled up her spine, but she kept her face impassive. "Trouble?"

Chuckling, he scuffed one shoe on the dirt as he continued, "They had some girls' pictures on their phones and got suspended. The girls sent the pictures and my boys didn't know they were doing anything wrong when they passed them around. You know how boys can be."

"No, enlighten me," she said, her voice cool and steady.

"Come on, Ginny. They're horny teenagers. Any chance they can get to look at a naked girl, they will. It's normal, teenage boy behavior."

A lifted eyebrow was the only response he received, so he continued. "If the girls didn't want the guys staring at them, they should have never sent the pictures."

"And if the girls were unaware the pictures were being taken? If they were taken against their will?"

Eyes wide, James scoffed, "I know some of those girls and, believe me, they'll pose for anyone, anytime."

Heart racing, Ginny forced herself to breathe slowly, struggling to maintain control. "Let me educate you, James. I saw the photographs. Many were not taken with the girls' knowledge or permission. What the boys did was not just *adolescent behavior*, which is often a fallacy perpetuated by our society. A woman is not an object, but a human, with the right to privacy. Those boys broke the law and the principal has assured me the expulsion will stay until they have their day in court." By the time she finished, she was shaking.

James' face turned red as he stepped forward menacingly. "You can't do this. My wrestling team will not lose because of some girls who just want guys to drop at their feet. It's an attention getting ploy—"

"You need to back off—"

A roar sounded to the side as Brogan charged in between Ginny and James. Quick on her feet, Ginny whirled around, placing herself in between the two men.

"Brogan!" she shouted. Repeating herself several times, she waited for his attention to turn from a murderous look toward James down to hers, concern now on his face.

"Brogan," she said, softer this time. "I've got this. Don't do anything that'll make me have to arrest you." Looking to the side, she saw a circle of their friends gathered, shielding any of the children from witnessing the scene. Her body quaking, she turned back to James, "You may think what they did was nothing, but I assure you, to those girls, it's horrific." Her voice broke on the last word as she swallowed deeply, her heart pounding out of her chest.

James stared a long minute at her before turning and pushing his way through the crowd. Ginny stood ramrod stiff, her gaze sweeping past Aiden, Mitch, and Grant, before the women led them away.

She knew Brogan was still at her back—she felt the heat from his body radiating toward her. Dropping her chin to her chest, she said, "Brogan, go home."

"No," came the rumble from behind. "I'm not leaving you."

11

Ginny stared out the window of Brogan's old truck as they rumbled over the gravel and sand driveway, stopping at a small beach house. Neither spoke as they sat in the cab, the sound of the surf crashing upon the sand in the distance, the only noise.

Finally, Brogan reached over and placed his hand on hers and said, "Wanna take a walk?"

Nodding in reply, she opened her door and hopped out, meeting him at the front. He held her gaze and said, "I'd really like to open the door for you when we're out together…that's how my Mama and Grandmama taught me. But, I get you're kinda…uh…raw right now. But maybe in the future…"

Silently, she nodded again, touched by the vulnerability she saw in his eyes.

They crossed the dunes in silence, Brogan's fingers twitching to comfort her. Battling with himself, he finally reached over and grabbed her hand as they began walking along the stretch of beach. Nervous, he let out a long breath as she moved her fingers so they were linked with his. Right...it felt right. Recognizing she needed time to process the morning's events, his lips curved slightly at the corners just knowing she chose to be with him.

After a few minutes, he moved to sit down on the sand, gently pulling her down next to him. They watched the seagulls flying about, occasionally diving into the surf before rising out with a fish in their beaks.

"I was naïve," she began, her words breaking the quiet.

He turned to look at her but she kept her eyes on the bay, so he followed suit and faced the water again.

Licking her lips, Ginny said, "My dad was Army. My grandfather was Army. Both career...stayed in thirty years before retiring. My brother joined the Navy after college and became a pilot. My mom was a true, red-white-and-blue Army wife. Packed us up every move, handled life when Dad was deployed, and when Dad said, 'Jump', she asked 'How high?'"

She looked down at their linked fingers and realized it had been a long time since she sat with a man like this. Somehow, that small gesture touched her heart. Sighing, she continued, "I never considered any other career than the military. I planned on college, but when I was in high school, my brother was killed in a plane crash." She felt the involuntary squeeze of his fingers, but plunged ahead, "I joined the Army as soon as I graduated from high school and made it to the Military Police. I think I just wanted to do something that made me feel close to my family and make my dad proud."

"And was he?"

Nodding, she said, "Yeah. He never saw any reason for me to go to college and when I graduated from basic training and from my MOS school, it was the proudest I've ever seen him be of me."

The surf continued its undulations, washing up on the shore and then back out to sea, as they sat, each to their own thoughts.

"I liked the Army…I like the job I did. It felt important and I was good at it. I was deployed to Afghanistan…to Kandahar. I was mostly on patrol or on gate duty, searching incoming vehicles for bombs." Seeing him in her peripheral vision as he nodded, she added, "I guess you spent some time there too."

Another nod was her answer and she continued. "I thought I understood people. The military is mostly men, especially over there. But I was treated with respect. Got along great with the others in my squad and platoon. There were only a few of us women in the MP, but we worked just as hard as the men. We worked hard, played hard, and had each others' backs."

Turning toward him, her voice imploring, she said, "That was the most important thing over there—having each others' backs. That could be the difference between making it out alive or coming home in a body bag."

At the pleading look in her eyes, he nodded his agreement. "You're right. Having the backs of your squad could make all the difference." He watched as her lips pinched and, with a quick, jerking nod, she faced the bay again. "I take it, someone broke that trust?"

Blowing out a long breath, she nodded. "Yeah…a lot of someones."

Brogan gave her time to gather her thoughts, not wanting to rush her story, but could feel his anger building. A slow ember began in his stomach and spread outward, wanting to pound anyone who had ever hurt her. The thought that it was fellow soldiers, made his vision blur. Careful to keep his breathing steady, he sat quietly.

"It seemed some of our platoon thought it was funny to rig up cameras in the women's shower—"

Ginny felt the immediate tension radiating from Brogan's body next to hers. She halted, uncertain if she should continue.

"Go on," his low voice growled, then he added, "Please."

Clearing her throat, she said, "It went on for a few weeks. Not just the shower I used, but several of the women's showers." With her eyes closed tightly, she relived the memory of when she first found out and her pulse raced. Willing it to slow, she said, "Come to find out, the cameras had actually been placed there by a woman who agreed to do it for the men. The pictures and videos began to circulate and it took a little while for us to find out. By then, there was a dedicated website where the photographs ended up."

Looking at their linked fingers, she slid hers back into her lap, wiping her sweaty palms on her jean shorts. "At first, it was hard to get anyone to take our complaint seriously. Our sergeant blew us off…of course, we later found out he was just as guilty as anyone else. We kept going up the chain, trying to get someone to listen to us. I took the lead in ferreting out the guilty ones, but by that time I had alienated almost everyone on my squad. The whole dining facility would silence as I walked in. My bunk was wrecked more times than I can remember. The picture of my brother was stolen." With that admission, her voice hitched as she battled tears, but she plunged forward, afraid that if she stopped the story, she might never be brave enough to face him again.

"I was called in and reprimanded for stirring up trouble. I was told that men will just be men and that this was normal behavior. That they were just blowing off steam and needed the diversion. I was told I was making a mountain out of a molehill. I was threatened…even received a note threatening me with sexual assault if I did not quit *making a stink*." Snorting, she shook her head. "My body, and the bodies of many women, were plastered all over the Internet, and I was *making a stink*."

"Oh, fuck, Ginny," Brogan breathed, no longer willing to sit by, not speaking. He wrapped his arm across her shoulders and pulled her into his side, kissing the top of her head. "Oh, fuck, I'm so sorry."

"It got so bad that some of the other women begged me to drop it. Let it go. They just wanted to forget, said my attempt to get retribution was making it hard for them. So, in the end, I had few friends."

Sighing, she continued, "It finally took one of the other women, an officer, to be exact, who had connections way up, to get the lid blown off the situation. It hit the news back in the States and suddenly it couldn't be shoved under the carpet anymore. A bunch of fellow soldiers were now facing charges. Some were arrested, some were dishonorably discharged, some received reprimands, and some escaped censure. All in all, it was a fucking mess and I seemed to be at the center. I was sent home to a base in the states to finish out my last months of service, for my own protection, but everyone knew. I went from wanting a career in the Army to only serving one tour and then getting the hell out."

"Where did you go?"

Another snort escaped as she confessed, "I made the huge mistake of going home."

Now that she was leaning against his chest, he could not see her face. Needing to peer into her eyes, he pulled back slightly as he craned his head to see her expression. She looked up, her dark eyes full of sadness, sending a sharp stab of pain to his heart. "Why was that a mistake?"

"Because I was a failure."

"Failure? Ginny, honey, you're not a failure. You're a goddamn hero," he growled, his voice rough with emotion.

Ginny stared at him for a moment, realizing that Brogan calling her *honey* only slid warmth through her, unlike when James said it. With James, it was a throwaway, meant to placate, but with Brogan's gravelly words that sent shivers of pleasure down her spine, she felt the endearment and wished they were talking about anything other than what they were.

"From my father's perspective, I was a complete and total failure. He met me at the door and said I had one week to find a new job and move on. In no uncertain terms, he labeled me a disgrace to the military and to our family." Swallowing hard, she added, "He even said that if God had been merciful, my brother would be living and I would be the one with the honorable death in combat."

"Oh, fuckin' hell, no!" Brogan exploded, his body vibrating with anger.

Ginny watched in fascination as this large man vibrated in rage for her. He jostled her as he jumped up and stalked a few feet away, his hands on his hips with his legs planted apart, staring at the bay. She stayed silent for a few minutes, waiting to see what he would do. Swallowing audibly, she sat staring at his broad back, the muscles in his body taut.

Brogan stared out, not seeing the beauty of the beach, his eyes only filled with the ugliness of her words. Family was everything—at least to a MacFarlane. Dropping his chin to his chest, he felt the sting near his heart once more.

Whirling around, with surprising agility for such a large man, Ginny watched in fascination as Brogan's blue eyes pinned her to the spot. "No fuckin way, Ginny, did your family turn against you. No fuckin' way." His voice was so shattered as to how family could turn their backs on a daughter, his anguish evident.

Standing, she brushed the sand from the seat of her shorts before walking toward him, only stopping when her toes were right at his. Not touching him, she lifted her head and looked in his eyes. "I left home the next day. My parents have not been in touch for the past five years. I moved in with some people I found on Craig's List who needed a roommate and, with my Army college fund, I got my degree in Police Science. Finished it in three years even with working almost full time. I've been here for the past two years. Never looked back... not at the Army and not at my family."

"What about the American Legion? Isn't that a constant reminder?"

"I wondered about that," she admitted, still holding his gaze. Shrugging, she said, "I met a lot of really great people in the Army. I got close to the other women who refused to give up the fight." Seeing his confusion, she added, "Yeah, some of the women were scared and decided to drop the pursuit of justice. But, there was a small group of us that kept fighting until we won."

"You should have been fighting the enemy," Brogan said, his voice still laced with rage, "not your own platoon."

She agreed, but knew no words were necessary, so she just continued to hold his eyes, refusing to look away. If he held censure there, she wanted to see it. But, all she saw was concern.

Brogan slowly lifted his hands and placed them gently on her shoulders, drawing her forward until her face planted into his chest and his arms wrapped around her, pulling her tight. His mind filled with his own memories of a good platoon, a good squad, but he also knew his share of assholes, some hiding behind rank. The idea of Ginny facing the abuse that had been heaped on her rocked him and he locked his knees to keep from falling to the ground, taking her with him. "God, you're the bravest woman I know."

Ginny kept her face buried as she felt the softness of his t-shirt against her cheek and the strength of his heartbeat pounding against her ear. Her arms curved around his waist, the breadth of him wide enough that her hands barely clasped. It had been a long time since she had been enveloped in a man's embrace and she wanted to curl up with him, warm and cocooned from the outside world. His scent filled her nostrils as she breathed him in deeply.

Reality quickly crashed in upon her—there was one more story to tell. And this one might make the difference to the man holding her in his arms. Leaning her head back again, she said, "There's something else. Something else that happened."

Brogan peered into her eyes, the unknown depths staring back. He felt, as well as heard, her quickened breath as she moved out of his arms and stood a few feet away. Ice cold water flowed through his veins as he waited, unmoving, willing some of his strength to go her way.

Sucking in a deep breath, she plunged ahead before she lost her courage. "I was assaulted...not raped...but assaulted by a fellow service member. He came in when I was sleeping...pinned me to my bunk...and pressed his erection against me. He wore a mask, but I recognized him. His eyes were greenish-brown and he had a little scar through his eyebrow. So even though he thought he was hidden, I knew who he was. He squeezed my breasts as he rubbed himself on me and told me that if I ever told anyone, he'd kill me."

"Jesus, Ginny," Brogan ground out, his heart aching for her and yet uncertain how to help.

She turned, facing him, the sea breeze whipping her dark hair about her head, a storm beginning to form in the distant sky. "I need you to know before you speak too highly of me...I never told anyone about what he did. I was so tired of it all…ready to be discharged…so demoralized…I simply could not fight one more fight."

His eyebrows lowered, as his jaw hardened to steel. "What makes you think I wouldn't speak highly of you?"

Swallowing back a sob, she said, "Because I gave up. I knew who he was and I never said anything. I was a cop, even in the Army. I should have stopped him. Now, for all I know, he's still out there, assaulting women, and I was a chicken-shit who did nothing."

Brogan reached out once more and pulled her sobbing body into his, cradling the back of her head with his large hand, while his other arm banded around her back. Feeling her shake against him, he felt as though they were still not close enough. Bending, he scooped her into his arms, stalking through the wind over the dune, not stopping until he landed on the front porch of his weather-beaten house. Bending, he threw open the door, kicking it shut behind them with his shoe.

Already having made up his mind, he continued to stalk down the short hall, passing the one bathroom and entering his bedroom. His bed was unmade, but clean, and he lowered her onto the mattress, following right along with her. Pulling up the covers, he wrapped his entire body around hers, forming a cocoon that he hoped protected her from the memories of the past.

Holding her, pressed against his chest, making soothing noises, he felt her sobs subside and her breathing even out as sleep claimed her. Lying in his bed with her in his arms, the tightness in his chest finally eased.

12

A knock on the front door had Brogan cursing under his breath, hoping whoever was there would leave. Another knock killed that hope. Sliding away from Ginny's sleeping body and out of bed, he walked quietly to the door, throwing it open and observing Grant and Jillian on the porch.

"Yeah, I've got her and she's fine."

Snorting, Grant said, "Hell, man, we didn't even ask anything." Wrapping his arm around Jillian, "Glad she's with you."

Stepping out on the porch, he pulled the door shut behind him. "She had shit she needed to get out and I'm damn glad I was the one there."

"She means something to you." Grant did not ask but, rather, stated the obvious.

Nodding, Brogan replied with a simple, "Yeah." Then, as an afterthought, he added, "Normally, I wouldn't say shit, but since she's one of your partners, I'll let you know that she's fine. Like all of us, got some stuff to deal with, but she's good…and I'm going to make sure she stays that way." Focusing intently on Jillian, he said, "It'd be good if she had some female support too. I'll have a word with Katelyn. She doesn't need anyone fussing, but I think it's been awhile since she's had girlfriends. Y'all might've driven me bat-shit crazy when I was a kid, but I know you'll take care of her too."

As Grant tucked Jillian in closer to his side, she said, "No problem, Brogan. We all really like her and we'll be there for her."

Nodding, he finished up, "Now, if there ain't anything else, I'd like to get back to her. She's sleeping right now and from what she says, that doesn't come easily. I want to be there when she wakes up." With a head jerk, he turned and walked back through his front door, missing the huge grin Grant and Jillian shared between themselves.

Blinking, Ginny tried to discern where she was. Her body was wrapped in warmth, a heavy weight across her legs. Her hand lay on a broad chest and as she lifted her head, she was greeted by a pair of sparkling, blue eyes. Blinking a few more times to bring everything into focus, a hand reached up and pushed messy tendrils out of her face before cupping her jaw.

"Brogan," she breathed, just before their conversation slammed back into her.

Feeling her tense, his deep voice rumbled, "Oh, no. You're not going back there. No shame…not with me.

No guilt…not with me. And, sure as hell, no regret…not with me. You gave it all to me and I'm gonna help you carry it, honey."

Unsure of his meaning, she hesitated slightly in silent question.

"I wasn't kidding when I said you were the strongest person I know. What you endured…what you fought for. You're fuckin' amazing. You're getting counseling and are right back in a career helping others when you could have said *fuck it* to everyone. And," he added leaning so close his breath whispered across her face, "you are not in this alone. Not anymore."

"I've carried it alone for a really long time—"

"I get that, but no more. You've got me and I'll help you move to a place where it won't hurt so much, if you'll let me."

Reaching up, she settled her palm against his face, the beard stubble rough underneath her fingers as she moved her thumb over his cheek. The worry creases in her face eased and a small smile curved her lips. "I'll let you," she whispered, realizing for the first time in years she did not feel alone.

He kissed her, cupping her cheek, moving his lips over hers, relishing the taste and texture of the petal softness. The desire to claim was strong. The desire to protect screamed at him. The desire to right all the wrongs she had suffered claimed him as they let words slip away, the only sound was the little moans from her lips and the deep growl in his chest.

Time stood still as they lay tangled together, lips locked as they explored each other's mouths. Brogan fought the urge to allow his hands to roam across her breasts, wanting to focus on her delectable lips, but almost lost his resolve as she pushed her hips forward, pressing against his straining erection.

"Babe, I want you so bad, but I want it to be a celebration of us...not a response to all the stuff you've been through."

Ginny knew he was right and flopped on her back, her kiss swollen lips still tingling. Smiling, she nodded. "Yeah, you're right."

"Come on, let me fix you breakfast." He rose from the bed and took her hand, gently pulling her along with him. Ginny made a detour to his bathroom as he headed to the kitchen.

A few minutes later, she entered the room, viewing a sight that would make any woman swoon—a bare chested Brogan, standing in his kitchen turning sizzling, aromatic bacon while a petite, black cat swirled about his legs. Before she had a chance to speak, she heard him softly say, "Come on, MB. Give me a minute and, once it cools, I'll give you some bacon, too."

"You have a cat?" Ginny asked, unnecessarily, bending to pet her. "Oh, my goodness, how sweet!"

"She was just a stray I found on the beach," he explained. "Came here and was so hungry and scraggly. I fed her and she stayed attached to me."

"What's her name?"

Brogan grinned, a slight blush staining his cheeks. "MB."

Still kneeling, she looked up, her brows furrowed. "Embee?"

"It's the initials," he explained. "M and B, together...MB."

Still petting the loving cat that was now preening under her ministrations, she looked up again and asked, "What does MB stand for?"

Blushing redder now, Brogan tried to turn back to the bacon, but she was relentless. "Oh, no you don't. What did the big, bad Brogan name his cat?"

"Midnight Beauty," he mumbled.

Standing, she walked over, placing her hands on his waist, turning him slightly so he was facing her. "Oh, that's so sweet," she said, her smile wide.

Shrugging, he admitted, "She was so straggly, I thought she might not feel very pretty. I guess I figured if she had a pretty name, she would like it."

Ginny's mirth slipped away as her heart filled, her fingers digging into his waist slightly. Blinking back tears as her eyes drank in the enigmatic man standing in front of her, she whispered, "Midnight Beauty…that's perfect."

The room was full, with the addition of the local law enforcement from the Virginia area of the Eastern Shore peninsula. Monthly, the area sheriffs and police chiefs rotated group meetings. Today, they gathered in the Baytown Police Department and included Colt Hudson, Sheriff of North Heron, Hannah Freeman, the Easton Police Chief, Liam Sullivan, the Accawmacke County Sheriff, Wyatt Newman, the Manteague Police Chief, and Dylan Hunt, Seaside Police Chief. As Mitch brought the first part of the meeting to a close, he turned it over to Ginny.

"I just wanted to let you know that I've been doing some research on peeping toms and escalating behavior. I wanted all of you to be aware." Receiving interested nods from all, she flashed information on the wall screen as she began speaking.

"The clinical term for this type of abnormal sexual behavior is voyeurism. It goes way beyond just a man wanting to get off by looking at a woman as she changes clothes or sleeps. And most importantly, it can, and does, escalate. Criminal profiling studies and researchers have learned almost all rapists and serial killers started their criminal activities with various levels of window peeping. To quote Vernon Geberth, author of *A Sex-Related Homicide and Death Investigation*, 'not all voyeurs become serial rapists or killers - but all rapists have been involved in window peeping as they criminally evolved.'"

"Holy shit," Sam cursed. Ginny looked his way, then watched the others, their eyes pinned to her data on the screen.

Continuing, she said, "Many sexual predators report that window peeping was a routine behavior but then they needed more enticing behaviors to become sexually stimulated. They are likely to escalate to burglary when residents aren't home, to cat burglary when people are home, and eventually to sexual assault. The number one deterrent, believe it or not, is closed blinds or curtains on windows."

"That simple?" Grant asked. "I'm trying to remember if we close our blinds in the living room at night. I know we usually do in our bedroom, but if it's a hot night, Jillian will raise them so she can open the window."

Burt, looking concerned, added, "My wife and I always close the blinds as soon as the sun goes down."

Ginny nodded, "That's good and it's a good thing to teach your children."

Wide eyed, Grant shook his head. "Well, damn, we might as well live in a box."

Ginny continued, "Most voyeurs are men, who tend to be more visual when sexually stimulated. A voyeur is less likely to be caught than a rapist. It's easier to offend against multiple victims, or even the same victim, numerous times."

"I gotta ask a question," Wyatt interrupted. "We know rape is a crime of anger and control…it's not about sex. But for a voyeur, isn't it about sexual stimulation?"

"Good question," Ginny acknowledged. "A voyeur needs this kind of stimulation to become sexual. But as they need more and more stimulation to maintain or initiate sexual satisfaction, they can become angry. They feel a lack of control because they can't have or maintain an erection with just voyeurism. So, it can escalate to sexual contact and rape." Looking around the room, she reminded them, "Don't forget though, not all voyeurs become rapists. But some do."

Hannah spoke, "You would think that with the Internet porn sites, someone would no longer need to peek in windows."

Nodding, Ginny said, "I looked into that also. Usually voyeurs are users of Internet porn, but remember, it is still about control. Some people can go into a strip club and watch a woman dance and take her clothes off for money. That can turn most people on, but there's no control there. In fact, the woman is in control. A voyeur needs control."

Mitch took over as he looked to the other law enforcement personnel present and said, "I wanted you all in on this. Colt, we're in your county, so there's a good chance if we have an active voyeur, it may branch out into your district. And of course, as close as we all are, you should all be aware."

"I'm really sorry."

Ginny looked over at Sam, his face more ruddy than usual. Not saying anything, she let him continue when he was ready.

"I never should have said that some behavior should be excused simply because someone is a man. Wrong is wrong. Peeking in someone's window is wrong." Blowing out a breath, "Sometimes I open my mouth and can't believe the shit coming out."

At that, a laugh escaped and Ginny said, "Apology accepted."

Arriving at the Baytown Elementary School, the two officers went inside to meet Jade. She met them in the counselor's office, her face red with anger.

"Jade, what's up?" Ginny asked.

After sitting, Jade said, "I've got a student that has reported that her neighbor watches her from his window. She says he watches her and her friends when they're in the yard playing. She said he is real friendly, described as a nice, old man. Then she said, when her older sister lays out in the sun in the back yard, the man is doing things."

Eyes narrowed, Ginny questioned, "Did she describe what she meant by doing things?"

Jade looked at Sam and blushed, but forged ahead. "It seems there is a treehouse in her backyard and when she's in it, she can see her neighbor at his window and she said his hands are down his pants."

At that comment, Sam leaned back as he said, "Oh, lordy."

"To be honest, what she said was he took his thingie out of his pants and played with it, using his hands."

Rubbing his hands over his face, Sam said, "Ms. Lyons, I know this was disturbing to the youngster, but without sounding crude, it's not illegal for a man to…uh—"

"What my fellow officer is politely trying to say, is that a man has a legal right to masterbate in his own home."

Blushing more, Jade nodded, "Oh, I know. But then she said that she was in her treehouse when her mother left for work and her sister was inside. She said he came through the hedge that divided their yards and went to her sister's room and peeked inside."

Ginny's eyes widened at that revelation and she heard Sam whistle under his breath. "Okay, Jade, you're right. That makes a difference."

They took down the information and with the counselor's promise to call the parents involved, they left to drive to the girl's home.

"You think this could be our peeping tom?" Sam asked. "Somehow I imagined someone younger."

"I don't know," she replied. "It would be nice if it was him, just so we would know we had caught the right person, but there's no way to tell right now. Let's go check him out."

Calling in the report, they headed back to Baytown, Ginny's mind full of what they might find.

13

"Mr. Barton? Mr. Al Barton?"

Brown eyes peered back at her from under bushy, grey eyebrows. "Yes?"

His one-word reply also formed a question, which wasn't surprising. Ginny was used to people being wary of the police knocking on their door.

"I'm Officer Spencer and this is Officer Stubbis. We'd like to ask you a few questions. May we come in?"

Nodding, the older man moved back, opening the door wider. Once inside, he led them to his living room, filled with comfortable furniture. Ginny's eyes quickly appraised the space, the length of the room allowing it to flow into a small dining area, with the kitchen at the back. There were three windows on the side of the house she was interested in and she noted a dining room chair was pulled from the table and placed near the window overlooking the house next door. The dining room table held a variety of papers, but she was unable to discern their contents.

"Will you have a seat?" Mr. Barton asked, indicating the sofa.

Thanking him, she and Sam sat down, watching Al as he took a seat in a chair opposite them.

"What can I help you with, Officers?"

"We're investigating a report that there was a man peering into the window of your neighbors...the Caldwells," Ginny began, lifting her hand to point to the house visible from the windows.

Bushy eyebrows lifted in unison, as Al responded in surprise. "You're kidding? I've never noticed anything untoward in this neighborhood. I know times are changing and we have so many rental visitors, but that's horrible."

"So, you haven't seen anything?" Sam asked.

"No, no," Al responded, shaking his head. "I admit that I'm often working, so I wouldn't have noticed much, but if I had, I would have reported it."

"Do you mind me asking about your work?"

Smiling slightly, Al said, "I'm retired, so I confess it's really a hobby...I draw. Mostly charcoal. I do sell some to a few dealers and even some for magazines."

Glancing over to the dining room table, Ginny inquired, "Is that where you work?"

Twisting his head to follow Ginny's line of vision, his voice tightened. "Uh, yes. Some. I also have a bedroom down the hall to the right that I use at times as well. This area has good light."

"What subjects do you draw?" she asked, suspicious that his chair was at the window instead of the table.

Lifting his shoulders in a shrug, Al said, "Oh, anything that catches my eye."

Sam leaned forward, a smile on his face, "Anything pretty around here catch your eye? Maybe from that window over there? Lots of pretty *scenery* around."

Ginny hid her smile, knowing Sam was using his *Aw shucks, good ol' boy* routine. And as usual, it worked.

Al seemed to relax slightly, saying, "Living here gives me lots of pretty *scenery*."

Sam's smile dropped off his face as he continued, "So, if I walk over to your drawing pad, am I going to see some of the pretty scenery from your neighbor's backyard? Such as their teenage daughter?"

Ginny watched Al's bushy eyebrows rise so high she wondered if they would disappear into his hairline.

Sputtering, Al exclaimed, "It's not illegal to draw what you see in public." Pinching his lips tightly for a moment, he then blurted, "And if girls are going to wander around in their bathing suits that leave nothing to the imagination, then that's on them."

"I'm curious about your chair angled at the window, facing your neighbor's back yard. Do you normally spend your time watching out that window? Maybe waiting for a glance to see your teenage neighbor who, being in her backyard that is reasonably hidden from view, is not technically in public?"

"No, that's not the way it is. Yes, I draw women… some with clothes and some nudes, but if I happen to see her lying in the sun, I use her as simply a way to study the female form. I use it in my art."

"Uh huh," Sam grunted. "Sure you don't get a little *excited* at the view?"

Al clamped his mouth shut and stared at the two officers. Taking a deep breath, he said, "I understand you have a concern about someone peeking into windows, but that was not me. And what I do inside my house is my business and definitely not breaking the law." Standing, he added, "I'd like to ask you to leave."

"And if we have a witness that the person peeking into the window was you?" Ginny prodded, standing as well.

Swallowing deeply, Al replied, "Then bring them forward and arrest me. If you have the proof." With that, he lifted his hand toward the front door.

Nodding, Ginny and Sam walked out and down the walk toward the neighbor's house. Once there, they began to scour the area outside the window. Ginny asked, "What do you think?"

"I think he's a dirty-old-man who gets his jollies by jacking off while watching his teenage neighbor out the window."

"So, you believe the child?" she asked, surprised by his response.

"Yes. That little girl's got no reason to make this shit up. But..." he leveled a stare her way, "Mr. Barton's right. There's no law being broken by him looking, drawing, or even masturbating to what he sees from the inside of his house."

Unable to find evidence, they nonetheless dusted the window and window-frame for prints before going to the front door to talk to the child's mother, who was expecting them.

Ginny did not need to turn around to know Al Barton was staring at her from his window. She could feel his eyes on the back of her head.

FINDING PEACE

Brogan walked to the Baytown High School football field and stood on the sidelines for a moment. He watched as James ran the boys through their paces. Any other time, his mind would go back to when he and the other original Baytown Boys played every sport they could. But not today...today was about the man in the middle of the field.

Not one to notice a man's appearance, he did catch that the cheerleaders near the bleachers were certainly noticing the coach. As James jogged back to grab waters for his players, he looked over at the girls and smiled. Huge. *What the fuck? A grown man flirting with a bunch of teenage girls?*

Even madder now than he was when he arrived, he waited until practice was over and the players had left. As James waved goodbye to the other coaches, he started walking toward his car, not noticing Brogan until he was almost upon him. Startled, he eyed the big man warily, but plastered on a white-toothed smile and said, "Hey, Brogan."

Brogan said nothing, but continued to stare, his arms crossed as he leaned with casual grace against the pole next to James' car.

"Listen, about yesterday," James began again. "I never should have approached Ginny. I was just upset over my guys being so stupid and now they're out for a lot of matches. This could really affect some of their futures, you know?"

If he was hoping to gain male camaraderie with Brogan, he was mistaken, squirming under Brogan's unrelenting gaze. "But, uh...I get that...uh...I shouldn't have—"

Pushing off the light pole, Brogan pulled himself up to his full height. "Let me tell you how this is going to go, asshole. You don't speak to Ginny. You don't talk about her. She's with me and I don't share."

James narrowed his eyes, a slow smile curving his lips. "Ginny know you're here? She know you've staked a claim? She doesn't seem like the type of woman who goes for the caveman act—"

Brogan's arm flashed out, his hand wrapped in James' collar as he whirled around and walked the man backward until he was pressed up against his car. "You're not a good listener, are you? You don't talk about her. And if I have to remind you one more time, you're not going to like the consequences."

Throwing his hands up, James cried out, "Chill, man, chill. Fine, I won't talk to her or about her."

Brogan let go reluctantly, the desire to send his fist into James' perfect smile almost overriding his good sense, his body quaking with the need to pound something. The thought of Ginny being disappointed in him had him stepping back, his gaze murderous. "You keep that promise asshole." With a head jerk, he turned and walked off, missing the venomous expression on James' face.

Brogan walked into his parents' house, the smell of home cooking tempting his nostrils. He realized that while working in a restaurant the odor of food wasn't always tantalizing, but his mother's Guinness stew always made his mouth water.

Stepping into the large kitchen, he wasn't surprised to see the whole family already gathered. His mother was at the stove stirring a large pot. Aiden, and their dad, Eric, along with Pops, were sitting in the den, arguing over sports. Katelyn was bent over pulling bread out of the oven and Gareth was at the counter, his eyes glued to her ass.

Walking by, Brogan shoulder bumped him, growling, "Eyes back in your head, man."

Gareth, without turning away from his view, replied, "Yeah, right."

Moving into the kitchen, he kissed his mom and sister before heading into the den to plop onto the end of the sofa.

Aiden turned toward him and said, "Hear you gave surfer-boy some love today."

Jerking his eyes over, Brogan said, "No one's business but my own."

Hands up, Aiden defended, "Hey, you got no problems with me. Ben dropped by and we had a good yuk over it. That prick's managed to grab up the last couple of girls I'd planned on asking out."

"You're just pissed because he's encroaching on your territory?" Katelyn asked, walking into the room, her arm around Gareth, pushing him into a chair and sitting in his lap.

"No, no," Aiden protested, his face resembling that of an adolescent pouting, before he grinned. "Well, yeah, kinda."

Eric looked over at Brogan and asked, "Was there trouble, son?"

"Nope," Brogan replied. "Just had a little man-to-man talk, that's all."

Katelyn's eyes brightened as a smile curved her lips. "This wouldn't have anything to do with Ginny's run-in with him, would it?"

At that, Corrine walked into the room, wiping her hands on a dishtowel, her sharp gaze pinned on her oldest. "Ginny? Ginny Spencer?"

"Jesus, Mom," Brogan complained, looking around to see his entire family's attention on him.

"Well, I don't want to be the last to know," Corrine complained.

Eric grinned at his wife and then shifted his gaze toward Brogan. "You and Ginny?"

Sighing heavily, Brogan shot Aiden a look, before replying, "We're…friends."

"Just friends?" Katelyn asked, her smile now wide. "From what Jillian said—"

"Are you shittin' me?" Brogan asked, leaning forward, pinning his sister with a hard stare. "Jillian's been sharing what she had no business sharing."

Katelyn left Gareth's lap to kneel on the floor in front of Brogan. Placing her hands on his knees, she looked up and said softly, "No, she hasn't, Brogan. She just said that Ginny was upset and you comforted her. She said that she's never seen you so determined to protect someone."

Dropping his chin to his chest, he felt her hands squeeze his thighs and unfamiliar tears prickled his eyes. Swallowing deeply, he lifted his head to see his family staring at him, concern in their eyes.

"She's the best of women," he said, then shook his head and corrected, "the best of people." Then, softly, he added, "I'm not worthy."

Corrine gasped, "Not worthy? But—"

"Corrine," Eric said quietly to his wife and, catching her eyes, shook his head.

Biting her bottom lip, she did what he indicated, her eyes full of concern.

"Corrine? That stew ready to eat?" Pops asked, scooting forward and pulling himself up from his seat. "My stomach's growling and I'd like to take care o' that problem."

Taking Pops' hint, they all made their way to the dining room, where bowls of stew and hot, buttered bread filled their plates. Conversation soon ensued, playful bantering flying back and forth across the table.

Once the dinner dishes were washed and the kitchen cleaned by all, the younger MacFarlanes began to leave. Katelyn said goodbye, hesitating at Brogan, wanting to say something, but was pulled gently away by Gareth. She stared for a second before she smiled and headed out the door, quickly tucked in tight to his side.

Aiden was next as he slapped Brogan on the back and said, "See you tomorrow. You open the bar, remember?"

"I made the schedule, I should remember," Brogan quipped, earning a laugh from his brother.

Pops looked up at Brogan, "Had a friend drop me off. Think you could take me home?"

"Sure thing," Brogan replied easily before turning to

his mom to offer a hug. Whispering in her ear, "Thanks, Mom."

Corrine looked up into his eyes and clutched his shoulders tightly. "Whatever's on your mind...we're here. And to me, you are one of the most worthy men I know."

A curt nod was his only response as he turned to his dad, who pulled him in for a handshake-hug. With a slap on the back, Eric said, "Always here for you, son."

Nodding, he and Pops walked out to his old truck. Watching to see if his grandfather needed assistance, he climbed into the driver's seat. A minute passed before Brogan could not stand the silence. "Okay, Pops, what's on your mind?"

"You were always a serious boy. Aiden was a mischief maker and Katelyn was a combination of princess-tomboy. But you...hell, boy, you were so serious about everything. But you were also loyal to a fault and fun-loving." Sighing, he continued, "You came back from the military. Still serious...but it was like something broke inside of you. Seen it in my own time in the service...seen it with your father's time. Figured it was just something that happens to some of us in war. But to hear you say you don't feel worthy...those words just about damn near broke my heart tonight."

Pulling into his grandfather's driveway, he cut the engine and stared out the windshield, sighing heavily. "I like her, Pops. She's smart, driven, and so fuckin' good. I'm gonna watch out for her. I want to lighten her load. Hell, I want to take care of her. But, I don't know about anything else."

"Well," the older man began as he opened the door to

the truck and climbed out. Slamming the door, he propped his arms on the open window, "she's always talking at the AL meetings about counseling. Sounds like you need to take her up on it…or at least talk to someone. Remember boy, you've got a whole family and group of friends that have your back. Always do and always will." Slapping his hand on the truck door, he waved as Brogan watched him walk to his front door and into his bungalow.

Scrubbing his hand over his face, he backed out of the driveway and headed toward his house. Thinking of the card on his kitchen counter with the Mental Health group number on it, he knew he had a phone call to make first thing in the morning.

14

"I assure you, nothing here will bite."

Brogan sat in the counselor's office, nervously looking around as his hands twisted in his lap. His gaze jumped to Charles, the counselor, and a wry smile slipped out. "Sorry. Guess I'm not used to doing much talking."

"Don't be sorry. Coming here is a huge step for anyone and, to be perfectly honest, for most of the military men and women we see, many say it's scarier to step into this office than to go into battle."

Brogan sought Charles' eyes, seeing understanding, and nodded. "In battle, you have adrenaline and your squad at your side. Here?" he looked around, "I'm all alone."

"But here is where you're not alone anymore," Charles said. "You're here because you've been all alone in your thoughts, your concerns. But now, with assistance, you won't be alone. And my job is to listen, help you discover what's on your mind and then assist you in finding a way to move forward in life."

"I notice you don't say you'll do the work."

Charles chuckled as he shook his head. "You're right. My job is to lead and guide you. You'll find the way on your own with my assistance."

The two sat in companionable silence for a few minutes and then Charles suggested, "Why don't you just talk to me. Tell me what's on your mind. Keep it as simple or as in depth as you are comfortable with today."

Brogan dropped his chin to his chest as his forearms rested on his thighs. "You've probably heard of the Baytown Boys." Looking up, he viewed Charles' knowing smile and shook his head ruefully, "Yeah, I guess everyone around here has." Sucking in a deep breath, he said, "I loved this town. I loved my friends. Thought it was the greatest life there was. Unlike some of my friends, who were chomping at the bit to leave, I knew I could settle here and be happy. But, by the time I was a senior, and a bunch had decided to join the service, listening to them talk about the world out there, the bug bit me and I wanted that too. Me, Mitch Evans, Grant Wilder, Philip Bayles, and Zac Hamilton finished high school and left for our boot camps right after graduation. The next year, my brother, Aiden, and Callan Ward joined as well." Snorting, he added, "We all made our way back here after finding out the world wasn't as grand as we thought it was." He paused a moment and added, "Well, all except Philip that is. I guess, in retrospect, we were lucky no one else came home to be buried."

Charles nodded his understanding, encouraging Brogan to continue. "Tell me about the Brogan who was a Baytown Boy back in the day."

Unable to hide the grin that slipped out, Brogan answered, "We all came from strong families. My parents and my grandfather are good people…taught me and my siblings right from wrong. The rest of the Baytown Boys were the same…best damn people I've ever known. We went from kids who ran around, biked, kayaked, swam in the ocean, had a clubhouse, and bothered the girls, to teens who played all sports together and good-naturedly battled to see who might get the girls. But we didn't fuck around. We never got into trouble. Like I said, we knew right from wrong."

Charles peered at Brogan intently. "Right from wrong. You've mentioned that phrase several times. That's important to you?"

Brogan's blue eyes jumped to Charles' face. "Hell, yeah. It's what we were taught. Honesty. Integrity. Loyalty. It was what my dad used to call *the measure of a man*." Seeing Charles nod, he continued, "It was what I was. It was who I was."

"And now?" Charles' asked, his voice soft.

Swallowing deeply, Brogan said, "Not so much."

The silence felt stiff for a moment until Brogan sighed. "Things changed over there. Things happened. I changed. And ever since, I feel like a phony. Like everyone thinks I'm still the same, but I know I'm not. I know I failed."

"And that failure makes you feel…?"

Looking up, Brogan answered without hesitation, sadness lacing his rough voice, "Unworthy."

Ginny watched as his feet pounded the sand, running hard and fast in the midday sun. Brogan had not seen her yet but the intense expression of his face as he neared the dune had her rethinking her surprise visit. And yet, she longed to take away the fierce anger that seemed to stay within him. She had bared her soul to him and he had taken the weight of it. But now, she wondered if it was too heavy…or perhaps an unwanted burden. Not wanting to startle him, she started walking down the dune, observing when he first noticed her. His eyes lit from within before darkening with whatever was on his mind.

Sucking in a deep breath, she smiled as her hand lifted in a wave. He stopped several feet from her, his breath ragged as his naked, sweaty chest heaved. She watched the play of muscles move as he worked to control his breathing, in part fascination and in part in longing to run her hands over his chest and abs. The tattoos on his arms and chest fascinated her. She had toyed with the idea of getting a tattoo, but could never decide on what she might want permanently inked into her skin.

Stepping a bit closer, she looked up and greeted him. "Hey. I hope I'm not interrupting."

Snorting, he took the t-shirt hanging about his neck and wiped his face before replying, "Nope. I'm glad you're interrupting me trying to kill myself with a heart attack or heat stroke."

Stepping another pace closer, she held his gaze as

she admonished, "Please don't do anything crazy like that."

"I'm a tough ol' bull," he said. "It'll take more than a long, hot run to do me in."

She looked down at her feet for a moment wondering how to ask what she wanted to ask. He lifted her chin with his forefinger and peered into her eyes.

"I can see your mind working," he stated. "What's on it?"

"I...well, I just..."

"Honey, as long as I've been around you, you've never been at a loss for words. Just spit it out."

"I was just wondering if you were all right."

He held her gaze before finally dropping his chin to his chest, placing his fists on his hips. "Who told?"

"Aiden and Katelyn were talking about the family dinner and she said something to Jillian, who saw you coming out of the counseling office when she was picking up Grant from his session."

"Fuckin' small town," he cursed. "No privacy. Everyone always up in everyone's business." He felt her cool hand on his overheated arm and looked at the delicate fingers against his tanned skin.

"Brogan, look at me," she ordered gently. As he lifted his gaze, she plunged ahead. "No one is talking about you. But your family and your friends care." Without hesitation, she added, "I care." She moved one of her hands from his arm up to his chest, feeling it rumble under her fingertips as he spoke.

"Ginny, I'm all sweaty."

A small smile slipped across her face as she slid her

other hand up his chest. "I don't care...you're all gorgeous and sweaty—"

Grabbing her hands in his, he stilled the movement, then apologized as a flash of doubt filled her eyes. "Sorry. It's not that I don't want your hands on me. Hell, the thought of your hands on me has been on my mind ever since you moved into town. But, uh...let's just say that I'm gonna have one hell of an erection if this keeps going."

Blushing, she tried—and failed—to keep her eyes from dropping to his crotch. And the visible bulge had her gaze jumping back to his eyes in time to see him close his as he dropped his chin to his chest once more. "Sorry," she whispered.

"Don't be," he said, a grin making its way through his irritation of being the subject of talk. Looking at her face turned up toward his, the care in her eyes, he said, "You want to come in? It'll only take a minute for me to shower and I can throw some steaks on the grill and we can talk."

"Sounds perfect," she said, loving that he kept her hand in his as they made their way back over the dune to his house. Entering, he told her to make herself at home and he headed back to his bathroom. She went into the kitchen and opened the refrigerator, seeing what she might fix to go along with steak. Finding corn on the cob and several baking potatoes in a bin on the counter, she took them out along with the meat.

MB walked into the room, swirling around her food dish and Ginny found some cat food in the cabinet. Putting a small amount down, she stroked the silky, black fur, enjoying the sound of purring emanating from the small cat.

By the time she started prepping dinner, Brogan walked back into the room. Seeing her in his kitchen pierced his heart, never thinking to see that sight. Hearing him, she turned around, her smile beaming at him and, once more, his heart felt the twinge.

Ginny's gaze took in his dark, wet hair, his face with its dark stubble covering his jaws. A clean, white t-shirt stretched across his biceps and chest muscles. His jeans were filled out in all the right places, from the tight thighs to the comfortably worn material over the crotch. As her eyes continued their descent, she took in his bare toes. *Damn. The man is gorgeous.*

"Babe," his voice rumbled.

Her gaze jumped back to his.

Chuckling, he walked toward her, kissed the top of her head, and grabbed the plate of steaks along with some bottles of seasonings. Walking out, he called, "Join me out here as soon as you can."

With the corn and potatoes wrapped in aluminum foil ready for the grill, she headed out to the weather-beaten deck off the kitchen, facing the bay. Admiring his backside as he stood at the grill, she smiled as she walked up next to him, setting the platter on the grill shelf. An hour later, the meal was eaten, the sun was setting, and the two sat on the deck in old, paint-chipped, Adirondack chairs watching the colors of the sky pass before them.

Licking her lips, she glanced out of the corner of her eye toward him, seeing his stoic expression firmly in place. "You know, you don't have to talk to me about anything. I just want you to be okay. And, well, I've been talking to a counselor about my situation and it's enough for me to know that you're getting some peace as well."

"I don't know if peace is what I'll find, Ginny."

She fingered the water droplets falling from her glass for a moment before looking over at him. "Brogan, you took care of me. You listened to me. You didn't judge me. You gave me the strength to face my demons." She held his gaze as she finished, "I'd like to do the same for you."

Shaking his head, he said, "I noticed you when you first came to town. You came in to the pub with Grant and Burt and were introduced to the crowd. Holy shit, Ginny, it was like looking at a ray of sunshine."

She snorted, "Me? A ray of sunshine?" Peering up at him, she queried, "With all the women in town? You noticed me?"

Holding her gaze, he said, "Ain't no woman in town that can hold a candle to you. You were in police uniform...the ones before Mitch came back to be Chief and let you all wear polos and khakis. God, you were sharp, looked so smart, and so pretty. So goddamn pretty. And I knew you were good. Clean. Pure. And I cursed myself because I felt like I'd never be good enough for you."

Ginny wanted to argue, but knew whatever demons ate at Brogan, he needed to get them out. As hard as it was for her to listen to his words, she remained quiet, attention focused entirely on him as her hand reached out to clasp his. As the sun continued to set, shadows were settling around them, wrapping them in their own private world on his deck.

"Lately, as we've gotten closer, I like having you in my life. But I can't live a lie. I've never told anyone what I'm about to tell you. Not my family...not my friends... not even the counselor today. I started the story with him, but only got so far. Then, decided that I wanted you to hear it first. I want you to see the man that you're with and know my worst."

Nodding, she said, "Okay. Tell me what's so heavy on your mind, Brogan. Please, give it to me."

He closed his eyes for a moment, relishing the feel of her hand on his, knowing it might be the last time he had that pleasure. Swallowing deeply, he began.

"Growing up, Mitch was always the stalwart one... son of the Police Chief, he always did the right thing. Philip Bayles was the peacemaker. Looking back, I realize he had such a good soul. Zac, Grant, Callan...all rock solid guys. Aiden," he chuckled, "was always just my brother, the jokester of the group, but I knew he felt things deep...just didn't show it. But me? I was like the one who always demanded the best outta all of us. Whether we were on the field playing, or just having fun. Who knew I'd end up not doing the right thing... and someone would get killed because of it?"

At his words, Ginny tried to keep her breathing steady, but her heart plunged to her stomach. Forcing her hand to stay on his, she willed him to keep talking, while her mind raced to wonder what on earth she would say to make something so monumental better.

He heaved a sigh as he leaned back in his chair, eyes closed, his mind back in the villages of Afghanistan. "You realize that once you hear this, you may never want to speak to me again?"

"We all carry pain…unburden yourself, Brogan, and we'll face it together," she vowed, squeezing his fingers.

15

"Had a buddy, Terry, that liked to drink. Weren't supposed to have alcohol over there, but…well…as military police, you probably dealt with your share of servicemen who managed to smuggle it in." Brogan did not have to look at her to know she understood exactly what he was saying. Unfortunately, some service members had no problem finding bootleg anything, and alcohol was just one of the many things.

"I wasn't the one doing the smuggling but confess that, a couple of times, I imbibed. Didn't get drunk. I was always afraid we'd get called up, and I wanted to think straight. But I knew he was doing it and did nothing about it." He heard her intake of breath, but he halted her words before she spoke. "Don't Ginny. Don't make excuses. A sin of omission is just as bad."

Scrubbing his free hand over his face, he felt the vast difference from his rough skin to her delicate fingers resting on his other hand. Light…darkness. *Jesus, could we be more different?* Determined to get it over with, he continued.

"Terry used to go into one of the local villages and get the hooch from a man who had access to it. Where the local stole it from or bought it from, I never heard Terry say...I didn't want to know. I really didn't think much about it being wrong. We were busy with our jobs in a shit part of the world in a shit war. So, a few drinks on the side seemed okay to this twenty-year old idiot."

Wanting to deny his assessment, Ginny kept quiet, knowing he needed to get his story out. Rubbing his hand gently, she hoped he could feel her encouragement.

"Anyway," he sighed heavily, "one day, Terry came by and said he needed to go into the village to get more alcohol. Said he had gotten a message for a pickup but hadn't been able to go right away and he needed some backup to go with him. Come to find out, usually another buddy would go into the village with him, a bit of backup firepower if needed."

At that, she let a gasp slip out, hating that it did, but she knew how dangerous that could have been. "Sorry," she mumbled.

He shot her a look that said no apology was needed, that he understood her surprise. "Anyway, a couple of us went. Terry drove to the house where he got the stuff, parked down the road and told us to wait. We just hung out in the vehicle and he went inside. He was gone for a while and I started getting nervous. We then saw a man go into the house and I wondered if Terry had just been in there waiting for him all that time."

Leaning forward suddenly, Brogan grimaced, his

eyes tightly closed as the memories slammed into him. Covering his face with his hands, he sucked in a deep breath. "The next thing we know, Terry comes running out, heading toward us, yelling, 'We gotta go. We gotta go.' Swear to God, I thought a bomb was going to go off. I was sure he'd walked into a trap and taken all of us with him."

"It wasn't?" Ginny asked, her heart now in her throat as she waited anxiously for the rest of his story.

"No. It was worse." Silence slithered between the two, only broken by the calls of the seagulls diving into the water. Finally, sucking in another ragged breath, he continued, his voice flat. "The man came out of the house dragging a woman. He began beating her and was quickly surrounded by villagers who began throwing stones at her as well. I jumped out of the vehicle about the time Terry came to us and he grabbed me to keep me from running to her. I fought him, but then two of our other buddies came and grabbed me as well. I might be big, but I was no match for all three of them.

He sucked in a shuddering breath. "Jesus, her screams...I can still hear them at night sometimes."

Ginny sat perfectly quiet for a moment, afraid to move, sure he could hear her heart pounding. His anguish was so palpable, she felt it to her core. Slowly, she moved her hand back over to rest on his thigh, rubbing gently, hoping he could feel her presence.

"I guess, since you were over there, you can guess what had happened. Terry, the dumbass that he was, didn't realize that waiting in a house alone with an Afghan village woman would cause her to be immediately accused of adultery. It was forbidden for her to be with a man that was not a relative, but especially not a foreigner." He paused again, before continuing, "Fucking hell. What a total, complete fuck-up. Terry and the others manhandled me into the back of the vehicle and they took off and didn't look back until we were through the gates and back on base."

Brogan opened his eyes and looked over at Ginny, expecting disgust and censure and steeling himself for her rejection. She was leaning forward, her hand still on his leg, staring deeply into his face...with *concern?* He opened his mouth to speak, but closed it quickly, not knowing what to say.

"Brogan," she began, still staring intently into his eyes, "I understand the horror of the situation...seeing a woman stoned and not being able to protect her would have affected anyone, especially a man like you. A man who feels right from wrong so strongly...who has a protective nature. But you've taken on the actions of someone else and made them your own."

"You don't see, do you, Ginny?" he said, sadness radiating from his eyes. "That woman was stoned because, first of all, a friend of mine was doing something he shouldn't have been doing and, second of all, I was there and didn't stop it. That woman was stoned to death right in front of me and I couldn't stop it!" The last statement was roared as he stood, pushing her hand off his leg. Pacing away, he stomped to the edge of the deck, his fists on his hips, and lifted his head, screaming into the wind.

After his primal roar was carried off into the evening sky, he dropped his chin to his chest, his heart aching with the loss of Ginny in his life. She was the best thing that had ever happened to him, but he had been a fool to think that she would be able to live with his past.

He jolted as small hands encircled his waist from behind, reaching around until they met at his front. He looked down, seeing her pale hands against his shirt. Holding firm. Not letting go. Confused, he nonetheless chose not to move, relishing the feel of her hands on him. Warm. Comforting.

After several minutes with her face pressed against his back, Ginny shuffled around, still holding onto his waist, until her front was pressed to his. She remained quiet, her cheek against his heartbeat, hearing it pound. Knowing his pain, she wanted to hold him as close as she could, hoping he would let her bear some of it.

Hearing him swallow, she lifted her face to his. Seeing his agony, she said, "Brogan, what happened was not your fault." Observing doubt in his eyes and knowing denial was about to spew from him, she reached her fingers up to touch his lips. "You have to listen to me." A shiver swept over her and his arms instinctively wrapped around her, pulling her in closer.

Brogan hated to invite her in only to have her leave in disgust later, but he wanted her to be comfortable, and it was getting chilly. "Come on, Ginny. Let's get you out of the breeze." He turned and walked with her tucked underneath his arm. Once inside, he hesitated, uncertain where to sit.

Ginny walked to the sofa, leading Brogan by the hand and, as she sat, she pulled on his arm. As he plopped next to her, she flipped quickly and straddled his knees, holding him in place. Knowing he could easily dislodge her, she prayed he stayed where he was. Cupping his tense jaws with her hands, she said, "You need to listen to me." Sucking in a deep breath before letting it out slowly, she began, "Terry made a series of bad choices. Terry. Not you. Terry."

His eyes jumped to hers but he stayed silent.

"He chose to buy illegal alcohol. He chose to get it from a local village which has so many stupid risks that I can't even begin to list them all. He chose to go into that house, which could have been rigged with explosives, where God knows what else could have lain in wait for him. He chose to wait in that house with an Afghanistan national female, not thinking of anything but himself. And he chose to run when things got hot. Run straight toward his friends which could have gotten them killed as well. And then he chose to keep you from going to help which, I have to say, at that point, was the only good decision he could have made."

Brogan's mouth opened to speak but she shushed him again.

"No, you talked and now it's my time. Honey, I know that culture. I know that area. I was there. And if you had run back into the villagers' frenzy, they would have killed you and probably all your buddies. And then there would have been an incident and the Americans would have had to retaliate. Think about it, Brogan…it could have been catastrophic!"

He shook his head slowly, but with less determination than earlier, turning her words over in his mind. She clung to his cheeks, holding him firm.

"Terry made so many bad choices, including dragging you into his mess. But that's on him, honey, not you." Seeing the doubt still in his eyes, she said, "Do you blame me for what happened to me?"

Jerking back, Brogan's eyes turned stormy as he barked, "Hell, no! Of course not. How could you even ask that?"

"Because, if I had kept my mouth shut and just tried to deal with the trauma of the pictures, I wouldn't have been accosted."

"Babe, that's on him," Brogan argued. "You did nothing wrong. That was all on those assholes!"

Rubbing her thumbs over the rough stubble of his cheeks, she leaned her face close into his, so that their eyes were in a direct line, just inches apart. "I know. I had a lot of guilt about what I did, thinking of all the different things I could have done. But, ultimately, I knew the blame was on those men who made the choice to take pictures and share them. And, then, on the asshole who accosted me. Just. Like. Terry. It's all on him. All those bad choices."

"It's different, Ginny," he said, his voice rough with emotion. "You did what you could to right a wrong, in spite of all the forces against you. I sat back and watched Terry involved in an activity that I could have reported. Then, I could have not gone with him that day, knowing it wasn't the right thing to do. And then—"

"I'm not excusing what you did about ignoring Terry's illegal bootlegging, but you were young and, again—that was his activity, not yours. But when he needed someone to guard his back, you were there. When you saw that woman in trouble, your instinct was to save her. You cannot blame yourself for the choices others make."

Brogan's fingers flexed on her ass as her words finally penetrated and all his anger and rage finally made sense. He realized how much he had hated Terry over the past eight years. Hated what Terry had been involved in. Hated Terry's stupid handling of the alcohol pick-ups. And hated Terry for running away from the dying woman. As he sat there with Ginny on his lap, he realized he even hated the husband and villagers for their treatment of women. All this time he thought his guilt was destroying him, but it wasn't the only thing. Drinking in a deep gulp of air, he let it out slowly, his eyes closed as he willed his mind to settle.

"Can I ask you a question?"

Hearing her soft voice so close, he opened his eyes, surprised to see her face still within inches of his. "Baby, I've got no secrets left."

"Is that the reason you don't drink?"

Snorting, he dropped his head, his forehead resting against hers. "Fucked-up, isn't it? A man who owns a pub and doesn't drink." Lifting his gaze back to hers, he said, "After that, I can't stomach alcohol anymore. Yeah, I've occasionally had a drink, but rarely and, honest to God, it sours in my stomach. I know alcohol isn't the problem. I can own, run, and bartend a pub. But I keep a close eye out on those who imbibe too much and have no problem cutting them off. They get pissed and go somewhere else, that's on them."

"Yes. That's on *them*," she repeated, her lips curving slightly.

Her small smile warmed him as much as her palms

still holding his face. "Yeah...that's the point you've been trying to make, right? I can't be responsible for the choices of others." He saw her smile widen and felt the weight on his chest lift slightly. Tilting his head, he added, "But I still fucked up myself. That's on me."

Nodding, she said, "Then deal with that part. You've learned from it by the way you run your bar, but you haven't actually forgiven yourself, so it still eats away at you. Keep going to counseling...talk about it...then let it go, Brogan. Don't be so hard on yourself."

She leaned in, her lips touching his. He held perfectly still for a moment, except for a reflexive twitch of his fingers on her ass again, letting her mouth do all the work. She angled her head before taking the kiss further, licking the seam of his lips and plunging her tongue inside when he opened his mouth on a groan.

He came alive, his hands roving up and down her back from her neck to her ass, before sliding her closer to him. Her core was pressed against his erection and her breasts pressed against his chest, heartbeat to heartbeat.

She leaned back slightly, her eyes glazed with lust and her kiss-swollen mouth moist as she licked her lips. "Brogan, when I told you about me you said you wanted our first time to be about us, not in response to what had happened. But this isn't like that. I see you, Brogan, and you see me...so, please."

His hips involuntarily moved upward, his cock eagerly seeking her core. Hands moving back to her ass, he growled, "You're right. This is different. But you gotta give me the words, baby. I gotta know exactly what you want me to do."

Smiling, Ginny licked his lips, loving the groan from his mouth that she swallowed as soon as she latched on once more. Mumbling while kissing, she said, "I want you to take me to bed. Make love to me…please."

Standing with her in his arms, his hands still holding on to her ass as she wrapped her legs around his hips, he grinned, "You don't gotta beg, honey."

16

Moving with Ginny, Brogan checked the sliding glass door and flipped the lock while holding her with one arm. Her arms wrapped tighter about his neck, her lips finding his as soon as the door was secure. Making it down the short hall to his bedroom, Brogan spent a second wishing he had made the bed and picked up last night's clothes, but as her mouth continued to plunder his lips, he gave up all thoughts other than the bed. Before laying her down, he stared at her for a moment, leaning back in to place a kiss on her lips. A whisper of a kiss this time. Reverent. Quietly saying nothing while saying everything.

Bending over, he placed her on the edge of the king-sized bed before standing and toeing off his running shoes. Jerking his shirt over his head, it joined the other clothes on the floor.

Her eyes dropped to his chest, massive muscles tapering to a washboard abdomen, silky chest hair that she ached to run her fingers through as it trailed off into his shorts. Before she had a chance to think more of his happy trail, his hands moved to his shorts and, with a quick motion, he slid them down his legs, snagging his boxers at the same time.

A sudden flash of uncertainty flew through Brogan's eyes as he gazed at the still-dressed beauty lying on his bed. She lifted her arms up toward him, beckoning him to her with a smile beaming his way. The doubt left instantly as he crawled up her body, his heavy cock bobbing, a drop of pre-cum already at the tip.

They stared at each other for a moment before he leaned down and captured her lips once again. This time, in the slow exploration of lovers. Her lips were soft and pliant under his, allowing him to control the intensity, the depth. Her taste was already familiar to him and as her tongue slid across his, he felt his erection painfully pressing against her hip. His hand moved from her cheek down to her neck where he could feel her pulse beating wildly. His lips followed the trail of his hand, moving to that spot in the hollow of her neck where he nipped and licked.

Ginny shivered with the sensations as he reached underneath her shirt and slid his hand upward, stopping at the underside of her breast. Taking the weight in his hand, he rubbed his thumb over her distended nipple, swallowing her groan as his lips stayed on hers. Her hips moved upward, driving his cock wild with desire. Moving his hand back down to the bottom hem of her shirt, he slid it upward and over her head as she leaned up to assist.

Immediately self-conscious about her plain underwear, Ginny noted that Brogan did not seem to lose the lust in his eyes as they roved hungrily over her body. Unsnapping her white bra, he slid it down her arms and tossed it away as well. Brogan's hand moved to her breast as he took in the beauty of her. Full breasts with rosy-tipped nipples begged to be sucked. Tweaking one nipple as his lips found the other, he alternated between her breasts, sucking, nipping, tugging, and licking until both nipples were elongated with need.

As his mouth continued its ministrations, he slid his hand lower until his fingers found her folds. Inserting one finger, and then two, he moved them slowly, exploring her sex, finding just the right spots to have her squirming and moaning. He circled his fingers deep inside before pulling them out to swirl them around her clit before plunging back inside. His lips made their way back to hers, his tongue mimicking his fingers.

Ginny felt strung tight as a bow, the waiting excruciating. Her hips undulated against his as her hand moved down toward his cock, wrapping it around the thick length. She barely began moving her hand up and down his shaft before her inner walls grabbed at his fingers deep inside.

Brogan watched as she leaned her head back, her eyes tightly closed, her body jerking in response to the orgasm ripping through her.

"Baby, let me see you," he whispered, eliciting her eyes to open. As she was coming down from her bliss, he moved his hand from her sex back up to her pants' zipper, drawing it down. Lifting to his knees as he bent over her, he grabbed the waist and pulled them down her legs, snagging her white panties at the same time.

She blushed, saying, "My underwear is boring. I don't really have any fancy lingerie—"

"Shh," he whispered, staring once more at the beauty in his bed, unable to believe the object of his fantasies for almost two years was here with him. "Do I look like the kind of man that needs his woman to wear fancy shit?" Moving his lips back over her breasts and down to her stomach, he muttered, "It'd get taken off just as fast."

His rough stubbled jaws scraped along her inner thighs and she widened her legs to give him more access. Her hand reached to his hair, her fingers sliding over his scalp. He kneeled at her apex and gently pulled her legs up onto his shoulders. Her sex glistened with moisture and he dragged his tongue along her folds. She tasted better than he could have imagined as he dipped his tongue inside, finally moving up to latch his mouth over her clit, while plunging his fingers in once more.

Ginny cried out his name as the electricity shot over her body from her core outwards. His beard scratched her sensitive skin as her body wound tight. "Brogan, I want you inside me," she pleaded.

"I know, babe, but I'm a big guy and you're tight. Let me do this for you to get you ready." He licked toward her clit, sucking it into his mouth while his hand slid up from her stomach to her breast and rolled her nipple between his fingers.

Finally, Ginny cried out again, this time her hips bucking as the orgasm vibrated deep inside, spreading outwards.

Brogan kept licking, feeling her juices spread over

his tongue. Opening his mouth wide, he felt her vibrations throughout, wanting them to last forever. They slowly subsided and he raised up, seeing her head back on the mattress, her eyes closed and a soft smile playing on her lips.

Letting her legs down gently from his shoulders, he took a moment to roll on the condom before crawling back over her body, grinning when she opened her eyes, filled with warmth and pleasure. With his dick at her entrance, he held her gaze and pushed in slowly, inch by inch. Her eyes hooded with passion, lips plumped from their kissing, her perfect teeth biting her bottom lip. "Jesus, baby, you're perfect," he groaned.

The urge to pound into her waiting sex was strong, but he maintained a steady pace. Wanting her to have pleasure again, he moved excruciatingly slowly out before plunging in quickly. Over and over he did this until he was not sure he could last another minute. Bearing his weight on his forearms, he held her head in his hands, rocking into her body with her hips matching his thrusts.

She spread her knees wider to offer deeper access and looked down to where their bodies were joined. They watched with fascination at their coupling as his cock moved in and out of her slick cavity. Lifting his eyes, her gaze captured his, a smile curving her beautiful mouth.

"Honey, I'm gonna come," he rasped. "Are you close?"

After two orgasms, Ginny wanted to say *go for it*, thinking she could never have a third, but as her mouth opened to tell him that, she felt her inner walls tightening with the friction of his movements. "Yes," she moaned against his thrusts.

As her orgasm flooded over her, his own release had him emptying himself deep into her warmth. His sated body fell to the side of hers, pulling her over with him. Arms wrapped around each other, they held on tightly, hearts pounding.

Brogan leaned down just long enough to grab the covers, pulling them up over their sweat-slicked bodies, making sure to tuck her in securely. Ginny's head lay on his chest and he pulled her tighter against him.

Ginny's limbs were weightless as fatigue overtook her. Closing her eyes for a moment she allowed the exhaustion of the day to ease her into slumber.

As the two slept peacefully, wrapped tightly in each other's arms, keeping the nightmares at bay, MB hopped up on the bed, and circled several times before curling up at their feet.

17

Another call about a peeping tom. Ginny's stomach knotted in anger as she and Grant knocked on the door.

"Ma'am, I'm Officer Spencer and this is Officer Wilder."

Ginny and Grant entered the rental home as Jerelle Simpkins stepped back to let them in. Having answered the 9-1-1 call, Sam and Mitch were still outside gathering evidence after their initial conversation with her.

Jerelle jerked her head in a nod as she led them to the sofa in the living room. Ginny noticed two little girls standing, wide-eyed, on the stairs, peering at them. She offered a smile but Jerelle said, "Girls. Back to bed. Everything's fine. Please, girls, just obey Mama."

The two little ones obediently turned and hurried back up the stairs and Jerelle stood still until she heard their door close. Turning back to the officers, she said, "I don't want them to hear anything and get nightmares. I just told them that I thought someone outside might need help and had called the police to take care of them."

Nodding, Ginny assured, "I think that's very wise, Ms. Simpkins. Can we sit and get your statement once more? I know it was given to Chief Evans, but I'd like you to tell it again. Sometimes things come back to you when you talk to someone different."

The three sat down as Ginny's gaze swept the room. It was a typical rental house in Baytown—an old structure, updated with brightly painted walls, beach-themed decorations, and furniture that was built to withstand multiple family visits each week during the season. Turning back to Jerelle, Ginny said, "Please, just start at the beginning and we'll take notes."

Swallowing, Jerelle began, "We've been here for about four nights. We've got another couple of nights on our rental, but I don't know if I can stay here again. I'm so spooked." Twisting her hands in front of her, she continued, "I'm recently divorced…it was ugly…and expensive." Shaking her head as though to restart her thoughts, she explained, "This is our first vacation in almost two years. The girls wanted to come to the beach and I knew we couldn't afford anything in Virginia Beach, so we came here. It's been great. They've had fun and we've had some good seafood. They love the town pier and the Seafood Shack. Love watching the boats and the sunsets." Shaking her head again, she cried, "Why did this have to happen when we were having such a lovely time?"

"Ms. Simpkins, I know this is so hard for you. But can you tell us about tonight?"

"Yes, yes, sorry. My mind just seems shaken."

Ginny's gentle smile was encouraging and Jerelle took a deep breath and let it out slowly before speaking again.

"We walked back from the beach after watching the sunset and I sent the girls up to take a bath. They're six and eight years old, so it's still easy for them to take a bubble bath together and I don't have to be right there with them. I spent some time shaking out the beach towels on the back deck and then hung them over the rail to dry overnight—"

"Can you tell us about what time that was?" Grant asked.

Jerelle scrunched her forehead in thought. "Well, the sunset was at 8:17. We looked it up on my phone and we had a good time as we watched it and, honest to goodness, it did set at exactly 8:17. So by the time we walked home and I got them upstairs, it was probably about 8:45."

Ginny nodded, "Go on, please."

"I shut and locked the back door. I'm real careful about that…it's just habit from my divorce days. Bill would occasionally try to come over when he wasn't supposed to, so I always lock the doors. Anyway, I heard the girls getting out of the tub and yelled up for them to get in their pajamas and make sure they wiped down any water that might have gotten on the floor. It was just a little after nine when I walked into the living room. And I know this because I looked at my watch to see if there was enough time for us to watch a Disney movie before they went to bed." She took a deep breath before plunging on, "And that's when I saw him. He was at the side window peeking in."

Jerelle stopped, her breath coming in faster pants.

"Ma'am, breathe slowly. Breathe with me." Ginny inhaled deeply, holding Jerelle's gaze until both women were breathing in unison. As Ginny observed the other woman's color returning to normal, she smiled. "Good, you're doing good."

Clutching her hands together again, Jerelle said, "Lordy, I feel so crazy. Nothin' like this has ever happened to me."

"Please describe the man for us," Grant encouraged.

"He was peeking in that bottom pane over there," she pointed. "He had a dark cap on, so I have no idea what color his hair was and his hands were cupping his face as he looked in."

"Did you see his hand? Did you see flesh color or was he wearing gloves?"

Licking her lips as she pondered, she suddenly looked up in surprise. "Gloves. The only flesh color I saw was his face pressed against the glass. And he was white." Sighing, she said, "But I have no idea if he was old or young. As soon as I saw him I let out a scream and he moved away. It was so dark outside, I had no idea if he was gone or just in the shadows."

Ginny stood and walked over to the window, her heart now pounding. *Some man in this town is terrorizing women...*and that fact pissed her off.

"He's taunting us," Ginny said, staring at the investigation board.

"Taunting us?" Sam asked, reaching his hand over to snag some carrots off the vegetable tray Mildred had brought in. She used to always provide pastries from Jillian's Coffee Shop, but Sam's wife had started bringing in healthy snacks and Mildred approved of the change. She still occasionally brought pastries, but now Sam had to contend with both his wife and Mildred watching out for his weight and blood pressure. Glancing at Mable standing in the doorway, smiling contentedly, Ginny figured Sam now had one more woman to watch over him as well.

"Why would he look into the living room window? For these older, two-story houses, the bedrooms are always on the second floor. There is only the kitchen, living rooms, and dining rooms on the first floor. It's as though he knows someone will see him...I mean, Ms. Simpkins' lights were still on! He had to know with his stupid face smashed against the window someone would see him!" Letting her breath out in a rush, she shook her head. "Sorry...I'm getting emotional and that doesn't help us."

"You're fine," Mitch assured. "We get pissed at criminal activity but we're also human and we feel the crimes very personally. We just don't want the personal involvement to cloud our investigation." He looked back up at the board as well, all the voyeuristic activity listed. "But, you're also right. What is he up to? How does Al Barton fit into this? Was he just looking into his neighbor's house because of the teenager there? If so, he's still a threat and I'm hoping we, or someone, can catch him in the act."

"And not just the little sister," Burt groused. "I

believe her, but with no proof, the DA will never go for it based on the word of a child."

Grumbles came from all around the table before they heard a commotion from the reception area. Corwin Banks and Silas Mills' loud voices could be heard arguing with Mildred before the two pompous men stormed into the police workroom.

"What the hell are you doing about these peeping toms?" the mayor yelled, his fist shaking in the air, his jowls shaking as well. "I told Celia to keep her mouth shut, but someone told the Baytown Herald and I got a call this morning from the editor that she wants an official statement about the possibility of a sexual predator in our town—"

"We're gonna start losing visitors," Silas interrupted, his eyes narrowing, "and the last thing this town needs is a bad reputation."

Mitch looked up and said, "You wanna tell me something I don't know?"

Silas sneered but before he had a chance to speak, Corwin jumped in. "I know you're working on it, but we gotta catch this bastard before he blackens the name of our little haven."

"We are trying to catch him!" Ginny shouted, standing while staring the two men down. "But maybe you should be more concerned about the women he's scaring and not just the town's reputation."

"Officer Spencer," Silas responded, his oily voice oozing sarcasm, "you manage to get your panties in a twist when something affects women. But if this town loses revenue, then maybe your job will be in jeopardy—"

Ginny, red faced and ready to throw down, opened her mouth, but Mitch got there first. Standing, he faced the two interlopers and said with force, "That's it! Outta my workroom so we can actually get on with the investigation." Leaning toward Silas, he added, "And if you insult one of my officers again, we're gonna have a problem. You got that?"

His Adam's Apple bobbing, Silas glared at the group, adding over his shoulder as he left, "Just do your jobs."

"Always have," Mitch countered, his discontent now penetrating Corwin, who had the good grace to blush before leaving.

The room was silent for a moment before Burt looked at Ginny. "We've never had a sexual crime here…at least not since I've been with the force. And even though I'm married with a daughter, this is hitting home in a way that I've never faced before." Seeing the others' eyes on him, he continued, "I'm realizing how much more difficult this job can be on you, Ginny."

She opened her mouth to protest, but he held up his hand. "No, let me finish. You take a certain amount of backlash, just for being a woman in charge. For being a woman in a uniform. Hell, for being a woman. You're every bit the officer that any of us are, but it's harder for you…at least, sometimes. Goddamnit, Silas would have never made a comment about us men getting our underwear in a twist."

At that, a light giggle slipped from her lips then bubbled out loud, her shoulders shaking. The others joined in, the lighthearted banter lifting the heavy weight of the discussion. As their mirth dissipated, she nodded. "You're right. And, I let him get to me, which I shouldn't have. But, yeah, the nature of the crime strikes home to me in a personal way." Seeing her fellow officers' eyes pinned on her in concern, she shook her head. "It's over and done. It was years ago in the military. I'm working on it and working through it. But yeah, when someone like Silas comes around, the desire to punch him in the face gets to me."

"I'd let you," Sam offered, to the grins of the others.

Mable popped her head around the corner, her bluish curls bouncing as she grinned. "I'm going to like working here!" Before the officers had a chance to comment, she disappeared around the corner.

"Okay, back to work," Mitch ordered, shaking his head before turning his attention back to the board. Hearing another voice from the front lobby, he rolled his eyes before smiling as Gareth and Katelyn walked in.

Gareth greeted the group and then stated proudly, "Katelyn came across something that she thought might help."

"I was doing a check on some of the new residents in the area for a case that we're working on, and I found a person who moved to Baytown recently. Torrin Shadwell. He's registered as a sex offender in another state, but when he moved here, he didn't register. As you know, Virginia has a lifetime registration."

"Good job, Katelyn," the others said, and Ginny quickly took the information Katelyn offered. "And, I've arranged for lunch to be delivered from the Pub, on the house."

Nodding his thanks to Katelyn, Mitch then turned to Ginny, "Ginny, go with me to visit Torrin." Seeing

Grant about to protest, he held up his hand. "We've got this. You check with the lab to see if we're getting anything back from our evidence sent in."

Nodding, Ginny inwardly wondered if she was ready for the interview, but knew Mitch was right. As mad as she still was at Silas, she needed to pull herself together so she would be professional to Mr. Shadwell. Closing her eyes, she knew she was not likely to be very pleasant to anyone.

Katelyn walked over and patted her arm, saying, "Why don't you come over to Tori's place this evening? We're having another Jillian wedding planning get together." Laughing, she said, "Just bring yourself and, if you want, a bottle of wine. See you about eight." Without waiting for a response, she flitted out of the room, leaving Ginny standing wide-eyed in her wake.

Sighing at the prospect of an evening with the girls, she hustled to follow Mitch to the SUV. Once inside, his lips twitched and she turned to face him full on. "What's so funny?"

"I know hanging with people isn't your thing, but honestly, I think you'll have a good time with Tori, Katelyn, and Jillian."

Leaning back, she looked out the window, staring but not seeing what was passing by. "I know I will…I'm sure I will."

"Tell you what," Mitch added. "If you're not laughing and dancing and half-drunk when I get there tonight, I'll take one of your evening shifts."

Grinning, she agreed, "You're on. Easiest bet I'll ever win."

Minutes later, they pulled up to one of the small

homes on the east side of town, viewing a neat, well-kept yard with a few toys scattered about. Walking up, Ginny saw two girls swinging on the porch slurping popcicles. She greeted them with a smile when they looked over, wide-eyed, with orange popcicle-stained mouths.

A woman came to the screen door and, wiping her hands on a dishtowel, opened the door, saying, "Can I help you?"

"We're looking for Torrin Shadwell."

The woman paused for a second and then said, "That's my husband. I'm Glenda. Um, he's working in the back yard." Forcing a smile, she added, "He's been mowing but is now trying to see if we have enough room for a garage or shed in the back. You want to come through?"

Ginny allowed Mitch to take the lead, wondering if he would go around the house or follow Glenda into and through it. He chose the latter and they entered a nicely furnished home, decorated simply with a few more toys scattered in the living room. Passing through the kitchen, the scent of baking filled the air and Ginny's mouth watered at the sight of homemade cookies cooling on a rack on the counter.

Glenda opened the sliding glass door leading to the back yard and called for Torrin. A tall, thin man looked over and waved at his wife. "Honey, these officers wanted to talk to you."

She stepped back, letting Ginny and Mitch pass her on their way outside, closing the door behind them.

Torrin, wearing a polo and shorts, dressed like a man who had just played a round of golf, walked over, his face curious, and a little guarded, as he said, "What can I do for you?"

Mitch introduced himself and Ginny before saying, "I'll cut right to the chase, Mr. Shadwell. We've come across your name as being registered as a sexual offender, but you did not register when you moved to Virginia."

Torrin's eyes widened, his mouth going slack, before his shoulder slumped. It was as though all the air was sucked from him. Ginny blinked at the unexpected response.

Torrin pointed to a group of lawn chairs on the patio and said, "Can we sit?"

Nodding, the three settled in the chairs but, before they had a chance to talk, Glenda came out with a tray containing lemonade and cookies. Placing it on the table, she served them and then sat in the chair closest to Torrin, placing her hand on his arm, offering him a little smile.

"Officers, you'll find my wife is very supportive and we can speak freely in front of her."

"Considering I had as much to do with your judgement as you did, I should be here."

Her curiosity peaked, Ginny said, "We're not here to judge you, Mr. Shadwell, but to let you know that Virginia has a lifetime sexual offender registration. When you moved here a few months ago, you should have registered."

Nodding slowly, Torrin said, "I understand—"

"Well, I don't!" Glenda bit out, her friendly face torn by anger and, Ginny noticed, sadness.

"Honey, it is what it is," Torrin said, but his face was

full of the same emotions as his wife. Looking up, he said, "Chief Evans, you're right. I really just did not think about it because in the state we came from, the time statute was shorter than life and I made the poor assumption that Virginia was the same."

"My father, the sanctimonious asshole," Glenda said, her body shaking with emotion.

Mitch and Ginny shared a quick glance, but it was noticed by Torrin, who said, "Let me explain. Glenda and I were high school sweethearts." He reached over and linked fingers with her.

"I fell in love with her when I was only fifteen and she was fourteen. I was a sophomore and she was a freshman. We hung out, then dated when she was allowed to go on dates—"

"My father was a conservative minister," Glenda interjected. "He preached hell fire and damnation from the pulpit on Sunday mornings, but managed to slap my mother around when dinner wasn't prepared the way he wanted."

Torrin continued, "I took care of Glenda as much as I could, always made sure I had her home on time, helped her mom and dad around the house, but," sighing heavily, "we had sex before we got married. I was eighteen and she was only seventeen…and her father pressed charges when he found out."

Glenda explained further, "I got pregnant. My father was furious because of his position in our little community. I cried, pleaded, begged…but he was insistent that Torrin pay for his sins. Torrin was arrested and then convicted of a sexual offense with a minor." With a rueful snort, she added, "By then I was eighteen. Torrin was given a light sentence and we got married, left home and never went back."

Ginny was stunned, the story not being at all what she expected. "You…you were convicted?"

Torrin shrugged. "I was eighteen, she was seventeen, still a minor. She was pregnant. As far as the judge was concerned, there was no way to not find me guilty. He gave me community service as my sentence, which I did. The day it was over, we got married and left town. Been together thirteen years now."

The four sat silently as Ginny struggled with their story. Cutting her eyes toward Mitch, she saw his face full of consternation as well.

Finally, clearing his throat, he said, "Mr. Shadwell, I appreciate your candor and, as you know, your story can be easily investigated for its accuracy, which we will do as a matter of record. Once I have corroborated your story, I'll find out what the next step is. If you do not have to register here since you have completed your registration period in the state of conviction, then I'll let you know."

Relief filled Glenda and Torrin's faces and Ginny hoped they would not have to be further tainted by their adolescent decision. Standing, they shook hands and walked around the house toward the front. Waving goodbye to the two girls still swinging on the porch, Ginny followed Mitch to the SUV.

Silent for most of the way back to the station, Mitch finally said, "Not what I was expecting."

Shaking her head, Ginny whispered to the window, "Me either. Not at all."

18

"I don't trust easily."

Ginny made the comment to June and waited for the counselor to speak. When she did not, Ginny continued, "And not just men."

At that statement, June nodded and said, "I can certainly understand the trust issues with men, although we have talked about differentiating between those who hurt you and all men. But tell me more about the not trusting women."

"I told you how we women banded together to gain justice. We filed complaints together, worked together and, I thought, really bonded. But in the end, most got scared…or tired of fighting. Anyway, one by one they started begging me to just let it drop. I didn't, but I felt really alone." Shrugging, she added, "I always thought women would stick together…should stick together."

"Everyone handles their pain differently. For each of those women, the pressures inside and from the outside would have brought out different responses. For some, flight. For others, like yourself, fight. As a police officer, you know that is why many women don't report sexual assault. The response is different for everyone." June watched Ginny fiddle with the stress ball in her hands before asking, "Why does this come up now?"

Ginny shook her head in derision and said, "God, the reason is so stupid." Continuing to squeeze the rubber ball, she finally placed it back on June's desk, heaving a sigh. "I'm supposed to meet up with some women in town…friends of mine, but I've never hung out with them before."

"And that scares you?"

"Terrifies me!"

"Because?"

Huffing, Ginny said, "What do I talk about? If I talk about myself, how do I know I can trust them? So, do I just sit there and listen to them talk about wedding planning and say nothing?"

June leaned forward and asked, "Do you want to meet with them? Do you have any feelings for them or do you feel forced to hang out with them?"

"No, not forced. And they're really nice. Always nice to me. Some are with my co-workers. Most are in the Auxiliary, so I know them from there too. But that's different. That's business. And they've been friends for a long time…I'm just a newcomer."

June smiled at Ginny as she leaned back and said, "I think you need to identify what about them bothers you. Why you are so nervous."

Hesitantly, Ginny replied, "It's…what if I really have a good time…and…you know…"

"What?"

"And then I really like them…and they…" huffing out a breath of air, Ginny sat up straighter and said, "This is dumb. I'm not afraid of a bunch of women. The truth of the matter is that they intimidate me. There. I've said it."

"But you are afraid of…?"

Pinching her lips for a moment, Ginny replied, "Tori, Jillian, and Katelyn all exude such confidence." Seeing June's wide-eyed surprise, Ginny hurried, "I'm confident as a cop…but as a woman? Fun small-talk with a group of women? What the hell do they talk about? I don't know fashion. Makeup for me is a swipe of mascara and lip gloss. My nails haven't seen polish since before the Army. My clothes include my police uniform, exercise clothes, and a few pairs of shorts and t-shirts. My shoes are steel-toed boots and running shoes. I have one pair of flip-flops and one pair of dress pumps. I think I own two dresses…one I bought for a funeral and one is a simple wrap dress bought for Tori and Mitch's wedding last year and re-worn for my date with Brogan." Huffing, her shoulders slumped at her admission.

"Wow," June said. "You hate being objectified as a woman and, yet, did you not just do that with the other women? Assuming they only talk about makeup and clothes?"

The small room became quiet as Ginny's mouth opened and closed several times, wanting to refute June's observation but unable to do so. June appeared satisfied to allow the silence to slide over them, giving Ginny time to consider her tangled thoughts.

Dropping her head, staring at her hands, she sighed

heavily. "Oh, wow. You're right. I did to them exactly what I hate being done to me."

"So…" June prodded, "what really bothers you… what really holds you back?"

"I guess I hate the idea of having a good time and then having them abandon me. By the time I got out of the Army, I was alone. Almost completely alone. Like I had some kind of contagious disease. I got used to being alone."

June nodded in understanding. "No one can promise that you won't meet others in your life that abandon you at times, but only you can decide if this group of women is worth the risk of friendship. Because friendship, like love, is a risk."

Ginny thought on those words as she left the counseling office. She had taken a risk on Brogan…now it was time to take a risk on friends.

The group gathered at Mitch's bayside cabin, which used to belong to his grandfather and was used as a fishing cabin many years ago. It was stark compared to the nice rental cabins, being furnished simply, but the family had enjoyed many meals on the wooden deck and sing-a-longs around the fire pit. Now, it belonged to Mitch and he used it to host parties and cookouts with his friends.

This afternoon, a group of friends, all belonging to the American Legion, met to have an informal officers' meeting. Mitch, at the grill, was arguing with Grant over the proper way to cook fish, while Callan, Jason,

Gareth, and Zac lounged around the deck drinking. Aiden and Brogan walked together, carrying a cooler of beer, setting it down amongst the friends. Ginny, as usual the lone female, carried out a platter of chips, a large salad bowl, and condiments.

Grinning, Brogan turned and took the platter from her. As he set it on the table, he noticed the stares coming his way. "What?" he groused, glaring at them. "Just 'cause we're dating shouldn't make a difference to you all."

"Hate to break it to you, Bro, but the way you've made goo-goo eyes at Ginny for the past two years, it's hardly new to us to see the way you two look at each other. Nice, but hardly new," Zac grinned.

Ginny blushed and Zac threw his arm around her shoulders and whispered loudly enough for everyone to hear, "If you ever get tired of dating the grumpy giant, just let me know." He kissed the top of her head before ducking Brogan's raised fist.

"Now, now, boys," Ginny called out, slipping out from under Zac's arm and sliding up to Brogan. "Play nice."

Brogan wrapped his arm around Ginny pulling her into his side. "I'll play nice as long as he keeps his hands to himself."

Zac threw his head back in laughter as he slapped Brogan on the shoulder. Taking his beer, he headed back to his chair. "Good to see you two happy."

Brogan glanced around, seeing the same expression on the others' faces, before he felt a slight punch to his gut. Looking down in surprise, Ginny's fist was still pressed against his abs. "You okay?"

Leaning over to place a light kiss on her lips, he grinned, "More 'n okay, baby."

"Fish is up," Mitch called and soon the group was sitting around the deck, plates filled with fresh caught and grilled fish. Shouting greetings to Lance, as he walked up from the beach, they shifted their seats, making room for him.

After discussing the upcoming practices for the AL teams and the agenda items for the next meeting, the conversation rolled to the news article that had appeared that morning in the Baytown Herald.

"You see the mayor's nephew in the picture, standing by Corwin? Says he's here studying small town infrastructure. Guy looks like he's never done a day's work in his life. And I've watched him eye the girls on the beach as he walks through town," Callan said, filling his plate before sitting back down. "And, hell, the teen girls are all over him. I noticed him at the harbor over the past couple of weeks as he goes out in his boat."

"Just what we need, another Banks strolling through town as though they own it," Zac said through bites of corn on the cob.

"Anything we should be on the lookout for?" Aiden asked.

"So far, we're looking for a white male, but have no prints, no age, and not much to go on, although we got a partial shoe print from the last reported sighting," Grant added.

"Yeah, but are you looking at more than one person?" Gareth asked. "What'd you find out on that one lead we found?"

"That appears to be a dead end. He's not a person of interest."

"I'm so frustrated," Ginny admitted. "It's like looking for a needle in a haystack. Even in this little town, we've got people who are out and about all the time, so it's not unusual to see a man or teen walking along the street, cutting through yards and alleys. We're a beach community with the only public beach in the area, so there are always visitors. On top of that, with the weekly rental, vacation houses, who knows who is walking around today and then gone tomorrow."

"It's someone here," a deep, soft voice said.

Everyone turned and looked at Lance, stunned that he had entered the conversation, unusual silence hitting the group.

"Someone who has had the time to scope out the places where he's most likely to find someone to stimulate him." Lance looked at Ginny, and added, "They need overt stimulation for masturbation to lead to an orgasm."

"Jesus," Mitch said, staring at Lance, knowing his proclivity for privacy. Looking at the surprised faces of the group, he said, "We met in the Army and worked together on a case when I was with the FBI." Gaining a nod from Lance, he continued, "Lance worked as a criminal investigator with CID in the Army."

Stunned, the group remained quiet, but Ginny was now fascinated. "Do they always peer in windows to find someone when they need to masturbate? Why would someone peer into a living room window, for example?"

"Could be they just want to check out the inhabitants. They might be searching for a young teen, a woman, a child—"

Gasps resounded from the others, but Brogan cursed, "Oh, hell no!"

Lance nodded slowly. "Whether you want to face it or not, some men are only sexually excited with a child."

Zac tossed his dinner back to his plate. "That's so fucked."

"I don't think that's what we're dealing with," Mitch said. "All indications are that he is looking for women."

"He'll slip up," Lance said. "Sometime, he'll make a mistake."

"I hope it's sooner than later," Ginny replied. "Before he steps up his game."

That night, Ginny walked hesitantly toward the front door of the Sea Glass Inn. Stopping on the wide, front porch, she looked around. Across the street from the large bed and breakfast was the town beach, the breeze blowing in from the Chesapeake Bay. She knew Tori had inherited the inn from her grandmother and when she came back to run it, had also run into her childhood friends. Mitch had been one of those and the two quickly took up where they left off over ten years ago. She and Mitch now lived in their own house nearby, but Tori was at the inn almost every day, even though she now had a live-in manager there. Glancing down at her shorts and flip-flops, she had second thoughts, realizing she would be grossly underdressed for one of Tori's get togethers.

With her hand halted in mid-air before she knocked, Ginny was surprised when the door opened suddenly and Tori grinned. "I thought I saw you walk up. Come on back," she invited and led the way through the beautiful old inn. "I've still got the kitchen, deck, and back yard as my private place where guests aren't allowed," Tori called out. "It makes for a nice gathering place."

Ginny's gaze darted around, noting the antique furniture, exquisite artwork, and homey touches from Tori's grandmother's day. Following Tori, she breathed a sigh of relief seeing Tori in denim capris and flip-flops on her feet, as well. Entering the kitchen, she grinned at the number of open wine bottles and accepted the glass handed to her by her hostess before they stepped through the sliding glass doors onto a beautiful deck. Flower pots lined the edges and the backyard held lights in the trees, offering a surreal, nighttime vision.

Suddenly nervous, Ginny blushed at all the eyes now staring at her. Jillian, Katelyn, Jade, and Belle were in loungers and, from the looks of their happy faces, were definitely not on their first glass of wine.

Belle was the only one in a sundress and, as though she could read Ginny's mind, she swept her hand over her outfit and said, "I'm in nursing scrubs all day, so whenever I can put on a dress, I do." Giggling, she added, "And since I buy them on sale at Walmart, I can have a closet full!"

"Come on, have a seat," Tori invited, her smile indicating to Ginny that she must have noticed her reticence.

"Uh, sure. Thanks for inviting me."

"Glad you joined us!" Jillian said, her eyes warm and inviting.

After a few minutes, Belle turned to Ginny and asked, "Before you came, we were talking about the article in the newspaper about the peeping tom. Should we be worried?"

Ginny looked at the pretty brunette, her shy nature seeming to lesson with her third glass of wine. "I think every woman should take precautions. Keeping your blinds closed or curtains drawn at night is key—"

"I also read that if you plant thorny bushes under your windows, especially the windows at your bedroom, it can help," Jillian said. "Although, Grant resisted, saying he didn't want to deal with thorns next to where he mows."

"A nice little cactus garden would work," Jade surmised, only to frown at the laughter coming from Katelyn.

"Girl, a peeper isn't going to be walking around barefoot. A little cactus garden would get totally stepped on by some pervert in boots. He'd be squashing your baby cacti and whacking off at the same time!"

"Why is the plural of cactus cacti?" Jillian asked, her fourth glass of wine kicking in.

"Who cares about cactus or cacti?" Tori said, turning back to Ginny. "I want to hear about the peeping toms. I can't stand the thought that someone is doing this in our town."

"That's like octopi," Jade said, looking at Jillian.

"I'll bet it's more common than we think," Belle replied to Ginny.

"I know!" Jillian enthused. "That's so crazy. But then I don't suppose it should be octopuses."

Jade snorted as she repeated, "Octopuses. That sounds like a female octopus."

Jillian fell back on the sofa, her laughter ringing out as Katelyn stared at Jade, saying, "What the hell are you two talking about?"

"I think they're still on cactus and cacti," Belle said, stifling her giggle behind her hand as her blue eyes twinkled.

"Well, we need to get back onto the same friggin' topic!" Katelyn huffed. "Ginny's not going to want to come back to one of our planning parties if we can't behave."

"Have we actually talked about the wedding yet?" Ginny asked, her smile lopsided as the wine hit her.

"Nope," Jillian said. Grinning, she added, "Actually, it's mostly planned. This just gives us a good excuse to get together, drink, talk, and have a good time."

"Getting back to what we were talking about before Jillian and Jade went on a sea-creature rant, what is happening with the peeping tom?" Tori asked.

"We're investigating as best we can. I just don't want him to escalate."

Those words had the effect of a bucket of cold water dousing the others, sobering their expressions quickly.

"Oh, Jesus," Jade said, flopping back, forcing the air out of her lungs in a rush. "I never thought about that."

"A rapist?" Tori whispered, as though the very words would bring one forth.

"Not every voyeur becomes a rapist, but almost every rapist spent time as a voyeur," Ginny explained.

"How can we help?" Jillian asked, her eyes flashing with anger.

Ginny smiled, "Stay vigilant, observant, and watch out for each other."

"I hear the mayor and town manager want to run an article refuting that there's a problem," Tori said.

"Those two jackasses are such weasels, they should be stripped and run through the town to see how they like being looked at!" Katelyn hooted.

Jillian snorted, spitting out her wine, laughter spilling from her lips. "Oh, lordy, what a vision you just put in my head."

By the third glass of wine, Ginny knew her smile was slipping out more often. She had dreaded the gathering, unused to a group of women talking and having fun. Their conversations covered the town, their jobs, the Auxiliary, and the upcoming plans for the block party.

She relaxed in the deep cushions of the outdoor furniture and watched as Jillian and Katelyn tried to teach Jade how to line dance. Jade was not very coordinated but began to get the hang of the steps, in spite of her tipsiness.

"Come on, ladies!" Katelyn called out to the others, running over to pull Tori up from her seat as Jillian pulled on Belle's hand. "Time for dancing!"

Jade planted her hands on her hips and looked at Ginny. "The fact that you're a cop is kind of intimidating, but if I have to make a fool of myself, so do you."

Much to Ginny's surprise, she allowed herself to be pulled up from her chair and began to dance, her laughter bubbling forth, mixing in with the other women's.

At the end of the song, she turned to the others, her cheeks blushing, and blurted, "I need lingerie."

The others stopped and stared, their silent questioning causing her to rush on. "I never worried about underwear, but now I'd like something pretty. All I've got is basic, boring white. No lace. Just plain Jane underwear." Looking at Katelyn, she said, "Since I'm dating your brother, I guess that weirds you out, doesn't it?"

Katelyn grinned sloppily and said, "Nope. It's about time Brogan got some and I like you. So, you can give it to my brother anytime you want."

Belle swayed, stumbling slightly, with a confused expression on her face. "Why is Ginny giving Brogan her underwear?"

Snorting, Jillian said, "She's not giving him her underwear! She's giving him sex."

Belle blushed, then laughed as Tori grabbed her hand and twirled her around to the music.

Jillian threw her arm around Ginny and said, "No worries, girlie. We'll get you sorted. We'll go shopping!"

"I don't get a lot of time off right now."

"Victoria Secret online!" Jillian shouted, throwing her hands into the air as she danced around in a circle.

Within a few minutes, Tori had her laptop opened to the VS website and the ordering began. Embarrassed, Ginny attempted to call a halt to the proceedings, but the others were on a mission.

"You've got great boobs, so show 'em off, sweetie," Jillian said.

As the other women stared at her chest, Ginny blushed, giving them her measurements. She watched in awe as Tori began clicking.

"Do you want demi, push up, or just sexy?"

"I never really liked padded bras," Jade said. "I always wondered what the guy would say when he got the girl naked and instead of getting what he thought was a big handful, all he got was small."

"I agree," Katelyn said. "Might as well let them know what they're getting right away."

Belle looked down at her chest and sighed. "Yes, but with my curves, sometimes I think that's all a man sees." Looking up, she added, "I try to minimize what I can."

Ginny's head darted back and forth, trying to keep up with the conversation, before giving up and leaning over Tori's shoulder, seeing what she was ordering. "Wait, wait," Ginny protested. "I can't afford all that."

Jillian's smile slid over her face as she threw her arms around Ginny's shoulders. "Sweetie, consider this to be an early birthday present from all of us. Or Christmas. Whatever."

Seeing Ginny about to protest, Katelyn leaned forward. "Look girl, if you're banging my brother, who was in serious need of getting some…and not just from anyone, but from you…this is truly a gift from a grateful sister!"

"Done!" Tori announced, closing her laptop with a snap, before draining her glass. "Now, dance time!"

Wondering if she should have tried harder to keep her mouth shut, Ginny began to dance with the others, secretly excited for the lingerie to be delivered.

Soon, the rumble of deep laughter met their ears as

they turned, slightly inebriated, to see who was on the patio with them. Brogan, Mitch, Grant, Gareth, and Aiden were standing with their arms crossed, each fighting a smile.

Aiden opened his arms and said, "Looks like I'll take care of these ladies' tonight," and hugged Jade and Belle as they fell into him. Looking to the others, he called, "I'll get 'em home safe," before leading them back through the house.

Katelyn stood on her toes and kissed her brother before falling into Gareth's embrace. With a giggle and wave, they left as well.

As Mitch collected Tori, he looked over at Ginny and said, "It appears I won the bet."

Ginny grinned and nodded, "Yeah, seems I was wrong about how much fun I would have." Looking at Tori, she added, "Thanks for including me."

Grant snuggled Jillian next to him as Ginny walked straight into Brogan's embrace. Before the others left, Tori said, "The girls are worried about the voyeur. Just thought I'd let you know."

Mitch nodded, "Yeah. I decided to do a press conference tomorrow and see what we can do with public awareness."

With a wave, the three couples moved out into the night, each heading to their vehicles.

Brogan looked down at Ginny, her smile warming his heart. "I was a little worried," he said. "Wasn't sure it was your scene."

Laughing, she replied, "I wasn't sure it was either. But I had a good time."

After getting Ginny settled, Brogan climbed into his old truck and asked, "How drunk are you?"

"Just a little tipsy, why?"

"I don't want to take advantage of you, but I sure as hell want you tonight," he said, grinning.

His deep voice curled inside of her, waking her up as her core immediately tingled. "Oh, that can be arranged," she agreed. "Just take me home, honey. Just take me home."

19

Parking in front of her small house, Ginny jumped from his truck almost before he had it in park. Laughing as she raced up the front walk, she squeaked as he followed her inside and lifted her from the ground, twisting her in his arms before throwing her over his shoulder. With a light spank on her ass, causing her to kick her legs until he spanked her again, he rumbled, "Don't jump out of my truck until it's come to a stop."

"I'm a cop…I've had to hop out of our SUVs just as they were parking," she protested.

"That's work. But my truck, my rules," he said, with one more pat for emphasis. Stalking to the back, he asked, "Bedroom?"

"Yeah."

Chuckling, he said, "I mean *where* is the bedroom, not if you have one."

Blushing, she amended, "Back left."

Carrying her with ease, her middle still balanced over his shoulder, he stepped into a large room. He knew the old houses had small bedrooms and could tell that two rooms had been combined to create a nice space. A door opened into a bathroom, but as he spied the double-sized bed, all other thoughts flew out of his mind. Stooping, he gave a little toss and Ginny dropped onto her back on the mattress, a giggle jolting from her as his weight landed next to her.

She rolled on top, her breasts pressed to his chest as she kissed him. Immediately opening, she welcomed his tongue into her mouth. Sucking on it, she pulled it deeper, capturing the moan that escaped from deep in his chest.

Moving her hips, she pressed her pelvis closer to him as she rubbed her core against his jean-clad leg, knowing she could dry-hump him to orgasm.

That was all the invitation he needed before getting her naked. Grasping the bottom of her shirt, he pulled it over her head, their lips parting only for the passing of the material between them. She sat up, straddling his hips, her heated sex still searching for relief.

Ginny's plain bra pushed up her breasts like a feast for his eyes...and mouth. Dropping his lips from hers, he flipped her over, trailing a path down to the tops of her breasts with his tongue. He grabbed the material with his teeth and jerked it down, exposing her rosy-tipped nipples, already hard for him. Sucking deeply on one, he rolled the other between his forefinger and thumb. Moving between her breasts he teased each one, nipping then soothing, sucking deeply until she pressed harder against his leg.

Twisting her body, she heaved him to the side as she

retook the top position. His grin met hers, as they vied for dominance. "You're overdressed," she complained.

"Then you are welcome to do something about that situation," he drawled, his deep voice rumbling.

Her hands moved between them finding his jean button. Unfastening it as quickly as she could, she maneuvered the zipper over his massive erection. Palming him with one hand, she pushed his jeans down with the other, before sliding down to straddle his legs. Eyeing him with a grin, she licked her lips before licking the length of him.

"Oh, God, woman," Brogan groaned, watching as her lips slid over his erection, taking as much of him into her warmth as she could while fisting the base. With one hand cradling his balls, she bobbed her head up and down, sliding her tongue as she went. Occasionally, dragging her teeth gently over his sensitive skin, he reached down to grab her hair, twisting his fingers in her silky tresses.

Her ministrations were sending shock waves from his cock, short-circuiting his brain, until the only thing he was aware of were her lips, her tongue, her warm mouth. Feeling the sensation in his lower back, he squeezed his eyes tightly shut for a few seconds, debating whether to come in her mouth. Deciding he wanted to be buried in her sex, he pulled out, looking at her disappointed expression as she licked her lips.

"Baby, I want to come in your mouth sometime, but not tonight."

Rolling her to her side, his hands quickly divested her of her pants and panties. Soon they were both naked, hands caressing as they explored each other's bodies. Her lips traced the tattoo on his chest before pulling his own nipple into her mouth. Hearing his sharp intake of breath, Ginny smiled, knowing she retained some control.

Suddenly, she found herself hoisted up in his powerful arms and flipped once more. His gravelly voice commanded, "On your knees, babe."

She grinned as she acquiesced and he moved behind her, pulling her ass up as high as it would go. Leaning down, he fingered her folds as his other hand reached around, palming her breasts before tweaking each nipple.

The electric charge sent shockwaves throughout her body as she writhed in need, wiggling her ass as she pushed it back toward him. "Hold still. No moving." Following his command, he gave her ass a small spank, barely leaving a pink mark.

She gasped, the slight sting quickly replaced by a warmth that had her longing for more. His fingers continued to slide through her sex, every movement from her earning another spank.

Holding perfectly still, she panted as her orgasm neared. The sensations of his fingers probing her sex as he also pinched and rolled her nipples threatened to send her into oblivion. *Sweet oblivion. With him.* Tired of always being in control, releasing that control to Brogan was freeing. Closing her eyes, she grinned as her inner muscles tightened.

Reaching deep inside, Brogan tweaked the place he had learned was the exact spot to trigger her release. Not disappointed, she threw her head back just as he moved his other hand back to press his fingers against her clit, crying out her release as the orgasm rocked through her, sending her farther than she could have ever imagined.

Watching Ginny come so hard and fast, Brogan almost came himself before even entering her. Quickly sheathing himself, he plunged into her still quivering sex from behind, feeling her walls stretching to accommodate his girth.

No longer able to consider anything slow and easy, he moved quickly, rocking in and out as hard and as deep as he could. Glancing at the mirror to the side, he saw her pert tits bouncing in rhythm to his pounding. She had turned her head as well and he captured her gaze in the reflection.

As tightly wound as he was, he knew it would not take any time for his own orgasm to explode. "Touch yourself," he growled, then watched in fascination as her hand moved tentatively to her clit. Immediately acquiescing, she reached down and moved her finger over her taut bud.

His hand came down on her ass in a light spank and her gasp had him growing even harder. After each spank, he soothed the warm skin with his palm, feeling his balls tighten. "You ready?" he bit out, trying to maintain control. Moving his hand to her breasts again, he gently pinched then pulled on her nipples, just enough to cause her sex to tighten on his cock.

Fingering her clit once more, Ginny felt the sparks rush to all her extremities as her inner muscles clamped harder on his cock than she had ever felt. As she screamed his name, Brogan roared, his release pouring into her. Pressing as deep as he could, he continued to let her milk him until every drop was gone. Falling on top of her, he rolled to the side as he pulled out and moved her so that she was facing him.

Her breathing ragged, she felt like the winner of a long race. Exhausted, but elated. Her limp body lay next to his as he tucked her in tighter.

For minutes they said nothing, allowing the air to cool their bodies and time to slow their breathing. She finally lifted her head to stare at his face in the moonlight. "Damn. If that's what the other women get at the end of girls' night, no wonder they like it so much."

Chuckling, he said, "Don't want to think about Gareth giving it to my sister, babe."

"Well, he does and from what she says, he does good—"

"Fuck, honey—"

"I'm teasing, Brogan," she laughed, rolling toward him so her head now rested on his chest and her fingers played with the spattering of dark, curly hair. "Anyway, I've got the best, so you don't have to worry about any lack of comparison—"

"Damn, woman," he growled, lifting himself over her body as his lips clamped over hers. Mumbling against her mouth, he said, "Do I gotta get creative to shut you up?"

Kissing him back, she gentled her lips against his as she ran her fingers over his back. "No, baby. You can just be as creative as you want. Always."

The call came in two hours later, just as Ginny was deep in sleep, her legs tangled with Brogan's and her palm over his heart. Trained to immediately respond when her phone rang, she jumped, arms and legs whirling as she tried to locate her phone. Elbowing Brogan in the chest, her knee coming precariously close to his manhood, she managed to dislodge herself from him and roll to the edge of the bed as he cursed, rolling toward her.

Grabbing the phone, she answered just as Brogan lifted himself on one bent arm, his head in his hand watching her.

"Spencer, go ahead."

"Get to the Baytown Park, near the Gazebo. A woman was attacked."

"Fuck," Ginny breathed as she stood quickly, taking a second to gain her wits. Bending to grab her bra, she slipped it on before grabbing a clean pair of panties from the drawer. Rushing to her closet, she pulled a pair of khakis and a BPD polo off coat hangers.

"Babe."

"Brogan, I'm sorry. I promise this really happens rarely, but I gotta go. Please stay here and just lock the door when you leave."

"Babe," the deep voice came again.

Rushing out of the closet, she stared at his reflection in the mirror as she ran a brush though her tangled hair, pulling it up in a ponytail before twisting it into a tight bun.

Brogan watched as her warm gaze hardened before his eyes, her mind now on her job. He took a second to consider how that made him feel, but realized she was who she was...and he loved who she was.

Swinging his legs over the side of the bed, he stood and stalked to her as she turned to stare up at him. "Babe, you're fine. I'd be a liar if I said I didn't still want you asleep, curled up next to me, but you go do what you gotta do."

Relief rushed from her as she expelled the breath she had been holding. Rising on her toes, she kissed him, soft and sweet, with the promise of more to come. "Thank you, honey. Please stay here...go back to sleep."

Running out of her house, Ginny jogged to the SUV parked in front and hopped in, reporting to Mildred that she was on her way. Driving away, she glanced at her house in the rear-view mirror, images of the man inside, filling her mind...and her heart.

Brogan watched her drive down the road before wandering back to her bedroom to change into his clothes. Awake now, he decided to head back to his place so he could take care of MB. Making Ginny's bed, he hated how little sleep she was getting. Or the irregular meals. His mind wandered to the possible danger she could be in, but he forced that thought away.

Is this what it's like to love a cop?

20

Ginny arrived and pushed her way through the small crowd gathering, past the yellow police tape. Grumbling about people rushing from bed to see what the commotion was, she knew curiosity was human nature.

Arriving at the scene, she found the others gathered, Mitch overseeing Grant, Burt, Sam, and two detectives from the North Herron Sheriff's Office. Moving straight to Mitch, she said, "Got here as soon as I could."

"You're off duty, no apologies. The ambulance is ready to head to the hospital. I need you with her every moment. Take the bags given and collect everything—"

"I know the procedures, Chief," she interrupted.

With a nod, he growled, "We'll be here collecting evidence and then I'll come to the hospital after I make a public statement."

She placed her hand on his arm, her concern bleeding through her words, "Chief…Mitch…this is not your fault."

She felt pinned to the ground, his stare was so hard.

"If I hadn't listened to the mayor and had gone ahead to make a public warning—"

"He's your boss. You tried it his way. It didn't work. Now we do it our way," she assured. Turning, she ran to the back of the ambulance and hopped in, all other thoughts pushed back.

The young woman sat on the edge of the hospital bed, the curtains pulled all around. Ginny stood near her—close enough for comfort, but not crowding. She closed her eyes for a second, allowing the fatigue and adrenaline drain to overtake her for a second. She was thrilled Carly had not been raped, but to have been attacked was horrible. She knew the young woman was shaken to her very core.

The questions had been endless and Ginny hated having to be the one to ask. *Where were you? Did he come from behind? Did you see his face? How did he touch you?* On and on. Ginny had taken each article of clothing and placed them in separate evidence bags, sealing them. She had sealed the scrapings from underneath Carly's fingernails, too, as well as the buccal swab.

"Carly?" Ginny said softly, so as not to startle her. When Carly's eyes met hers and she continued, "This may not be very professional, but I'm going to tell you something…woman to woman." Seeing Carly's questioning gaze, she plunged ahead, "You will get through this. I know." Leaning closer, so that their faces were but inches apart, she repeated, "I. Know."

Carly's eyes widened in understanding, but a knock

on the door panel interrupted before she could respond. Ginny checked to see who it was, inviting June to come in.

When June looked to her for approval, she nodded once. Turning to Carly, June said, "Carly, my name is June Sisco. I'm with the Eastern Shore Mental Health Group and I am one of the Sexual Assault counselors. I work with the police and as a private counselor."

Carly lifted her gaze dully to June and nodded, sucking in a ragged breath, as June stepped closer and placed her hand on Carly's.

"What you need to know is that you are not alone. What happened made you vulnerable, but you are no longer alone. There are those who will help and I'll be with you every step of the way." Ginny watched as Carly held June's gaze for a long moment, before sliding her eyes to her. A slight nod followed.

"I'm going to step outside the room with Officer Spencer and ask her a few questions, if you don't mind. If you do, I'll be more than happy to meet with her at a different time and can stay with you now."

"No, it's fine," Carly said. "Is it about what happened?"

"Yes. I'll have the officer tell me your statement, so you don't have to repeat it so soon. We'll certainly talk about it later, but for now, if you like, she can give me the details."

"Yes, please," Carly nodded. "I'd rather not repeat it right now."

With a pat on her arm, June motioned for Ginny to step outside the doorway and shut the door behind her.

In the hallway, June's warm eyes bore into Ginny's and she asked, "How are you?"

"Me?"

"Come on, Ginny," June cajoled. "This cannot be easy for you."

Placing her hands on her hips, Ginny pinched her lips as she stared down at her shoes. Heaving a sigh, she said, "No. No, it's not. But this isn't about me. This is about her." Lifting her eyes, she said, "I've had several years to work through what happened to me. Several years to…not forget, but to…put it in a place where it doesn't affect my every thought. And, I'm getting help." A slight smile toward June slipped from her lips, soon to be replaced with a stoic, professional expression.

"Okay, the quick details. She was walking from a friend's house to hers, walking across the park. She had had a glass of wine but was not intoxicated. Her test put her under the legal limit, but of course, she wasn't driving. She said she's always aware of her surroundings, and had just passed the gazebo and was hustling to get to the next street light. She said she heard footsteps behind her, but they were already close and she had no time to turn around. She was grabbed from behind, one hand on her mouth and one arm around her upper body, clamping her arms to her sides.

"He took her to the ground, face down. His body weight on her back kept her from being able to get up and run. He talked to her, saying things like *'You're hot.'*, *'You make me want to come'*, *'I've been watching* you*'*, things like that. She said she tried to scream, but he shoved a rag in her mouth and even though she tried to push it out with her tongue, it was too much. Then she became afraid of choking, so she focused on breathing through her nose.

"He pressed his genitals against her bottom, rubbing himself on her, thrusting. Her pants and his stayed on, but he slid one hand underneath her shirt and managed to grab her breast. He had to be forceful, with the weight of their bodies on the ground, and she does have marks on her stomach and breasts."

During Ginny's recitation, June took notes on a pad of paper, her lips tight. Looking up, she nodded for Ginny to continue.

"She said he kept talking the whole time and then finally he grunted loudly and she said he must have ejaculated in his pants."

"Any semen on her clothes?"

"There was a tiny stain on the seat of her pants but I don't know what it will produce. Everything's been sent to the lab."

"Anything else?"

"She said she thought he was going to kill her, but he said for her to keep her face away from him and to stay on the ground for five minutes. If she didn't, he knew where she lived and he'd come for her."

"Shit, Ginny," June said, her mouth drawn in a tight line.

"Listen, just so you know, we've had reports of a voyeur in town. The mayor put the kibosh on Mitch talking about it, but the news is out now. Mitch'll be taking care of that. Just want you to know...it can stir up memories for past victims, so the Mental Health Group might be getting more calls."

"Right...thanks for the warning." June snapped her

notebook closed and placed it in her oversized bag. "Okay, let's go back in."

Bone tired. Not entirely a new experience for Ginny after having served in the Army's Military Police or as a police officer even in a small town. But right now, she was not sure she could remember the last time she was this tired.

Two hours of sleep, several long hours with a very emotional victim, returning thoughts of her own victimization, and a conference in the police station had her dragging. And the day was just starting.

Mitch had stood outside the police station with the local press, including several from the Virginia Beach area, and made a public statement concerning the reports of voyeuristic behavior and now an assault. The obvious questions about why he had waited rained down and his tense stance and short responses gave indication of his anger. Standing next to the blustering mayor, who assured the public that their fair town was safe, Ginny thought Mitch's teeth would crack under the pressure of his grimace.

Finally, with the circus gone, the law enforcers were back in the workroom. Mildred and Mable hustled in with coffees. "Compliments from Jillian," she said. The group took them gratefully. Mildred put her hand on Sam's shoulder and said, "Your wife called. She's worried, but I told her you were fine."

Sam grumbled good naturedly, "Worrying woman,"

but the soft smile on his face told the story of a man in love with his wife.

Ginny turned her attention to Mitch, knowing the pressure of his job right now was bearing down on him. "You okay, Chief?"

Standing by the white board with his hands on his hips, he nodded as he lifted his gaze to her. "Yeah. Kicking myself for not going with a public announcement earlier, but what's done is done. Now, we move forward and find this asshole."

Grant spoke next, "I canvassed the area to see who was seen out last night. Got an interesting list." Using his laptop, he projected the list on the white board. Ginny recognized several names of men in town, but a few she did not know. Grant explained they were vacationers. As her eyes dropped down the list, she reared back.

"Yep, I wondered when y'all would notice that. Robert Banks. The mayor's nephew. And, on top of that…Silas Mills."

"What was Silas doing out in the middle of the night?" Burt asked. "Or, for that matter, Robert Banks?"

"Looks like we're gonna find out," Mitch said. "But before we go out questioning the people on this list, let's look over what we know."

The group spent the next hour poring over the details of both the voyeur reports and the assault.

Mitch finally looked around and asked, "Who needs a break?"

Ginny quickly offered, "I had a couple of hours of sleep, so I'm better than Sam. I'll go question."

"Hell, Ginny, I ain't no old foggie," Sam muttered,

stifling a yawn behind his hand.

The others laughed, and Mitch ordered, "Sam, go home, get some sleep. At least a couple of hours. Ginny, I know this is hard, but I'd like you in on the interviews. You've got a different perspective than the rest of us and it'll give us a chance to question these men with a woman present. Got no idea if it'll make a difference, but I'd like you on them anyway. You and Grant talk to Robert, and then you and I'll talk to Silas."

"He's gonna be pissed," Grant warned, but winked at Ginny, knowing they all disliked the town manager.

"Not my job to keep him happy," Mitch said. "Okay, let's roll."

People crowded around the bar, conversations flowing about the latest news in town. Brogan glanced at Aiden, noticing his brother's normal loud laughter had not resounded today. Aiden's face appeared to mirror his own—tight lips and hard eyes. Sighing, Brogan pulled another beer and set it on the counter, wishing for the regular talk of fishing, weather, and sports to fill the air instead of the topic of Mitch's public statement.

Katelyn walked behind the bar after delivering a plate of food and sighed as she picked up a tray of drinks to take.

"You don't gotta do that, sis," Brogan said. He cast his practiced eye over the crowd. "We have plenty of servers."

"I know, but Gareth's doing some work with Mitch and I closed up the PI office early to come here." She held his gaze and shrugged. "I just found myself wanting to be near people instead of at the office by myself." Seeing his jolt of concern, she quickly added, "I wasn't afraid, I just felt so sad at what was happening in our town. But, I've got to admit, everyone's conversation is a downer."

"Some are bitching about the mayor not letting Mitch announce things earlier…others are blaming the police. Others are on a witch hunt for whoever they don't like, and a few…" Aiden sighed as he cursed, "fuckin' hell, a few are blaming women for leaving their windows open and walking at night."

Katelyn's eyes flashed as she announced, "Well, they better not say that around me or they'll go somewhere else!"

Nodding in agreement, Brogan moved down to the other end of the bar, refilling a few drink orders, but his thoughts were on Ginny. He knew she must be exhausted with only a few hours of sleep. Seeing Callan and Jason walk in, he jerked his chin in greeting.

"What a fuckin' mess," Jason said. "How's Ginny?"

"Haven't talked to her today, other than a text saying she'd be working late." He did not add that her text also said that if he wanted, she would try to meet with him tonight since she would love to fall asleep in his arms again. That thought sent warmth through him, as the memory of her soft body tucked next to his fired his blood.

"Mom. Dad," he heard Katelyn call out. Looking over, Brogan saw his parents coming in, his mother's face full of concern and his father's tight with anger. They slid into one of the booths in the back, Katelyn sliding in next to their mom, leaning her head over as Corrine wrapped her daughter in her arms. Aiden and Brogan soon joined, setting drinks in front of them.

"I was just talking to Mitch's parents and they're just as upset over Mayor Banks acting like he's above all of this mess saying that the town is fine," Eric said.

Mitch's father was the police chief for a long time before his retirement, so Brogan knew Ed had had his share of run-ins with Corwin and Silas.

"Where's Gareth?" Corrine asked Katelyn.

"He's in Virginia Beach on a case, but don't worry. I'll stay here until Aiden or Brogan can take me home."

"You're done here," Brogan stated, brooking no argument. "No need to stay. Mom and Dad can see you home."

"Are you sure?" Katelyn asked, her gaze moving across the crowd.

"We got it," Aiden assured, kissing the top of Katelyn's head before he headed back to the bar.

Nodding, Katelyn frowned. "I hate this. I hate not feeling safe here."

Corrine pulled her daughter in tighter. "I know, baby girl. I agree."

As Brogan watched his family leave, he rubbed his hand over his face, fatigue pulling at him. He considered closing the bar early, but knew patrons would not go home, instead hitting somewhere else to drink. A place where there was no one who cared how much they drank. Moving behind the bar with Aiden, he collected a few tabs as he cut some of the heavier drinkers off.

Looking at the clock one more time, he counted the hours until he had Ginny in his arms once more.

21

Boring. That was how many of Ginny's days were as a Baytown Police Officer. Maybe boring was too harsh of a word. *Uneventful. Yeah, that's better.* But today's investigations had her running ragged while Sam and Burt took on all the town patrols. Mitch had apologized ahead of time, but she understood why he wanted her there. Now all she felt was bone tired, as the interviews played over and over in her mind.

She and Grant had found Robert Banks at the mayor's residence, the door being opened by Corwin's, wife, Phyllis. Letting them in, she called for Robert. Corwin came from his study, his eyes narrowed on them. Turning to his wife, he groused, "Why did you let them in without a warrant?"

Phyllis glared at her husband, "Seriously? We have a possible rapist on the loose in this town and you're quibbling about your nephew answering some questions?"

"There's no evidence of a rapist," he argued back,

"just some woman who got felt up in the park when she probably—"

"Not. One. More. Word, Corwin," Phyllis announced, her finger in his face. "You are too good of a public servant to say what just ran through your mind." Successfully shutting her husband up, she turned to Robert as he descended the stairs, his eyes darting between the different persons in the foyer.

Ginny watched the self-assured young man. His dark hair was brushed to the side and he had that cute look that probably appealed to the young girls, with his almost filled out body and height. Wearing a light blue polo and checkered shorts, he appeared as though he could grace the cover of Teen Golf magazine—if there was such a thing.

"Robert, this is Officers Spencer and Wilder. You may speak with them in the living room and your uncle and I'll be in the kitchen. I trust you will cooperate fully and completely with all their questions."

"Of course," Robert said, nodding politely.

"Phyllis, one of us should be with him," Corwin said, pulling out his phone. "Let me call our attorney."

"I'm sure that won't be necessary," Robert said. Looking up at Grant, he asked, "Would it be alright if either my aunt or uncle were with us?"

"Certainly," Grant nodded.

"Aunt Phyllis?" Robert asked. "No offense, Uncle Corwin, but Aunt Phyllis remains a bit cooler, if you know what I mean."

"Of course," Phyllis replied as Corwin humphed and turned to leave.

After settling, Ginny began, "We understand you

were near the park late last night. We are simply trying to identify anyone in the area who might have heard or seen something that might aid our investigation. Can you please tell us of your whereabouts and times?"

"Certainly, Officer. I've been in town for about three weeks now, on a break from college. I'm taking a semester to study a small town and have previously studied a large city, as my major is Public Administration. I figured it would give me a chance to connect with my uncle and aunt again, watch a small town Mayor in action and, well," he chuckled, "also give me a break from classes before I go back to finish.

"I've just started meeting some people and have to say that there really aren't very many here that are my age. I've found a few that I've hung around with. Last night, there was a party at the apartments…uh…condos, off Franklin Street."

"Who was having the party?" Ginny asked.

Scrunching his brow, Robert said, "There are couple of teachers who share a place there. One is Ben, but I'm afraid I don't know his last name. The other is James. I don't know his last name either, but I know he works as a PE teacher at the high school."

Ginny kept her expression neutral, but knew who he was talking about. Offering an encouraging nod, she focused on Robert.

"Tell us about the party," Grant commanded in the tone he used when he wanted information but still made the person think they were just talking to a friend. Ginny held her smile knowing, at this moment, Grant was using his *hey, I'm just a guy, too* persona.

"It was good," Robert smiled. "Plenty of booze, but

nice, you know. Not like some frat party where everyone was just getting trashed. There was a game on TV and they had a nice set-up with a wide-screen. They had the table set up like a buffet with food, drinks on the kitchen counter."

"Did you recognize anyone else there?"

"Oh, sure, but I hardly know their names. I saw a couple of girls who work at the Seafood Shack there and a few more from the beach. Same with the guys...a few I recognized from some of the restaurants in town."

"And after the party?" Ginny asked.

Robert reddened slightly, his eyes cutting to his aunt who was sitting quietly in one of the upright chairs. "Well, I kinda hit it off with one of the girls and she invited me back to her place. We walked to her apartment that was a few blocks over, at the far end of the park. I stayed there for a bit and then had to walk back across the park to get to my car, which was left at the condo."

"What time was all this?"

"Uh...we left the party about midnight and I left her place about 1 a.m."

Phyllis lifted her eyebrow as she eyed Robert. "Didn't stay long, did you?"

Fully blushing now, Robert said, "Just long enough to...uh...have a drink...and talk a bit."

"Uh huh," she said, then settled back in her chair, shaking her head slightly.

"We'll need her name, of course," Grant said. "And what you saw as you walked in the park."

"Her name was Cindy Snyder," Robert said. "She'll corroborate everything I've said. But as to what I saw in the park...nothing. Honestly, nothing. I didn't see anyone or hear anyone at all. I was back to my car in only ten minutes...uh...fifteen minutes, at most, and then drove home."

Holding his gaze for a moment, Ginny and Grant only had a few more questions and then they left. Standing at their SUV for a moment, they discussed the next course of action, missing Robert pulling back the curtain in the living room watching them with narrowed-eyed interest.

It only took a few minutes to find Cindy's apartment and her at home. Still hungover, she looked a bit worse for the wear, but her statements matched Roberts'. Of course, he had no witnesses to what happened after he left her apartment and headed back to his car.

Later in the afternoon, she and Grant drove to the high school to meet with James and Ben. "James Smithson is a new teacher here at the high school...this is his first year here. Benjamin Hudgins is also fairly new, but he's been working here almost three years."

Grant grunted his acknowledgment and they walked up to the fence lining the football practice field. Grant shook his head, saying, "Man, this is nicer than what we had about fifteen years ago."

Looking up, she thought about the original Baytown Boys and smiled, imaging a ninth-grade Brogan, Grant, and Mitch. "So, you all had to rough it in the old days," she joked.

Chuckling, he said, "Well, we didn't have our own practice field. So, we had to share it with whoever else was practicing at the time. I think the girls' field hockey had to share it with us. "Of course, back then, the chance to watch the girls run around in shorts didn't exactly upset us."

"Anyone I know?"

"Busted," he laughed. "Jillian always caught my eye, even back then. Everyone always thought of Katelyn as the athlete but, let me tell you, Jillian had a mean swing."

Laughing, she turned and watched as Ben jogged over to the fence. His ready smile greeted them and she could see why Jillian had gone out with him a couple of times before Grant got his act together and went after her. Tall, muscular, but lean—more of a runner's build. His sandy blond hair was covered with a ball cap, which he took off to swipe his brow before replacing it back on his head. A sideways glance told her that Grant was not thrilled to have the reminder that Jillian had finally gotten tired of waiting on him standing right in front of him.

"Hey, the team manager said you needed to talk to me and James?" Ben asked, as he leaned on the fence. "Do you want to talk here or go sit somewhere?"

"This is good," Grant said curtly. "We need to know about the party last night. Who you were with and if you noticed when people came and left."

Ben scrunched his face to the side in thought and said, "Truthfully, I don't remember too much about the times. It was supposed to be a football game party. We have a large, flat screen TV and had invited about ten or so friends over to watch the games. But, like most parties, more and more people showed up."

"Did you stay at your place the whole time?"

"Yeah—uh, no. I had to make a snack run to the grocery at about nine or so. We were low on chips, dip, that kind of stuff. It probably took about thirty minutes to get there and back."

"And you didn't leave any time after that?"

Ben hesitated for a moment before sighing. "I'd like to ask what this is about, but I got a bad feeling that something happened to someone." Shaking his head, he answered, "I walked two of the women home. They had dropped by and when it was time to leave, I didn't feel right about them walking by themselves."

"Can you tell us where you walked them and what time?"

Rubbing his chin, Ben replied, "Both lived on the other side of the park. One was on the south side, in one of the vacation rentals, and then I walked the other one to the east side, to one of those condos. Time? The last game was over and they'd stayed for a while, just hanging out. I'd say it was close to midnight." He blushed and said, "I sound l like an old fogey, but with today being a work day, I was ready to call it a night. I'd preferred the party had just been some of us friends watching football, not a full-blown party." Jerking his head toward James, who was ambling over, he laughed, "Now, my roomie over there had no problem with a few women showing up."

Just then, a group of cheerleaders wandered by, giggling and shouting, "Hi, Mr. Smithson!" James threw his hand up good naturedly and waved at the girls, his smile wide and white.

Ben rolled his eyes and grinned. "Anything else I can answer for you, officers?"

Ginny knew Grant still had his *don't fuck with me*

face, so she smiled pleasantly and asked, "What time did you get back home and can anyone verify that?"

"Hmm, I guess it took about forty-five minutes to escort both women home and then back across the park to our place. Yeah, yeah, it was near one in the morning...well, this morning, because I was glad a few of our friends had stayed to clean up. When I got back, the place was in good shape and they were leaving."

"So, you and James were both there as the last people left around one a.m.?" Ginny asked.

"Well, James wasn't there. I figured he was in his room with...uh...well, with one of the girls. So, I said goodbye to the last of our friends, locked the front door and headed to my room and crashed. Hell, we have to get up at about 6:30 a.m. for work, so I can't pull the all-nighters anymore. But I did hear James come in later."

"I thought you said he was in his room—"

"That's what I thought, but I heard the front door later and happened to roll over. It was about two then."

"Did you ask him about it this morning?" Ginny inquired.

Ben laughed, "'Fraid not. We're roommates, that's all. We go and come as we please."

James made it to the fence and slapped Ben on the back. "You hanging in there? Jesus, I know I'm getting older when I'm dragging my ass from being up so late." Sliding his gaze through Ginny, he turned his attention toward Grant, saying, "Heard you needed a word."

After Ben rattled off the names of the guests, he waved and took off running after the boys on the practice field and Ginny and Grant began the questioning over again.

Forthcoming, James told them he had stayed in during the party, corroborating the times that Ben was gone to pick up food. As to the end of the party, he grinned, "I admit to a hookup." His gaze shifted to Ginny for an instant before moving back to Grant. "Ben had gone to walk some girls home, he's such a good boy scout. Anyway, most of our friends had left and there was a girl I had an eye on, so we hooked up."

"At your place?"

James leaned back, a hand on his heart, "Good God, no! Despite what you might think, our party was not some kind of college, frat-boy orgy! I drove to her place and we had a good time. Kissed her goodbye a little before two in the morning and drove back home."

"Did anyone see you when you got in?"

"No, but Ben's door was closed so, I assumed he was already in bed."

Ginny pinched her lips together, listening to his flimsy alibi. Grant showed James the list from Ben of the men who had attended the party and James confirmed.

"Can you tell me what this is about?" James asked, angling his ball cap to keep the sun out of his eyes.

"A woman was attacked in the early hours of the morning. We're following up on anyone reported to have been out in the area," Ginny said.

"Damn," James cursed. He looked to the side where the cheerleaders were practicing and said, "I've been toying with the idea of working with some of the girls about physical safety and protection. You know, things we often wait until college to even talk about. I figured these teenage girls could use some tips." He looked back to Ginny and smiled. "Would you be interested in helping?"

A tight-lipped smile formed on her face as she, noncommittedly, said, "If you get it started, let me know and I'll see."

As Ginny and Grant made it back to the SUV, he turned and said, "That's kind of like putting the cat in charge of the bird cage, isn't it?"

"No kidding," she said, climbing inside.

"Would you really work with him?"

"I might need to, if for no other reason, to see what he'd actually teach the girls," she replied, sucking in a deep breath to relieve the sinking feeling rushing into her stomach.

The sinking feeling had now turned into acid as Ginny faced Silas. She and Mitch had walked to his office and he had made them wait in the Town Hall lobby for fifteen minutes after the receptionist had told him they were there.

Now, sitting in the chairs facing his desk, his glare heavy on them, Ginny felt her anger slicing through her gut once more.

Mitch, cutting to the chase, said, "We need to know where you were last night."

Silas' eyes widened slightly before narrowing. "You have got to be kidding."

"Not at all. We're talking to everyone who was reported to be in the area of the park late last night. You're name was reported. So, I'll ask again. Where were you and I'll go ahead and throw in the next questions—what time and who did you see?"

"I don't have to answer any questions," he replied, his nose in the air, and Ginny was reminded that Jillian had referred to him as a weasel. She always thought it was because of his personality, but now she realized it was his physical appearance also. She remained quiet, knowing Silas would only respond to Mitch, because he was the Chief, but also because he was a man. The thought only mildly irritated her—she trusted Mitch to handle Silas but she also itched to spar with him. Refocusing, she watched with interest as Mitch's silence began to unnerve Silas.

"As town manager, I—"

"You know that no one is above the law," Mitch interjected.

"Don't try to intimidate me, *Chief*."

The sarcastic emphasis on Mitch's title did not go unnoticed by her but appeared to be completely ignored by Mitch.

"Silas," he continued, "I've got a sexual assault case on my hands and you, of all people, must want it solved as soon as possible. The news is now on it and every step we take is being watched. You think, for one minute, that the person who reported that you were seen out last night in the vicinity of the park, will stay quiet. Answer me now and this can end. I can report that we followed up on all sightings and determined they were not who we are looking for. The alternative is that reporter from Virginia Beach, the one you're always cozying up to when she's in the area, will be reporting on you."

The more Mitch spoke, the more Silas' lips pinched together. His gaze jumped from Mitch, to her, and then back to Mitch. The silence stretched interminably, but she knew Mitch was patient. They could wait.

Finally, Silas leaned back in his chair, anger vibrating from his being. His pen tapping on the desk, he said, "Fine. I was out. I was visiting a friend. I didn't want my car to be seen in front of he—uh, their house, and so I parked several blocks away. I…visited, and then walked back to my car."

"Time?"

Pinching his lips again, he replied, "About one in the morning."

"Did you see or hear anything while you were walking by the park?"

"No. Certainly not. When I heard there was an attack, I was horrified. Don't you think that if I knew something, I would have come forward?"

"No, I don't. But then, that's why we're here."

"Listen, I don't have to put up with your insinuations." He reached for his phone, adding, "In fact, I think I'll phone my attorney."

"No problem," Mitch said. "By the way, who were you with last night, so we can corroborate the times?"

Silas' hand stilled on his phone, his fingers slowly pulling back. "Who?"

"Yes, we need to verify your story and the times."

Ginny noticed the slight shaking of his hands as well as the pitch of his voice, which was rising. Silas leaned forward, baring his teeth, and she could now say without a doubt that he was indeed a weasel in every sense of the word.

"How dare you not take my word," he seethed.

Mitch sighed as though talking with a recalcitrant child. "Silas, I want to put this to rest. You think I want to be chasing false threads to this investigation? Hell, I want to get this over with so that I can continue finding the person responsible."

Ginny kept her gaze straight ahead but was surprised at Mitch's words. At this stage, Silas was still a suspect, but Mitch was acting as though he believed Silas was innocent. Before she had time to process this further, she noted Silas seemed to relax slightly and she understood. Mitch was a master interrogator. Right now, he was playing good cop which, she realized, made her bad cop. And that thought had her struggling to hide her smile.

Silas' gaze jumped between the two of them and he leaned toward Mitch slightly. "I was…uh…with a woman."

"Nothing wrong with that," Mitch acknowledged, a slight smile on his face. "I know you've been dating Holly Prescall. Congratulations. In fact, I heard that y'all are picking out china already. We'll just check with Holly and—"

"It wasn't Holly," Silas admitted, his words forced between gritted teeth.

Sighing again, Mitch said, "We're gonna need a name, Silas."

The silence once more hung heavy over the office.

"Celia."

Ginny managed to keep her face neutral, hoping the widening of her eyes had gone unnoticed.

"Celia Ring…your receptionist?"

"Yes," he bit out.

"Okay, we'll talk to Celia on our way out." With that, Mitch stood and, with a nod toward Silas, he stepped to the side, allowing Ginny to walk out in front of him.

Celia was sitting at her desk just outside the mayor's office and her eyes hit them as soon as they moved toward her. Casting her eyes toward Mitch, she purred, "Hello, Chief Evans," ignoring Ginny. "Do you want to see Corwin?"

Ginny knew the town talked about Celia when Corwin first hired his secretary. But she also knew Phyllis controlled the family money and Corwin would not chance an affair. *But Silas, the weasel?* Out of the corner of her eye, she saw Mitch stand back and she knew that was her cue to step in.

"Celia, we need to corroborate a story from last night and early this morning." Celia's cat-like smile dropped from her face as her eyes cut over to Silas' office door, firmly shut.

"Uh…I…uh…"

"We need to know who you were with, what time they arrived, and when they left."

"Uh..I…"

"We are investigating an assault in the park, Celia. After reporting your concerns, I know you want to do anything you can to assist us in checking on the reports of people in the area."

Celia's eyes flashed irritation mixed with resignation. "Yes…sure, yes. Silas Mills came by last night about eleven. We had…uh…business to discuss. Business that was…couldn't wait."

"And he left at what time?"

"About one…one this morning."

Thanking her, Ginny and Mitch turned to walk away when they noticed the mayor's door slightly open with Corwin standing at the opening, listening. Continuing to walk through the back corridor that led to the police station, neither spoke until they were back in their workroom, once more staring at their board.

22

Now, parked in front of her house, her legs too tired to move, Ginny leaned her head against the headrest and closed her eyes, thoughts of the day's interviews overwhelming her.

The sound of her door opening next to her caused her to yelp as Brogan leaned across her, unbuckling her seatbelt. His large frame filled the space and before she could protest, he reached in and pulled her gently out, cradling her against his chest as he carried her toward her front door. Throwing her arms around his neck, she protested feebly, "I can walk, you know? All my neighbors are going to think that you always carry me into my house." She felt his chest rumble against her and she could not help but smile. "Of course, this is a more dignified way to be carried than over your shoulder like last night. God, that seems like days ago."

As they entered, he kicked the door shut, bending to flip the deadbolt. "Right," he said, "and that's why I'm taking care of you now."

Brogan stalked straight to her bedroom and, bypassing the bed, marched into the bathroom. He discovered the former owners had indeed combined two small bedrooms, to create a nice master-bedroom suite. The bathroom was well appointed, with white tile and a full, soaker tub and shower. The toilet and linen closet were behind a door, offering privacy, and the long counter held double sinks.

He settled her feet on the plush floor mat, while he bent to turn on the water spigots. Hot, steaming water filled the tub quickly and he spied a box labeled bath bombs setting on the side of the tub. He picked it up and sniffed, the floral scent filling his nostrils. Throwing in a few, they immediately began to bubble and fizz, causing him to do a double-take, making sure it was okay.

Giggling, Ginny looked over at his surprised expression. "Did you even know what bath bombs were before you threw them in?"

Blushing slightly, he shook his head. "No, but anything with the name bath on it and, smells like flowers, must be good." Turning back to her, he began to strip her, pushing her hands out of the way. "This is all on me, babe." Peeling her polo and then bra off, he bent to slide her pants and panties down.

She held on to his broad shoulders as she stepped out of them, shivering as his hands trailed slowly up her legs.

"Damn, you're a temptation, but this is not about me and definitely not about sex."

Ginny peered down at him as he continued to kneel on the mat. "Then what is it about?" Her head lifted as he stood and she maintained eye contact, his Irish blues staring straight into her.

"This is about me taking care of my woman. Sounds caveman-ish, I know, but it's been a rough twenty-four hours for you. Come on," he said, offering his hand.

Taking it, he wrapped his warm hand carefully around her, and she allowed herself to be pampered, an unusual feeling, as she stepped into the tub and sank into the watery depths. Moaning as she laid back, she closed her eyes as her head hit the bath pillow.

Brogan sat on the floor next to the tub and stared at her for a long moment. He could not believe this woman was with him. This beautiful, kind, strong, caring woman. He had given everything to her—his painful past, his anger and guilt, and she had taken it all, telling him to let go of his demons. Unsure if he could, he knew he would cherish her, as long as she allowed him to.

Her slightly tanned face held a few freckles captive across her cheeks and nose. Her shiny, straight hair was still in its bun, tamed as always when she was in uniform. He wanted it to fall about her shoulders but figured that, for now, being up kept it dry. Her eyes were closed and a crescent of thick lashes rested on her upper cheeks. Her mouth, with its slash of pale lipstick, was lush and moist, slightly open as she breathed. Her arms floated on top of the water and as his gaze drifted, her rosy-tipped breasts were barely visibly, but he already had their shape and feel memorized.

Her eyes opened as she rolled her head toward him. "This feels so good. Why don't you join me?"

"If I do, then I'll—"

"Yep, and that's exactly what I want," she grinned. "A hot bath and some hot sex...perfect sleep recipe."

Grinning, he stood, jerking off his shirt. "Well, I aim to please, ma'am."

As he crawled into the tub behind her, she laughed when the water moved higher. Soon, forgetting about the water level, she allowed him to take the worries of the day away.

Ears open, Brogan listened as the man at the end of the bar continued to talk.

"Yep, nice little town you got here. I come a couple a' times a year. Once a year, I'll bring my wife, but the other times, I tell her I'm on a business trip and escape here to do a little fishin'. 'Course with the women around here, I don't tell my wife what I'm fishin' for."

He laughed at his own joke and Brogan pinched his lips tighter, wishing the man would leave.

"Yes, indeed. This little ol' town's got some mighty fine ass. Teens in bikinis with their pert little tits all up and high. Older women with asses that are big and firm. I keep looking for a woman with pert tits and a big ass, but—"

"You drinking or talking?" Brogan interrupted.

The man blinked a few times, then looked down at his empty drink. "Sorry, man. I'll take another. Fill 'er up." Snorting, he said, "That reminds me of a joke. What did the gas attendant say to the wh—"

"Shut the fuck up, man," Brogan said, moving away from him, disgusted. He glanced down at the credit card in his hand, making a note of the name, realizing that a vacationer could easily be the culprit the police were looking for. Martin Tobaski. Nodding toward Aiden, he headed to the back. Placing a quick call to Ginny, he could not keep the grin off his face when she answered with, "Hey, honey. What's up?"

Giving her the name, he said, "Just a thought that your culprit doesn't have to live here, and this guy says he comes several times a year to get away from his wife. He's been talking and, while I'm battling the desire to punch the fucker's mouth, I've heard him, and he's been observing, in great detail, the women while here."

"Thanks, honey. You're in a position to hear a lot so I'll take whatever intel you have."

Disconnecting, he heard a commotion and walked out just in time to see Aiden showing Martin to the door, with several angry customers around. Stalking to the front, one of the servers caught him by the arm.

"I'm sorry, Brogan. Please don't fire me. I really need this job."

He looked down at the young woman and asked, "What the fuck happened?"

"That man has been making crude comments to me when I pass and then he slapped me on the ass and said that if my boobs were bigger he'd show me what he could do with them." Ashley's face was bright red, but she held her body steady as she peered up into Brogan's angry face.

"That fucker—"

"Don't worry, Bro, I took care of him," Aiden said, walking over to offer Ashley a hug. "Go on home, darlin'. We've got it and you'll get paid for a full shift."

"It's okay," she shrugged. "I know I can face this kind of thing when working in a bar."

"Not in our bar," Brogan said. "Aiden's right. Take the evening off and take care of yourself."

She smiled her thanks and headed to the back, leaving both MacFarlane brothers standing in the middle of their bar, fists on their hips, anger pouring off them.

Early, the next morning, Ginny's phone rang again. Answering, she rubbed her eyes as she stared at the clock. 4 a.m. Grunting, she said, "Be right there."

Turning around, she watched as Brogan sat up in bed, his naked chest holding her attention as she tried to focus. She had more sleep than the previous night, but her body still felt sluggish. Staring at the muscles and tats as he twisted around to look at her, she knew her body craved his more than sleep.

His sleep rough voice rumbled, "Babe, you don't get enough shut-eye."

Her eyes focused on his face and, ignoring his observation, she asked, "Doesn't Ashley Tabor work at the pub?"

Brogan stared, his mouth tight as his stomach flip-flopped. "Yeah," he replied. "Why?"

Leaning forward, Ginny placed her hand on his arm, sympathy in her eyes as she answered, "Oh, honey, I'm sorry, but she was attacked tonight."

Another long day. Another day where the Baytown Police Department had all hands on deck as they worked the cases, desperate to find the man before he struck again.

Ginny stared at her fifth cup of coffee setting on the table as her stomach burned. Rubbing her sternum, Sam looked over.

"You got an ulcer?"

Shrugging, she dropped her hand, determined to plow through more of the intelligence. Since Ashley lived in a house just over the town line and officially in the North Herron County district, they now had the full support of the Sheriff's Department, since that crime was in their jurisdiction. The added deputies were needed and several of them were now at the station, reviewing the evidence in front of them.

Ginny had spent another few hours with Ashley at the hospital, grateful that she also had not been raped, but this assault occurred in her home. The assailant had forced her on her stomach also, feeling her up as he jacked-off on her back.

She had looked at the background of Martin Tobaski, who had conveniently left town, then she accompanied one of the North Herron Deputies to Virginia Beach to question him about his whereabouts the night before. He had not been pleased to have the police show up at his doorstep.

Closing her eyes, she thought back to their interview with the evasive Mr. Tobaski.

He had been visibly furious when they arrived, his eyes darting to the curious stares of his neighbors. "Come in and get off my stoop. Jesus, my wife is at the store and I want this done before she gets home." Seeing Ginny's lifted brow, he added, "She's not well and I don't want her upset."

Ginny stared at the forty-four-year old man—balding, medium build, with a slight potbelly hanging over his pants. A glance at the wedding picture on the mantle from what must have been about twenty years prior, showed a handsome man, blond, with a white-toothed smile. Shifting back, she thought that life had been hard on him, but buried the grin at the thought of his philandering ways bringing him some discomfort. She recognized the slight revenge streak in her, but dismissed it as the Deputy began questioning.

Martin first denied being in Baytown, but the credit card receipt from Finn's Pub blew that excuse. Then he denied being kicked out of the pub by the owners. Faced with the statements from Aiden and three other patrons, all claiming he made the sexual comments to the server, he leaned back in his chair in frustration.

"Come on, she's a barmaid. Jesus, she knows what it's like. She wears tight jeans and gets more tips. I was just giving her what she wanted—attention."

"What kind of attention were you willing to give her?" Ginny asked, her eyes never leaving his face as beads of sweat dripped from his forehead.

"I don't want my wife to know this," he moaned. "Can we get this over with?"

"If you start giving us straight answers, then yes. If not, we'll take you back to the station for further questioning."

At that, Martin blanched, "Fine, fine. I like a little on

the side, so sue me. I go out to Baytown because no one I know would ever be at that little shit-stain town."

Ginny inwardly flinched but maintained her outward composure, willing for him to keep digging a deeper hole.

"Not my wife, not her friends, not my co-workers... nobody. I walk around the beach, the town, checking out the women. I drink at the bar or at one of the restaurants, just to see who might be up for a romp."

"And if no one seems interested?"

"Oh, you can always find someone who's interested. They might just play a little hard to get."

"Is that what happened last night?"

"Look, I'm telling you that piece of fluff was interested, she just needed at little convincing. I tried the subtle way, but she was making me work for it. Hell, her ass was great but her tits were small, so I thought I'd get her juices flowing talking about what I'd like to do to her. Bitch got upset and then some big brute got up in my face and kicked me out of the bar. Me? Seriously? He kicks me out? You should have seen some of the red neck townies still in there. What a no-class dump."

"How'd that make you feel? Angry? Mad at the server?"

Leaning forward, Martin said, "Oh, hell, I was pissed and don't mind telling you. I've got a job that makes more money than anyone in that bar and yet I'm the one they gave the boot to? And you should have seen her eyes. She wanted it, but I think she just liked jerking my chain. But, when it comes to the ladies, I'm in control."

Ginny's neutral expression stayed plastered on her

face as she asked, "What did you do after you left the bar?"

"Oh, I got me some all right," Martin bragged.

"Where and with who?"

His face lost some of it bravado as his eyes narrowed. Nervously glancing out of the front window, he said, "Look, I want to know what this is about. I'm not answering any more questions until I know why you're asking."

"The woman you insulted," Ginny said, "was assaulted last night. Curious that, after she rebukes you, she's attacked."

Martin jerked back, his mouth open and eyes wide. "Me? You think I did that? No, no way. I...I—"

"Then I suggest you cooperate."

Looking out the window once more, he cursed, "Fucking hell. My wife is coming down the street—"

"Then talk quickly," Ginny prodded, secretly wishing his wife would hurry.

"I went walking. Ended up at the restaurant at the harbor...Seafood something. They had a band and I saw some women sitting outside on the deck. Scoped them out, asked one to dance, and then she took me back to her place. I was back here by about 1 a.m."

"Name of woman?"

"Jesus, I don't know. I wasn't interested in anything other than the fact that she had big hooters and a place easy to get to." Rubbing his sweaty forehead, he said, "Uh, Sherry...or Sheryl...or Sherilyn. That's it! Sherilyn."

Recognizing the name, Ginny wrote it down. "Where does she live?"

"Uh, close. We only had to drive a few minutes. It was off the road near the cemetery heading toward Route 13. It was a one-story...white house...had a fence in the front."

Nodding, Ginny snapped her notebook closed and looked at the deputy doing the same.

The front door opened and an attractive blonde stepped inside. Although twenty years had passed, they'd been much kinder to Mrs. Tobaski than her husband.

"Martin? What's going on?"

"Darling, these officers were just finishing. I had some business on the Eastern Shore and there was an accident. They wanted to check up on anyone who had been in the area."

She appeared confused for a few seconds as she looked from Ginny, to the deputy, then over to her husband. "Eastern Shore?"

"They have two great golf courses and I wanted to check them out. I had a drink at one of the restaurants there and they wanted to question me about some of the people there."

His excuse was laughable at best, but Ginny nodded as she turned to walk out the front door. "We'll be in touch if we need more information," she said, seeing Martin's glare burning straight toward her. As she stepped out onto the porch, she could hear his wife's strident voice from inside, questioning Martin about where he had been and who he had been with.

"Is it a bad thing that I'm glad his wife is giving him hell?" the deputy asked as they climbed into the North Hampton cruiser.

Chuckling, Ginny shook her head. "Personally, I was hoping she'd come home in the middle of our questioning. I wanted to see him squirm a little more." Closing her eyes as they began the drive back over the long Chesapeake Bay Bridge Tunnel, she dreamed of her tub filled with warm water, a bath bomb, and Brogan.

23

Looking up, Ginny said, "Are we dealing with a man who can't have sex? Or is afraid of sex? Or…oh, hell, I don't know!"

Mitch walked in, Lance with him, surprising everyone in the room. "I've asked Lance Green to assist with a possible profile."

The gathering of law enforcement personnel turned with interest, eager to listen to what Lance could offer. He stood, tall and ill at ease, the expression on his face screaming he would rather be somewhere else, preferably by himself. Ginny thought his profile was handsome, but realized she had never seen him smile. Blinking as he began to speak, she focused on his words.

"The typical voyeur is male, and the behavior generally begins before the adolescent years. This would make it difficult to determine the age of who you are looking for, if it weren't for the heights of the windows involved. Based on what Chief Evans has said, you are probably looking at an adult male, instead of an adolescent or pre-teen. The latest behavior is called Frotteurism, which is touching or rubbing against a non-consenting person. and generally involves the suffering or humiliation of the other person."

"So, it's not sexual—it's about humiliation and control?" Grant asked.

"Yes, it's about control, but the humiliation is a big part of it. Voyeurism is a crime when the perpetrator steps over the bounds and watches someone against their will," Lance added. "Many people need added stimulation such as porn, nude magazines, etc. Voyeurs usually start with watching someone at home, their parents having sex or a sibling taking a bath, for example. They need the external stimulation of peeking at someone to become sexually stimulated."

"Age?" Burt asked.

Shrugging, Lance said, "No particular age. Sorry. But keep in mind that not all voyeurs take the peeping any further than just getting stimulated when they illicitly peer at someone. Frotteurism is taking it to a different level. It could be someone who's getting their jollies standing in a crowded subway and their crotch just happens to be at the level of someone's rear end. But, taken to extremes, it can become sexual assault when the person attacks someone with the express purpose of having control over their victim and using their body to cause orgasm."

By the time Lance was finished and left the station, Ginny's head was about to explode. Rubbing her forehead, she said, "Mitch, I need to check on the final plans for Finn's block party. Is the mayor still on board?"

"Oh, yeah. He and Silas want it to move forward to

counter the bad publicity of our attacker. Looking at his watch, he said, "Go on and talk to Brogan, then call it a night." Looking at the others, he said, "We meet back here first thing in the morning. Let's hope we have a quiet night. Sam, you have the first evening shift and then Grant, you're on call after eleven."

Grateful for the reprieve, Ginny waved goodbye, heading down the street toward the pub. Passing Jillian's Coffee Shop and Galleria, she darted inside, reminded that she needed to speak to Jillian.

Stepping into the cool interior, Ginny took a second to let her eyes adjust and to admire the shop. Antique tables and amber sconces on the walls to soften the sunlight that came from the front gave the quaint shop its ambience. The old building had originally been a store in the late 1800's and fell into disrepair over the years. The store passed through multiple owners and eventually ended up bought by Jillian's parents. Determined to return the store to its former glory, they kept the solid wood paneling, carved wooden support poles, and the glass display cases on the sides of the long room downstairs. They turned the rest into a coffee shop and Jillian's mother began baking pastries to sell along with the coffee.

Once her parents turned it over to her, Jillian restored the second floor to the same glory as the coffee shop downstairs and showcased local artists' paintings on the dark paneled walls.

Directed upstairs, Ginny rounded the banister and observed Jillian on a stepstool, hanging a piece of sea glass art that was exquisite. Jillian grinned at her and climbed down.

"Wow," Ginny said, staring at the perfectly balanced piece of work. "That is breath taking."

"I know," Jillian gushed. "All his work is gorgeous. I'm so glad Lance lets me display it." Turning her appraising eye toward Ginny, she said, "You know the sea glass story, don't you?" Seeing Ginny's quizzical expression, she reached over to a small bowl on her desk and plucked out one of the many pieces of sea glass. Handing it to Ginny, she said, "Sea glass comes from the ships out in the harbor. They still use glass bottles and plates. They can just wash to reuse, of course, and when they break, they can toss them into the sea, unlike paper refuse. The shards drop to the bottom of the sea, churned by the sand and surf until all the edges become smooth. By the time they wash up on shore, they're beautiful pieces of sea glass."

Ginny rubbed her fingers over the deep green glass in her hand, admiring the way the delicate glass was as smooth as it was strong. Smiling, she handed it back to Jillian, who shook her head.

"Oh, no. That's for you. To always remind you that it is not the calm seas that shape us, but the rough and tumbles in life that make us who we are."

Ginny blinked back tears as she swallowed deeply. Shoving the sea glass into her pocket, she nodded her thanks, not trusting her voice.

Smiling, Jillian, ever perceptive, said, "You look like a woman who needs a good cup of coffee."

"Oh, yeah, that'd be great."

Calling down to her barista, Jillian ordered two coffees and then ushered Ginny to a little table near the tall windows overlooking Main Street. "I get the feeling you're here officially. What can I do for you?" Leaning forward, her eyes alight, she added, "I hear good gossip, you know." Leaning back, she pretend pouted, "Although, when Katelyn worked at the diner, she got great gossip!"

Chuckling, Ginny said, "I actually need to ask you what you thought about Ben Hudgins or James Smithson." Seeing Jillian's surprised face, Ginny quickly explained, "Nothing's wrong with them, but I need to get a read on their personalities. Grant and I had to interview them and I...well, I know you had gone out with Ben."

"Oh, lordy, you and Grant talked to Ben? I'll bet Grant was real happy about that!" Jillian said, rolling her eyes.

A server brought the coffees to them and Ginny took a grateful sip.

"To be honest, Ginny, I don't have a ton of information to give you. I met Ben when a group of new teachers were brought in on a tour of the town. James wasn't with them...he might have been hired a year later. Anyway, I only know James by sight, but we've never talked, other than just *hello* when he happens to come by. Ben was a real sweetie and we kind of flirted." She fiddled with the tablecloth for a moment and said, "That was a dark time for me and Grant. He'd been back in town for over a year and never made a move on me... in fact, he made it a point to make sure he wasn't with *me*, if you get what I mean." Sighing, she continued, "Anyway, Ben seemed interested, nice, and God knows, he's handsome. So, we went to dinner a couple of times. No major sparks and I didn't sleep with him. We kissed, but that was about it. I asked him to take me to Tori and Mitch's engagement party and that was when Grant first saw us, acted like an ass to Ben, and then he and I began our big fight, makeup, and trying to figure out what the hell we were." Grinning, she flashed her engagement ring and said, "From then on, it was Grant."

"How did Ben take that?"

"He was fine. He and I talked and he admitted he knew we weren't true loves. He even said that he hoped Grant and I were happy."

"And nothing about James?"

"Other than he's got a reputation?"

"What have you heard?"

Jillian's lips turned down slightly, as she said, "Ginny, this is only hearsay. Just gossip."

"I understand and I'll take it as that."

Nodding, Jillian said, "Well, I remember Ben mentioning a few times about James and women. How he likes a different one all the time, rarely sees someone two times in a row. How he brags about variety. I remember Ben making a comment once about how James is so friendly with women out in public…kind of flirty, you know? But then he talks really badly about them in private." Sighing, she continued, "I know Grant certainly dated around, but he never trashed talked anyone."

"Jade seemed to think—"

Jillian immediately interrupted, "I know Jade said James was professional, but she works in the elementary school, not at the high school with him. She tends to think the best of everyone, but I've heard he can be overly friendly. So far, not with the students, but with others."

Ginny sipped her coffee, her mind processing Jillian's comments...and an uneasy feeling crawled up her spine. Nodding, Ginny sighed, pushing her chair back to stand, but Jillian's twinkling eyes stopped her. "Was there something else?" she asked.

"I just wondered how the new underwear was working out for you?"

Pink stained Ginny's cheeks but she was unable to keep the smile from her face. "It just came in but I've been so busy, I haven't worn it yet. I'll be honest, though I don't see how you manage to match your panties and bra every day—"

"Oh, honey," Jillian said, "that's just for special occasions...or romance novels where the heroine always manages to have things match. I suppose someone with money can also do that daily, since they probably own a bunch of matching lingerie. But, for most of us ordinary women, we do what we can with what we have!"

Ginny laughed, enjoying the ease of their conversation. "Good. Hopefully, I can soon report that Brogan approves whole-heartedly."

"And just remember, men don't honestly give a hoot what you're wearing under your clothes, because all they can think about is getting you naked," Jillian laughed. "That lingerie is for you to feel pretty and special—men just want it off!"

"That's certainly been the case so far," Ginny admitted, her heart light as she shared an intimate conversation with a friend. A few minutes later, she was back on the sidewalk, sliding her sunglasses on her nose, heading toward Finn's.

Ginny could not remember having so much fun. Sitting in a booth at Finn's, tucked into Brogan's side, surrounded by their friends. After living a somewhat solitary social life since she had been in Baytown, relaxing with friends was a welcome change in her life. Feeling a squeeze on her shoulder, she twisted her head around to look up at Brogan. His eyes were focused on her, warm and gentle.

"Having a good time?" he whispered in her ear.

Nodding, "Yeah."

"Good. I wanted you to have a chance to relax."

Jason, Callan, Zac, and Aiden had a cut-throat game of darts going near the front, showing off for Jade and Belle. Jillian and Grant, Tori and Mitch, and Katelyn and Gareth filled the booth in the back, easy conversation and banter flowing between them. As if they had agreed to a moratorium on discussing the events of the past week, no one mentioned the case. Instead, the excitement about Finn's block party the next night filled their conversation.

"I'll be working, you know," Ginny said to Brogan, watching his smile turn to a scowl.

"I know," he grumbled.

"That's what we get for being involved with the police," Tori said to Jillian before looking over at Brogan. "Whether you like it or not, Brogan, you've now joined our club."

"Great, just great," his deep voice rumbled against Ginny's side, winking down at her.

"Hey," Ginny twisted around, pretending to glare. "You knew that when you started dating me!"

Kissing her hard and fast, he groused, "I know and I'm proud of you. But that doesn't mean I have to like the danger you are in."

"Honey, in this town, there's not a lot of danger."

"Any amount is too much," he whispered against her lips, before kissing her again.

"Don't worry," she assured. "You'll be too busy tomorrow night selling drinks and food, you won't even miss me." Grinning, she teased, "You better save some for me!"

"Babe, for you, I'll save anything you want."

"Hmm," she purred, "I'll have to get creative then. Fish and chips won't be near enough!"

"Ginny, can you spare a few minutes?"

Recognizing Katelyn's voice, she replied, "What's up?"

"There's a meeting with a bunch of Auxiliary women, who were gathering to make sure we had what we needed for our block party booth tonight and, of course, the topic of conversation turned to the recent events. Some of the women are scared and I know you're slammed, but if you had a few minutes, could you talk to us?"

Glancing at the clock on the wall near her desk, she replied, "Sure. I'll be right there."

Within fifteen minutes, Ginny was facing a group of almost twenty women of all ages, concern etched on their faces.

"You know we have no definitive information other than what Mitch has given at the announcement, but the most important thing to understand is what you need to do to be safe. And there are very definite things you can do to ensure that."

All eyes were glued on her, anxious and eager, for any information she could impart. Ginny realized how much terror this individual had created and she grew angry at that loss of control for these women.

"Number one, do not walk alone, especially at night. Sexual predators look for opportunity and a woman alone, gives them that opportunity. Number two, be aware of your surroundings. Don't just blindly walk to your car or down the street without looking around. They don't want to risk getting caught, and a woman whose head is up, looking around, with a firm grip on their phone or purse, is not someone they want to tangle with."

"What about at home? The peeping tom?" one woman asked.

"Ladies, you must lock your doors and windows," Ginny implored. "Keep your blinds closed and curtains closed at night. And don't change clothes in front of windows or in a room with open windows."

"You know what I hate about this?" Jillian's mother, Claire Evans, said. "I used to love leaving the windows open so the bay breeze could flow through the house. In the last week, I've kept the house locked up tight. I should have control over my own house, not some pervert!" Applause broke out in agreement.

Swallowing deeply, Ginny nodded. "I agree. You should have control. You should have control over your house. Control over your life. Control over your body. But the reality is that there is someone out there who wants that control and doesn't mind taking it."

"You're all so strong," Belle said softly, looking around the room. "I'm such a ninny and have always kept my doors and windows locked, even before this." Shrugging slightly, she added, "It seems like I've been scared my whole life." As her eyes cut over to Ginny, she said, "You're especially strong, Ginny. I can't image you being afraid of anyone."

Rubbing her hand over her face, Ginny leaned against the table in the front of the gathering. The butterflies in her stomach threatened to take flight, but she plunged ahead. "I know that kind of fear. I know that loss of control." The women's eyes were trained on her, almost fearful as she continued. "In the military, I was the victim of a sexual harassment situation where cameras were placed in the women's showers and then the videos were posted online and passed around."

Gasps were heard as jaws dropped and every woman's eyes widened in shock.

"No fucking way," Katelyn cursed, her face a mask of anger.

"And when I protested and filed complaints, I was harassed. And then, one night, assaulted in my bed."

"Oh, Jesus, no," cried Corrine MacFarlane, her eyes full of tears.

"I wasn't raped, but I was assaulted." Shaking her

head gently, Ginny realized she no longer feared saying her story out loud. These women needed to hear her story...know that a woman can be strong in the face of adversity...know that a woman can survive even when control is wrenched away. Pushing away from the table, she stood proudly and pointed to her chest, saying, "But I survived. I continued to fight against the injustice of it all. The Army conducted a huge investigation into the shower video scandals. I had left the Army by then, but I knew that I had a hand in taking back the control for women soldiers. For taking back my control."

"You didn't give up," Corrine whispered, pride shining in her eyes.

Ginny looked down at Brogan's mom and replied, "Yeah, I did. Admittedly, I grew tired and, by the end, I just wanted out. Stopped fighting. Almost stopped caring." She realized at that moment that she had never spent any time with Corrine since she and Brogan had begun dating. Licking her lips, she wondered what the woman thought of her, but one look at her face and Ginny smiled softly as Corrine held her gaze.

The group thanked Ginny for taking time to talk to them but she pushed aside their praise. "Hey, you all are here doing the Auxiliary work for the block party, so I want to do my part too."

"Oh, you'll be doing your part," Tori said, "since you have to work tonight."

Shrugging, Ginny smiled. "It's all part of the job." Heading back to the station, her heart lighter, she remembered how much she loved her job.

24

I hate my job.

Ginny's good will had come to an end as she managed to push her way toward the edge of the crowd, away from the band. Closing her eyes, she hoped Brogan was having a good evening because, as a cop, she was tired and grumpy and it was only ten p.m.

The crowd was more than what was expected, but she shouldn't be surprised. The local bands were good so the promise of good music, good food, and alcohol had pulled in hundreds more people to keep an eye on.

Finn's block party to raise money for the American Legion and Baytown Fire Department was in full swing with two blocks of town closed off to traffic and people were milling about in great numbers. The food trucks lined one end and she had seen Mexican, Barbeque, Chinese, and Cajun. Then there was the dessert trucks with funnel cakes, snow cones, donuts, and fried Oreos. The scent of food was tantalizing, initially, and after her fourth trip around the perimeter, she was starving.

The other end of the blockade was a temporary stage for the evening's entertainment and quite a few people were dancing on the street, just in front of it. As she walked along the sidewalk in front of the closed businesses, in the old, brick buildings that lined the town's business end, she could not help but admire the history of Baytown.

The sound of teenagers rang out and she quickly moved through the crowd to check out the situation, only finding a group calling out loudly to each other as they danced and laughed. Children scooted among the adults and she saw a few parents darting behind them. Looking to the side, she saw Torrin and Glenda Shadwell, their two daughters walking with them. The family looked happy and, as she passed, she offered a smile, pleased when she received one in return.

Making her way to Finn's large tent behind the pub, she stood to the side for a moment, admiring the MacFarlane's set up. It had been Katelyn's idea and it was a good one. The customers had to go to one side of the tent where they showed their ID to get an alcohol wrist band and their name was entered into a database. Each time they went through the line, the bartenders used a marker to make a black slash on the sturdy plastic. Keeping up with those who came back often, Brogan or Aiden would cut them off. It made for a few pissed off customers, but Brogan was determined to cut down on the number of drunks staggering around. Most of the town was very impressed and as a police officer, she had to admit it was a great plan.

Brogan caught her eye and grinned, making his way

toward her. Bending down, he kissed her lips, whispering, "How you doing, babe?"

"Fine, although, would you be pissed to hear me say that I'll be glad when it's over?"

He chuckled, "Nah. To be honest, it's been bigger and better than we expected, but I'll be ready at midnight to shut it all down as well."

"Oh, God, two more hours," she mumbled against his lips.

"Hey, Romeo, wanna get me a beer?" someone shouted from the line.

Brogan kept his lips on Ginny's while flipping off the customer. Leaning back, he grumbled, "I gotta go."

"Me too. See you later."

With a wave, she continued around the perimeter of the masses, observing that the evening was going well. Families were out, their children dancing to the music. Couples were circling the dance floor, as well as moving along, hand in hand. She nodded to the other officers and deputies as she walked.

"Officer Spencer," she heard and, turning around, spied Helen rushing over to her, wearing a blouse with a bright blue cat embroidered over the breast pocket.

"Helen," she greeted.

"I just wondered if that peeping man had been caught yet."

"No, ma'am. But we are working the case diligently."

The older woman patted her arm, "Oh, I'm sure you are. If you ever want some of my cookies, dear, just come by anytime."

Smiling her thanks, Ginny watched as Helen wandered off in the crowd. Turning around, she spied

Al Barton wandering along, his beady eyes jerking around. Eyeing him for a moment, she determined there was no reason to try to follow him, so she continued walking down the sidewalk.

Looking to the side, she almost ran into Corwin Banks and his wife. "Mayor, Phyllis," she greeted, noting his apparent good humor.

"Officer Spencer!" he shouted, making sure to be heard over the crowd.

"Corwin," Phyllis said, "you don't have to shout. It's not an election year."

"Just wanted to be sure the good Baytown officer, here, could hear. I'm sure her ear is trained for any unruliness."

Rolling her eyes, Phyllis smiled sympathetically at Ginny before moving on to greet someone else.

"Well, I have to say that I didn't think your boyfriend's plan would work, but this is bringing in quite a bit of money," Corwin said, his chest puffed out. "I know the proceeds from the sales here go to worthy causes, but with so many out-of-towners, the hotels and inns are full, and I've heard the town restaurants have had full houses today. Excellent, excellent."

Ginny smiled, not wanting to belabor her conversation with the mayor and hating the way the word *boyfriend* left his lips, but his nephew walked up and smiled at her, halting her escape.

"Officer Spencer, nice to see you again," Robert said, his gaze drifting down to her chest.

"Robert," she said, realizing how much like his uncle he was. *Wow, to be such a smooze at a young age.* "Are you enjoying yourself?"

"Oh, yes. I find the quaintness of the town to be fascinating." His gaze drifted to the side as a group of young women walked by in tank tops and short shorts, twirling their hair and popping their gum. "And the diversions to be exceptional."

As he turned to follow, she called out, "Those happen to be teens, Robert." He looked back at her before his eyes cut over to his uncle, who had now engaged someone else in conversation, then hesitated. "Just make sure to check the ages of anyone you decide to…uh…party with. Age of consent is eighteen in Virginia."

His wide-eyes narrowed suddenly as he stepped back closer to her. "I appreciate the warning, Officer. I'm sure I can handle myself."

With that, he walked away, but she noticed he walked in a different direction than the young girls. Turning, she decided to head toward the food trucks but had only made it half a block when she ran into Silas. And from the pinched expression on his face, he was no more glad to see her than she was him.

"Officer Spencer," he said, making her name sound like something unpleasant he stepped in.

Knowing he had been against the block party, she smiled and said, "Isn't it exciting how successful this endeavor is? And everyone is having such a good time!" She added the last in a sickly-sweet voice, just to irritate him, knowing it was childish. It was all she could to do to keep from sticking her tongue out at him.

"We'll see, we'll see," he sneered. "By the time we add up the expenses for the extra trash removal and," his gaze swept her from head to toe, "the added *police protection*, who knows if this was profitable to the town or not."

"Part of the proceeds go to the town's fire department," she reminded, "and the added police protection is on a voluntary basis. So, I think when you crunch your numbers, you'll be impressed."

He said nothing for a moment, his Adam's Apple bobbing, before turning to walk away, tossing out, "There's very little that impresses me about the police or the pub. Very little." With that, he walked away, leaving Ginny to fume in his wake. She was surprised to see Celia make her way to him, but even more surprised to observe Celia place her hand on his arm, which he shook off before hustling away. The pissed expression on Celia's face almost made up for the irritation Silas had cause. *Lordy, this job is making me so catty.*

Her stomach grumbled again and she continued down the block. Coming to a food truck, she recognized a few of the workers, the tantalizing odor of spicy Mexican food meeting her nostrils. One called out to her and, as she made her way over, they handed her a soft tortilla filled with flavorful meat and beans, with a hint of queso.

"Just like you like it, Officer Spencer?"

"Oh, Manuel, thank you," she gushed, her stomach ready for some food. Taking a big bite, she grinned, the flavors mixing in a delightful way on her taste buds. Pleased that he remembered she did not like food too spicy, the delicate blend of flavors was perfect. Grinning as she grabbed a napkin to wipe her chin, she continued along her patrol, her mood much improved.

Brogan looked over the crowd, amazed at how many people came to the block party. It seemed as though most of North Hampton County had come, as well as some people from the Virginia Beach area. He knew the main band they had booked was local, but gaining popularity, and for the little fee they charged, it was a steal. Marking another customer's wrist band, he also marveled at Katelyn's idea. He, Katelyn, and Aiden had spent time trying to figure out the best way to control the flow of alcohol at the event, while still turning a profit. Working with Mitch, they decided to keep track of those who drank so that they could not cut off their wrist band and apply for a new one. The customers were told when they showed their ID that the bartenders would have ultimate say in who could and could not buy more beer. So far, it was working.

As his gaze traveled over the crowd, he observed couples, from teens to elders, strolling around, hands held tightly. Sighing, he wished that he and Ginny had the opportunity to enjoy themselves instead of both working.

A couple of teenage girls came up to him, attempting to buy beer. They flashed their eyes and one leaned forward so that she almost flashed her entire breasts to him, in an effort to gain his favor. "Keep moving," he barked, his brow lowering as he glowered at them. "You want beer, you go over there and prove you're old enough. Then, and only then, will I even consider serving you."

"Bastard," one grumbled under her breath.

"Girls, what are you doing here at the beer tent?"

Brogan looked up and saw James standing nearby. The girls giggled and rushed over to him.

"Oh, Mr. Smithson, isn't this a great party?"

"What are you drinking? Care to share?"

More giggling ensued and Brogan rolled his eyes. Barely noting the customer in front of him, he watched James carefully. If that man so much as even looked as though he would share his alcohol with those teens, Brogan would be over the bar in a flash.

"No sharing, girls," James said, moving back slightly to add more distance between he and the girls.

"Hey, Brogan."

Brogan's attention was diverted by Ben, up for another beer. "Hey, Ben, how's it going?"

"You got a great thing going here, man. This is fabulous."

Handing him a beer and marking his wristband, Brogan nodded. "Thanks. 'Preciate it."

Ben turned, taking a sip, and saw James with his groupies hanging around. "Geez, I see it at work and damned if I don't see it when I go out."

Brogan's attention was pulled away by the next customer and when he looked up again, the girls were gone and so was James. *Good riddance.*

Loud voices at the other end of the beer tent grabbed his attention and he hustled over to see what was happening.

"I'm telling you, your name is already on the list," Katelyn was saying. Gareth was standing at her back, his stance protective.

"I ain't got no band on my wrist, so I ain't been here yet," the man yelled, staggering slightly.

"Just because you took it off after you were shut down at the bar does not mean you get to start over," she said, her voice firm.

"Mister, you need to move on," Gareth said, just as Brogan and Aiden made it to the table.

Ginny walked up, assessing the situation, her gaze jumping from the man to Brogan. With a slight nod his way, she placed her hand on the man and said, "You need to move on, now. They're not serving you anymore. In fact, it looks like you've already had enough."

He whirled, his face red with anger. "Shut up, bitch. This ain't got nothing to do with you."

In a flash, Brogan scaled over the counter, his size not hindering the speed with which his arms pressed down and his legs swung over. Ginny blinked at his agility, before jerking her gaze back to the inebriated man.

"Oh, the big guy's gonna come over here now," the man sneered, staggering more. "You ain't gonna do nothin' with this bitch cop standing next to me."

"No, I'm going to do something," Ginny said, reaching for his arm as she spoke into her shoulder radio, calling for assistance.

The man made a swing as Brogan stepped forward, but Ginny tried to place herself between the drunk and Brogan. Unable to duck in time, the blow caught her on the jaw, knocking her backward.

Brogan roared as he saw red, grabbing the man by

the throat. Regaining her balance, Ginny moved quickly, pushing her body into the fray.

"Brogan, let him go. I've got this." With zip ties, she secured the man's arms, still yelling at Brogan. "Let him go, or I'll have to arrest you too!"

He dropped his gaze to hers, his growl emanating from deep within, "No one hits what's mine."

Standing to her full height, which still left her eyes having to look way up, she narrowed her eyes and said, "I may be yours, but right now, I'm a cop. Let. Him. Go. Now."

"Bro," Aiden's voice came from behind, calm and gentle. "Do as Ginny says. She's got him."

He loosened his fingers and the man fell backward, Ginny taking his weight, stumbling slightly. "Yes, ma'am. By all means, do your *job*, Officer Spencer." As soon as the words left his mouth, Brogan dropped his chin to his chest, regretting the sarcastic tone. "Ginny, I'm sorry, that's not what I meant—"

Grant made it to the tent and, taking the man's other arm, said, "Come on. Time to sleep it off."

Brogan looked at Ginny, a red bruise on her cheek forming, blinking to battle the tears, and the hurt in her eyes, as she glanced back at him. "Fuck, Ginny, I'm sorry." She gave a curt nod and walked off with Grant and the drunk, the crowd parting for them.

Brogan looked over the gathering, his mom and dad looking on, worried expressions on their faces. Turning he saw Katelyn and Aiden standing behind him and he bit out, "Can you handle this?"

Both nodded as Gareth said, "I'll take your place. Go on. Take a walk and cool off."

"I need to go to her—"

"Let her do her job, right now, Bro," Aiden said, his voice still calm as he placed his hand on Brogan's shoulder. "She's fine and you need a breather."

"I need to fix this—"

"Brogan," Katelyn said, stepping up to him, her blue eyes pinning him in place. "You and Ginny are fine. Shit happens. Arguments will occur, but it's okay. You and Ginny love each other and you're still learning to be a couple."

Brogan sighed heavily, his hands on his hips and his eyes staring at his boots. "I've never told her I love her," he confessed. "But I do."

"Then I suggest you rectify that situation tonight… along with your apology."

He lifted his head and said, "But what if…" His voice trailed off, unable to put words to his fears.

"No ifs, Bro. She loves you. She's doing her job right now, but if I had to guess, she feels as badly as you do."

Uncertain they were right, he nodded toward Gareth. "Thanks for filling in. I'm just going for a walk, but I'll be back for cleanup." With that, he walked away from the block party, leaving the noise, music, and laughter behind. With no particular direction in mind, his feet eventually took him down Main Street to the town pier. Walking along the wooden planks, the dark, moonlit waves washing against the pylons, he sat down heavily, leaning back against the sides. The memories of his first date with Ginny on this very pier assaulted him.

Rubbing his hand over his face, he cursed his temper and the look on Ginny's face when he made a snide comment as she was doing her job. Chuckling ruefully, he thought back to his last counseling session, when he had discussed his anger and sense of guilt. Charles had been so proud of him for telling his story to Ginny and encouraged him to continue to work on letting go of guilt. *Now, I fuck up and have more guilt to deal with. And this time, it is my fault. God, is this what dating a cop is going to be like? Knowing she could get hurt at any time. And if I step in, then I take away her control and authority?*

After thirty minutes, he grew tired of his pity-party and knew it was time to head back. The music from the band could still be heard and, he had to admit, they were talented. The crowd appeared to have had a good time and the money raised for the American Legion and Fire Station was beyond expected. Trying to focus on the positives, he knew it was a losing battle, as long as things were unresolved with Ginny.

Stepping off the pier onto the sand leading to the street, he saw a dark shadow nearby. Halting defensively, he opened his mouth to speak, but the shadow spoke first.

"Hey."

The soft voice curled around his heart bringing peace as his breath caught in his throat. "Ginny," he whispered, his low growl carried away in the night breeze.

She stepped into the light of the nearest streetlamp and looked up at him. Her left cheek was bruised and slightly swollen. He wanted to roar before going to the police station, pulling out the drunk and seeing how he felt having a bigger man punch him in the face. Sucking in a deep breath, he pushed that thought out of his mind.

Ginny stepped closer, still keeping her distance, uncertain of Brogan's feelings. "I wanted to check on you, when they said you left."

"You went back to the block party?"

Tilting her head to the side, she said, "Yeah. Once we got the drunk into the tank, we went back. The party still has another thirty minutes until it's over and I know there will be some cleanup, as well as making sure the crowd disperses."

Swallowing, he nodded, "I need to get back. I…uh… took a walk."

A light chortle slipped from her lips as she said, "I kinda got that." Sobering for a moment, she said with less lightheartedness, "Well…I better get back. I just wanted to check on you." Turning, she was halted as his quick steps brought him next to her, his hand on her arm.

"Can I walk with you?"

Nodding slowly, but without smiling, she replied, "Of course."

Silently, they walked the three blocks to the corner where Finn's stood proudly, the beginning of the party. Brogan looked over at the alcohol tent, now closed for business during the last half hour of the concert, seeing Katelyn, Gareth, Aiden, and others putting the alcohol away while swaying to the music. He knew he needed to be over there helping, but hated leaving Ginny's side with so many emotions unsaid.

"Ginny, I owe you a big apology for the way I spoke to your earlier. It was rude and uncalled for—"

"Shh, Brogan. We can talk later." She smiled up at

him, jerking her head toward the tent. "Go on. You've got work to do and so do I."

"Will I...uh...see you...later?" His voice sounded strange, even to his own ears. Swallowing deeply, he steadied himself for her rejection. Instead, his eyes jumped down as she placed her hand on his arm.

"Of course," she replied. "We both have a lot to do, but I'll see you when I get home."

"Home?" he asked, his voice hopeful.

"Yes, silly. Home." Her brow creased as she said, "I was thinking of my house, since it's closer, but would you prefer yours?"

The weight on his chest lifted as he said, "If you don't mind, I'd rather wait and go with you. Either house...doesn't matter, but...I'd...uh...really like to just be with you."

"Okay," she said, her smile warming his heart once again. "We'll go home together."

25

Brogan stirred from sleep, his mind groggy with fatigue, but instantly smiled at the feel of Ginny's warm body snuggled in close to his. Her head rested on his chest, her small hand placed over his heart in sleep. One leg was thrown over his thighs, perilously close to his twitching cock.

He watched her sleep, trying to focus on her peaceful beauty and not the bruise on her cheek. Granted, it was only slightly reddish in the morning light and not nearly as dark as he assumed it would be, but he knew it had hurt and the idea of someone hurting her still made his teeth clench.

Forcing the negative thoughts from his mind, he focused instead on the woman in his arms. After the crowd had dispersed without incident, the food trucks had driven away, Finn's beer tent had been taken down, the money had been put away in the safe for Katelyn to do an accounting the next day, the kegs and crates had been taken back into Finn's storage rooms, and as the town street sweepers had made their passes to collect the garbage, the city block once again retaining its normal appearance, Ginny had met him at the corner under the streetlamp at the door to the pub.

They decided to go to his place, just so they could wake up the next morning to the sunshine reflecting off the bay, the peace of the beach dunes, and the gulls and herons as their only company.

Both tired, they fell into bed, slumber coming almost immediately for both. Now, with the morning light shining in, Brogan knew there were things that needed to be said.

Ginny stirred slightly, her eyes fluttering as she adjusted to the light streaming in the window, the sound of the surf in the distance. Seeing Brogan's blue eyes, she smiled, licking her lips as she mumbled, "Morning."

Matching her smile, he leaned over and kissed her. Light. Gentle. "Hey, honey," he muttered against her lips, his hand sliding to the bottom of her t-shirt.

She mumbled incoherently again, her mouth opening as her tongue tangled with his. Feeling his cock twitch against her thigh, she shifted over his body, straddling him so her core was now pressed firmly on his erection. Holding on to his shoulders, her bedhead hair streaming down creating a curtain, she grinned.

His fingers gripped her ass tightly as he closed his eyes, all the blood rushing to his dick as the heat from her sex knocked all thoughts from his mind other than *me, her, now.*

Giggling, she whipped her t-shirt over her head, her breasts bouncing with the movement. His hands smoothed over her ribcage until both held her breasts, their weight filling his palms. Pushing them together, he jerked up, sucking first one nipple and then the other, deeply into his mouth. Ginny groaned at the sensation, wondering at the nerves that sparked between her breasts and her womb. Rubbing her panty clad sex on his erection, barely contained in his boxers, she sought the friction desperately needed.

"Fuck this," he groaned, his large hand grasping her hips and lifting her up enough to snag her panties. He noticed they were black and lacy and stopped just long enough to grin up at her.

"Your sister took me shopping," she said, grinning back.

"Well, I hope you have more, 'cause I can't wait," he said, just before he ripped them on one side and pulled the scrap of material away.

Before she could protest, his lips latched onto one nipple again as his fingers found their way into her warm sex, tweaking the right spots to have her wiggling and writhing in need.

Rolling them to the side, Brogan leaped from the bed just long enough to drop his boxers and free his massively erect cock, stroking it with his hand for a second as he looked down at her naked body, wide open for his perusal. Rolling on a condom, he grinned as he leaned over the bed.

With no restraint, he lifted her calves to his shoulders, centering the tip at her opening and, seeing her bright, lust-filled eyes, he plunged to the hilt in one swift motion. Her tight, warm channel accommodated him as he groaned in satisfaction.

"Fast and hard, baby?" he grunted, already moving inside of her.

"Yes," she cried out, her fingers grabbing onto his shoulders to hang on for the ride.

Thrusting into her, he buried his frustration, his fears, and worries all into the movement of his cock rocking into her luscious body. Opening his eyes, he watched as her breasts bounced in rhythm to their movements. Looking down at their coupling, he stared at his cock, slick with her juices, sliding in and out of her sex, the scent filling the air.

Realizing he had not made her come before they got started, a sliver of guilt hit him, but the light in her eyes and smile on her face took it away. Shifting his weight to one forearm, he slid his free hand over her breasts, pinching her nipples slightly before moving down over her mound and fingering her clit.

Her orgasm hit hard as her body bucked underneath him. He rolled quickly and, with her on top, ordered, "Ride it out, baby."

With his hands on her hips, he watched as she moved up and down on his shaft, her orgasm still causing her inner walls to clench him. She smiled in open abandon as she bounced, her hands gripping his shoulders again.

Throwing his head back, his neck muscles corded and his veins stood out prominently, his growl starting deep in his chest before it roared from his body. Pumping upward until every last stream of his orgasm was deep inside her, he collapsed back onto the mattress, her body landing on his with a thump.

They lay, exhausted but exhilarated, for several long

minutes, until their breath was less ragged. His hand smoothed over her skin from her shoulders to her ass and back again. Her unmarred cheek laid on his chest, the thick muscles cushioning her face.

Slowly, she lifted her head and peered down at him, a smile curving her lips. "We good, honey?"

"Oh, yeah, Ginny. We're good," he grinned in return, knowing they would talk later. But, for now…they were good.

The man lay flat against the dunes, his binoculars trained on the naked couple in bed, the beautiful Ginny on top of that brute. He had watched her rosy-tipped breasts bounce as the barman pounded into her. Holding the binoculars with one hand, he had slid his other hand down his pants, working his cock, but he could not come. Furious, his impotence enraged him. It was taking more and more to get him off. Watching her lift her hand to stretch, the man's cock still buried inside her, made him even angrier.

Ginny jerked her head toward the window and he realized the glass in the binoculars might have sent a reflection toward the house. Dropping to the sand, he slid down the dune, completely out of sight, and ran down the beach until he could get far enough away that, to anyone else, he would just appear to be an early beach comber. Seeing a few people up ahead looking for sea glass, he smiled. *Just a man out on a beautiful morning, enjoying the views.*

Ginny lounged in the Adirondack chair on Brogan's deck, her shower-wet hair drying in the breeze. The unsettled feeling in her gut she had had since their morning romp had disappeared, seeing nothing on the beach but gulls, herons, and the occasional black pelican. MB sauntered out onto the deck, stretching before winding herself around Ginny's legs, followed by Brogan, a tray in his hands, full of steaming cups of coffee, toasted bagels with cream cheese, and a plate each of scrambled eggs and bacon.

Her empty stomach rumbled, giving evidence to her pleasure at his offerings. "Oh, this is wonderful," she gushed, taking a sip of coffee. "Thank you."

The two sat in companionable silence for several minutes, enjoying the breakfast and the beautiful day.

As Brogan finished, he set his coffee on the deck and leaned forward, holding her gaze. "Honey, I gotta apologize for last night. Well, for part of last night." Seeing her eyes not wavering, he plunged on. "I'm a man, and a certain kind of man. They say a man learns how to treat a woman by how his father treated his mother. And, I gotta say, I learned from the best."

She reached across the space and laid her hand on his arm. "Yes, you did," she agreed softly.

Nodding, he continued, "My dad would have flattened any man who dared to lift a finger toward my mom. So would Pops. In fact, all the men I knew in my childhood would have done that. Mitch's dad, Jillian's, hell, even Zac's dad if he wasn't too drunk to stand up—" Seeing her quizzical expression, he shook his head and said, "another story for another day, babe."

Sighing, he continued, "But I know you were working. I've got no problem with you being a policewoman, Ginny. Nothing but the deepest respect for what you do. Hell, if I'd had a problem with your job, I wouldn't have been panting after you for two years."

At that, a smile slipped across her face, but Ginny remained quiet, knowing he needed to talk, and so pleased he was not holding it all in.

Wringing his large hands, he said, "I saw that man arguing with you, calling you a bitch…babe, I wanted to pound him into the ground. I kept telling myself you were working. I know you're a cop. But he clocked you, babe, and I saw red. Pure, fuckin' furious red."

"It's okay to want to protect me, you know."

At that, his eyes jumped to her, his brow lowered.

Swinging her legs around, so that she was facing him, she said, "In uniform, I'm in control, but that doesn't mean every situation can be handled according to plan. When dealing with belligerent persons, it's good to have backup there. Last night, I'd called for help on my radio but he took a swing at you and I fucked up by trying to get between you and him."

"Jesus, babe. Never put yourself between someone and me. Not when your safety…or honor, is in question."

"My honor? Honey, as a cop, I've been called worse than bitch. And as a woman, I've heard it all. That doesn't make it right and, as a cop, I do what I have to do." Chuckling, "as a woman, I might just knee them in the balls if I feel the situation warrants it."

The two sat quietly as he placed his large hands over hers, rubbing them gently. "It's hard for me, to be honest," he admitted. "I never wanted some wimpy woman, and you being a cop is not a bad thing. But, I hope we don't find ourselves in another situation like last night, 'cause I can't promise that I'll hold back."

"I don't want you to be anything other than what you are, honey," she said, her gaze warm with the sunlight catching the golden hues of her hazel eyes. "I'll always act like a cop when the situation warrants it, but otherwise, I can be your woman."

"There's one other thing I realized last night that I need to rectify," he confessed. Leaning closer, so that his lips were a breath away from hers, he whispered, "I love you, Ginny Spencer."

Her gasp was swallowed as his lips met hers, his hands pulling her closer so that she wrapped her legs around his hips as he stood and walked back inside. Grasping his face in her hands she pulled back slightly and smiled. "I love you, too, honey."

With a huge grin, he shut the door and laid her down on the bed. Just as he was about to climb in with her, she looked over. "Sweetie, you better pull the blinds. I don't want anyone being able to look in."

Ginny stared at the canoe on the water, determined to keep her feet on the sand. "That's not going to hold both of us," she said, backing away.

"Don't be afraid," Brogan encouraged. "You'll love it."

Her dubious expression stayed in place as she looked

at the hand he was holding out. "I've always been a *feet on the ground* sort of girl."

"You got this, honey."

Finally giving in, she stepped in and sat, nervously grabbing the sides. Looking up, she said, "I can't hold the paddle if I'm holding on for dear life."

Unabashedly staring, he looked down at her long legs, bare in her boy-shorts bathing suit. The tied bikini top was tantalizing, but he wondered if he should have insisted on her wearing a t-shirt over it to protect her shoulders from the sun…and to keep his eyes in his head.

Stepping into the water, he walked the canoe out until he was waist high and then swung his leg over, pulling himself in. Settling quickly, he laughed as Ginny screamed as the front lifted in the air with his weight in the back. Shifting slightly toward the center for balance, he began paddling them out past the sand bar before turning along the coast.

After a few minutes of watching her attempt to contribute, he called out, laughing, "Baby, put the oars down. You're paddling against me and we're just battling each other."

"Fine," Ginny said, blushing slightly at her lack of canoeing skills, and relaxed to view the shoreline from the bay.

They paddled south, getting closer to the Baytown public beach, when she noticed a cluster of kayaks paddling toward them. It seemed to be a group of teenagers, but then she spied James in the lead.

James' eyes shifted between Brogan and Ginny before he flashed a smile as he paddled by. "Hello," he called out, his voice as friendly as his smile. "Enjoying the water this morning?"

Ginny nodded and called out, "Looks like you've got a quite a group."

"I sponsor the Kayak Club at the high school and we try to go out a couple of times a month when the weather's nice."

Ginny noticed the teenage girls giggling as they looked over at muscle bound, tatted Brogan. *Look all you want, girlies, he's mine.* Shaking her head at her adolescent thought, she heard Brogan call her name.

Twisting around, she looked at him with her head tilted.

"You were shaking your head," he said. "I just wondered if you were all right."

"Yeah. I was just having an adolescent pang of possessiveness when those teens were staring at you. My mind was telling them to back off."

Chuckling, Brogan said, "Not interested in teens, babe. In fact, not interested in anyone but you."

She leaned back as he leaned forward and their lips met briefly before the canoe rocked precariously. With a yelp, she jerked back into place, her hands firmly gripping the sides. As she righted herself, Brogan looked over his shoulder at James, in the midst of a bunch of teens, where more than half were girls. Turning back, he wondered if the man was just a good mentor...or something less noble. "I'm just glad he kept his eyes in his head as you rowed by."

As they turned and headed back toward Brogan's bungalow, they came across Katelyn and Gareth out on kayaks. Greeting each other, Katelyn looked at her brother and said, "You know there's a family dinner tonight." Then, grinning at Ginny, she added, "And you're expected. Don't try to get out of it. It's time you made it official by joining all the MacFarlanes at one time."

"Oh, lordy," Ginny breathed.

"Don't worry," Gareth said, paddling by. "I survived."

As they made it to the beach outside Brogan's property, Ginny looked back. "By the way, did you know about dinner tonight?"

"Uh…yeah…" he said hesitantly, hearing the warning sound in her voice.

"And you didn't tell me?"

"Well, it's not dinnertime yet."

Whirling around in the canoe, making it rock from side to side, she said, "You weren't going to say anything until it was time to go?"

"It's just my family, honey. You weren't going to have to get fixed up or anything."

"Are you daft?" she yelled. "Brogan this is your whole family…your parents. That's a big, fucking deal!" Scrambling out of the canoe, she bolted so quickly he did not have time to right it before it flipped, sending him into the water.

Standing on the sandy bottom, grabbing the oars, he tossed them into the canoe once he had it righted. Looking up, he saw her stomping up the beach. "Ginny?" he called after her, shaking his head.

Once he hauled the canoe up the shore, he saw her standing at the top of the dune. Huffing, she said, "I'm sorry. Here, let me help."

"Got it, babe," he said, easily lifting the canoe over

his head, and carrying it up the dune and to the shed at the side of his house. Securing it, he turned to stare at her standing on his deck. She had donned one of his t-shirts, twisting the bottom as it hung to her thighs. One of his ball caps sat on her head and, while he could not see her eyes behind her glasses, he knew they were aimed right at him.

Looking down, she repeated, "I'm sorry. It's just the idea of parents…grandparents. That's a lot of pressure."

He stood with his hands on his hips, staring at her uncertain stance—this competent cop, an unafraid, strong woman, and he dropped his head. *Family. Parents. Fuck.* Lifting his head as he lifted his arms, he said, "Honey, come here."

She hesitated for only a second before rushing into his arms. He wrapped her tightly in his embrace, one hand at the back of her head, holding her cheek to his heart. Kissing the top of her head, he wanted her to take his strength, as much of it as she needed.

"Babe, I'm so sorry about not saying anything. I honestly didn't think about it because you've already met them all."

"I've met your parents and Pops as a police officer or a member of the AL or Auxiliary. Not as your girlfriend. I want them to like me but, after my parents' rejection, I don't think I'm so good with parents."

He grabbed her shoulders and pushed her gently back, just far enough that he could peer into her eyes. "Babe, you gotta get that outta your mind. Your parents suck. I know that's harsh, but it's true. You are the best—the best of cops…the best of women…hell, the best of people. If they can't deal with what happened to you, that's on them. Remember what you told me. That's on them. You don't take on that reaction and, please, don't project it on my parents."

"Oh, no," she rushed, eyes wide. "I would never think that of your parents." Gulping in deep breaths, she blinked back the tears. "You're right, Brogan. I've taken my parents' rejection and applied it across the board. I don't want to do that."

He pulled her back into his chest, once more offering her his strength.

Ginny's arms held tightly around his waist, his heartbeat steady against her ear. She thought of Corrine and Eric MacFarlane and let out a long breath. They were nice and she knew would be nice to her. Squeezing him before letting go, she looked up. "Do you think they're happy we're together?"

Chuckling, the rumbling coming from deep in his chest, Brogan replied, "Baby, they're over the fuckin' moon about us together."

26

"'Bout time Brogan brought you over…although Spencer's an English name. Don't 'spose you've got any Irish blood in you at all? Even a little bit?"

Ginny stared at Pops, suddenly uncertain, not knowing anything about her heritage. "Uh…"

"Dad, leave her alone," Eric commanded, walking from the back of the house to engulf her in a bear hug. He whispered in her ear, "Welcome to the family, Ginny. Good to have you with us." As he stepped back, his eye caught the make-up covered bruising on her cheek. His gaze jumped to Brogan's, but he said nothing, his warm smile staying in place.

Breathing a sigh of relief, she smiled up at the large man, so easy to see where Brogan and Aiden inherited their physiques. Eric was a big man, still muscular but now with a slight thickness around the middle. His dark hair was sprinkled with grey, but his blue eyes twinkled as much as his sons'.

"Humph," Pops complained, pushing past Eric. "I'm

not messing with her," giving her a hug as well. "But you can't blame an old Irishman for trying." Standing upright, he eyed her and then Brogan. "Good bloodlines. You'll have strong children," he added, thumping his chest.

Ginny blushed, but could not help laughing, seeing the love the elder, white-haired MacFarlane had for his family.

Corrine pushed her way to the front, an apron tied about her waist. "Oh, these men," she grumbled. "They'll worry you to death, so stay strong, Ginny." Drawing her into a hug as well, she pulled back, patting Ginny's cheek gently. "Such a beauty. So glad you could join us," she said, winking at Brogan. "Come on back everyone, supper's almost ready."

Brogan pressed his front to Ginny's back, offering his support as they watched Dad and Pops follow Mom down the hall toward the rear of the house. His hands on her shoulder gave a little squeeze. "You okay, honey?"

Nodding, she said, "Yeah, I think the worst is over."

He was not sure, but wisely kept his mouth shut. With a gentle push, they followed the others.

The large den held comfortable chairs and they were greeted by Katelyn, Gareth, and Aiden who had already arrived. Ginny slid easily into the kitchen with Katelyn and Corrine.

Corrine checked the dish in the oven and, as she stood, turned to Ginny. "My dear, please don't think we always have the women in the kitchen while the men lounge. Actually, Eric and I share cooking duties, but for family night, when Pops demands my Guinness Irish Stew, then I'm in charge of the meal."

"It smells delicious," Ginny responded truthfully.

Katelyn pulled the soda bread from the oven, the scent clearly teasing the crowd, as they heard the men in the den moaning. Ginny had to admit, her stomach growled at the sight and smell of the tantalizing bread too.

Soon, the lively group was seated around the large table, the food being served in heaping portions. Katelyn laughed when she viewed Ginny's wide eyes at the amount of food. "Don't worry, Ginny, it's better to have it on your plate to begin with before all these men start fighting over the food."

"We never fight," Aiden quipped, his mouth full of buttered bread. "We just know how to make sure we got our fair share."

"Your fair share?" Corrine asked, arching a brow. "I seem to remember sending you away from the table a time or two until you learned your manners."

"I was just an enthusiastic connoisseur of your cooking, Mom," he protested.

Brogan's spoon halted on its path to his mouth as he turned a narrowed eye toward his brother. "Connoisseur? You tried to stick a fork in the back of my hand when I reached for seconds—"

"Me? What about the time you threatened me with a knife when Mom offered me more pot roast?"

"I never threatened you with a knife," Brogan argued. "I was making a point and just happened to have a knife in my hand at the same time."

"I call bullshit," Katelyn argued, her laughing gaze

darting between the two. "You both dove into Mom's food so quick, there was precious little for me unless I got there first."

"I'll have you know," Aiden began, his smile overriding his attempt to be serious, "I have never—"

"No arguing at the table," Corrine dictated, her eyes wide as she shook her head, also attempting to hide her smile. "Gareth, you're used to this motley crew, but Ginny, I'm terribly sorry for my children's table manners. It seems I have failed as a mother."

Ginny laughed as she said, "Corrine, the food is delicious and the company is…enthusiastic."

Brogan's hand dropped to her thigh, a gentle squeeze offered as she turned her eyes up to his. He winked before returning to his meal.

"Well, I for one, never minded the kids messing about at the table," Pops declared, scraping the bottom of his stew bowl with his bread, sopping up the last goodness. "When y'all got in trouble and had to leave the table, who do you think got to finish their meal in peace and eat as much as they wanted?"

Katelyn stared at her grandfather for a moment before asking, "Is that why you used to tell me to steal Aiden's bread?"

The gathering burst into laughter as Aiden protested Pops' conniving ways. Ginny could not remember the last time she had laughed so much at a meal. After the stew and bread, Corrine carried out a huge platter of apple tarts and compliments to the cook called out from all.

A few minutes later, Ginny looked on as Brogan

finished his second tart, and rolled her eyes. "Where do you have room for all that?"

He looked at her half finished first one and shook his head. "Eat up, babe."

"Honey, I'm stuffed." Looking around to make sure no one was watching, she slid it to his plate and he gobbled it up with no problem.

"So," Pops said, "Did your parents let so many shenanigans go at the table?"

Her smile dropped from her face, her thoughts racing as she tried to think of what to say. She felt Brogan's hand on her leg, offering a reassuring squeeze.

"Pops, not everyone's family needs to be dissected," Brogan said. Looking at his mom, he diverted, "Dinner was great, as always, Mom."

Ginny realized everyone noticed the swift change of subject and, as her eyes landed on Brogan's grandfather's kind eyes, she blurted, "I was an Army brat. I'm afraid my dad didn't allow much talking at the table."

Brogan turned to her and said softly, "Honey, you don't have to say anything. It's all okay—"

She looked up into his face, the concern for her so evident. "I know. But I want to be with you, and your family is important to you, which means they'll be important to me. I don't want to have to hide my family situation."

She turned to see equally concerned expressions facing her, and Pops said gently, "Girl, just ignore me. You don't gotta talk about anything you don't want to."

"No, Mr. MacFarlane, it's fine. Just being here tonight has reminded me what family is…or can be. And to be honest, it's nice. A little overwhelming, but nice." Swallowing, she said, "My dad was Army…military right down to his bones. We moved around a lot. My brother was Navy and a pilot. I joined the military right out of high school. Uh—" she felt Brogan put his arm around her and she leaned into his side, his large body's warmth seeping into her. "My brother was killed in service and my parents never recovered from that."

"Oh, how horrible," Corrine said, pain lacing her voice. "I'm so sorry."

"I am sorry, darlin'," Pops said.

Ginny hesitated once more. She knew she could stop talking. Katelyn and Corrine knew more to the story but, while she understood the men did not have to know, looking around the table at the sympathetic gazes and understanding nods, having experienced all the fun that had been a MacFarlane family dinner, she wanted to share. Had to share.

So she blurted, "Katelyn, Corrine, and Brogan know I was the victim of sexual harassment and assault while in the military. My Command wanted to cover it up, but I pressed charges. I refused to stay a victim and stay quiet. So, I caused quite a ruckus until my superiors had to deal with the mess. It went bigtime anyway and…and I got out at the end of my tour."

The table was quiet and she felt her breath leave her in a huge sigh. Somehow the unburdening was easier now that the words had already been out of her mouth. Come what may, they were out.

"Honey," Brogan said softly, his hand on her shoulder pulling her in tighter to him. "Please, you don't have to say anything."

"Don't you see, Brogan," she said in a rush, looking into his blue eyes. The same eyes that peered at her from everyone around the table, with the same concern. "I've finally realized that holding on to this for so long has given it power over me. But now, I'm taking back my control."

Looking at the faces of Brogan's family, she said, "My father was disgusted with me for not dropping the inquiry, assuming women brought harassment on themselves, and then again for getting out of the military. My mother wouldn't go against him, so they told me to leave and not come back."

"Oh, sweetheart," Corrine gushed. "I'm sure they didn't mean it. No parent would ever mean that—"

"Mom," Brogan started, shaking his head.

"I know that's how you feel about your children, Corrine," Ginny said, "but my family is different. My father said that he wished my brother had lived and I had died in his place."

Ginny leaned back against Brogan, exhausted from her confession, but strangely at peace. Looking around, she began to second-guess her decision as she observed the horrified expressions on their faces. Before she could speak again, the entire table erupted.

Curses, tears, angry voices all spoke at once. Corrine jumped from her chair and rushed over, pulling Ginny into a huge hug and she felt tears sting her eyes as she realized she had missed a mother's arms around her. Aiden slammed his hand down on the table, cursing, "Fucking hell," while Eric's face was thunderous as he exclaimed, "No man who's any kind of a man would turn his back on his child." Katelyn followed her mom, hugging Ginny as she said, "You're right. You are empowered now."

"Okay, okay," Brogan said, pulling Ginny back into his embrace, peering deeply into her eyes as he took the pulse of her emotions. Wiping a stray tear, he said, "I'm so proud of you."

"I'm kinda proud of myself," she whispered in return.

The family pushed back from the table and the men did the cleanup while the women headed into the den. Ginny flopped back on the sofa, suddenly exhausted. Katelyn sat next to her, leaning her head onto her shoulder.

"I'm glad you're with Brogan. He needed you."

"I needed him," she whispered, her heart so full, she was almost afraid the spell would break.

Corrine sat on the coffee table in front of her, taking her hand in hers and, with tears in her eyes, said, "Oh, my darling girl, what you've been though. And to come out so much stronger. We women do that you know. We carry our families, bear our children, and often carry the weight of the world on our shoulders…and we are stronger together. And you…oh, Ginny, I could not have chosen a better woman to be with my Brogan."

In that moment, Ginny realized she had held back from people for so many years—afraid to make friends, afraid to let others in. And now, to be enveloped into this loving family, she blinked back the tears. Just as her heart was full to bursting, Brogan came over and said, "Babe, let's go home."

She stood, accepting hugs from everyone. When she came to Pops, his eyes misted over as he said, "All kinds of people in this world, darlin'. Some good from the start but they let life tear 'em up and they get nasty. Sounds like that's happened to your parents. Coulda happened to you, but it didn't. 'Cause there's others in life...they take what comes...make the world a better place. That's you, darlin'. And I'm glad to have you part of us." He wiped his eyes and then added, "Humph. I'm sure you got some Irish in you."

With a laugh and final hugs, she snuggled close to Brogan as he tucked her into his side. "Come on, honey. You've got to be exhausted."

Looking up, she asked, "Take me home?"

"Oh, yeah, babe. No place I'd rather be than home with you."

27

Ginny sat in the workroom, staring at the board, along with the files open on the table in front of her. They had gotten lucky with the DNA from on the back of Carly's pants, but it did not match anyone in the system, so that ruled out Torrin Shadwell. At least for that offense—who knew if they were looking at more than one assailant. Though, to be honest, he wasn't too likely in any case.

Al Barton was still a possibility, but Ginny did not see the older man as physically accosting the women, wondering about his strength, or lack of it. But, if she had learned anything as a cop, ruling out someone based on an assumption was stupid.

Martin Tobaski. She looked at the name and wished she could nail him for being a jack-ass, if nothing else. Rubbing her eyes, she sighed, recognizing her professionalism was taking a back seat to her fatigue. Long days of work paired with nights of passion with Brogan were making a happy, but tired, policewoman.

Sam walked in, his face slightly red from being outside. "Hey, Ginny," he greeted. Unscrewing the cap to an ice-cold water bottle, he took a long swig as he leaned against the counter. "How's it going?"

"Brain is fried," she admitted. "You know what's so frustrating? These names up on the board. They're just a few names we've come across, but honest to God, it could be anybody! Someone we haven't looked at. Someone who lives here, works here, shops here, vacations here...the possibilities are endless—"

"Hey, hey, calm down, Ginny," Sam said, walking over and sitting next to her. "You're right, but you gottta take this one step at a time and not get so worked up. You'll end up with an ulcer, like me...high blood pressure, like me...hell, overweight, like me."

She stared at him for a moment, really looking at him for the first time in a long time. Not as a fellow officer, but as a man. A man whose wife was worried about him. Placing her hand on his arm, she said, "Sam, how are you doing? Really doing? Not the bullshit you give us here."

"Damn, cut to the chase, why don't you, Ginny?" he chuckled, then sobered after a moment. Sighing heavily, he said, "This stays between us?" At her promise, he confessed, "Been a cop for most of the past twenty years, after doing a ten-year stint in the military. Love this job. Love this town. Loved working for Mitch's grandfather when he was chief and then for Mitch's father when he ran this place. I'm now on my third Evans as a chief and still love it." Leaning back, he ran his hand over his face, taking another long swig of water. "But, it's taking its toll. Physically. Wife's been after me to work on my diet and exercise. And, she's brought up retirement."

The idea of the Baytown Police Department without Sam struck her, realizing that, in some ways, Sam was a bit of a father-figure to her. Sucking in her lips, she stayed quiet, understanding this was about him…what he needed.

"Anyway, I've said nothing to anybody…not even to my wife, knowing she'd start planning our retirement trips." Smiling, he said, "I married a good woman. Married my high school sweetheart and never regretted a moment. She's taken care of me for many years."

Understanding slammed into her and she squeezed his arm. "You want to make sure you're around to take care of her, don't you?"

He smiled at her comment, nodding. "Yeah, I do. I want to make sure I'm around to do all the things we've always promised each other we'd do."

The two sat quietly for a moment before she said, "When will you make your decision?"

"Not sure, so that's why I don't want you to tell anyone."

"Absolutely," she promised again.

"But, I feel the winds of change blowing, Ginny. It may be sooner than later."

"I'll support you whenever you make the decision and be proud to have served with you."

His smile lit his worn face as he stood and tossed the empty bottle into the recycle bin. With a last glance at the board, he said, "I'm back out on patrol. Your shift was over a while back.

Don't make yourself crazy over this, Ginny." And with that, he was gone.

She turned back to the board and continued to stare for a few more minutes, wishing something would jump out at her.

Brogan stood at the podium, his heart in his throat, as he faced his fellow American Legion members. His sweaty palms gripped the edge of the wood, the microphone appearing to rise snakelike in front of him. Dropping his gaze to the front row, where the other officers sat, his eyes found Ginny, smiling at him, encouragement and love shining in her eyes. Swallowing deeply, he took a breath and began.

"Never figured I'd be up here, but always appreciated y'all brave enough to tell a little about your experiences. 'Specially those that weren't so good. We like to wave the flag and we nod and smile when people say they're thankful for our service. But sometimes, I kinda want them to leave me alone, 'cause there were things that I'm not so proud about.

"Most of it was good...I did my job, did what I was told to do, and came home to my family. Pretty successful, I guess. But there was some fucked-up—uh sorry... uh...oh, hell, there was some fucked-up shit that happened and I witnessed something in a village that not only stayed in my head, but stayed in my nightmares."

He took a deep breath before lifting his eyes again and staring out into the faces of the gathering. Instead of reproach, he saw slight nods. A few men wiping their eyes, their own memories slipping back. His gaze moved to his father and Pops, as well as the other Baytown Boys' fathers, and he wondered what their generation in the war had seen and done.

"Anyway, I know Ms. Spencer has talked about the importance of talking about things that happened and I always figured that was kinda worthless. Talking about something isn't going to make it go away. But, I got to where what was stuck in my head was messing with me to the point that I wasn't enjoying life anymore. Didn't feel worthy." Shaking his head slightly, he concluded, "But I finally listened, talked to someone…well, actually it's ongoing counseling, and I have to admit that I'm finally learning that what I saw was not on me. I didn't cause it and couldn't stop it. So, I've still got memories, but I don't beat myself up over them anymore. They come, I deal." Shrugging, he glanced back down at Ginny and said, "Uh…I guess that's it."

Walking back down the short steps to his seat, he was stunned as Pops stood and started clapping, quickly joined by the others. Blushing as he reached his seat next to Ginny, he complained good naturedly, "Leave it to Pops. Fuckin' crazy."

The evening sun hung low in the sky, the glistening water of the Bay the perfect backdrop for one of Mitch's beach parties. Ginny had participated before, but always as a single and, she had to admit, being part of a couple was a lot of fun.

She and Brogan, along with Katelyn and Aiden formed one team for beach volleyball with Jillian, Grant, Zac, and Callan on the other. Katelyn was a killer athlete and drilled the ball over the net as many time as Aiden did. Not a bad athlete herself, Ginny still found her shorter height to be a barrier with the much taller players. Finally, after missing the ball a couple of times as it sailed over her head, she yelped as hands on her waist hoisted her up into the air allowing her to slam the ball back over the net, surprising their opponents who let the ball drop at their feet.

Laughing as Brogan slowly let her down, she turned in his arms, his hands still skimming her waist. Looking up, she was mesmerized by the way his eyes reflected the sun over the water. Twinkling blue stared back at her. Her hands clung to his biceps as his fingers flexed against the soft skin at her side. In the distance, she heard Mitch call out that the food was ready, but her mind was purely on the man in front of her.

A slow smile formed on Brogan's lips as he bent to kiss her. A soft touch of lips, then deeper as she leaned into his body. He pulled away, wanting to take the kiss so much farther, but he knew there would be time later tonight for that.

Whispering against her cheek, he said, "We better get in line before it's all gone, babe."

With a grin, she nodded and the two of them walked up onto the deck of Mitch and Tori's cabin.

Settling down a few minutes later with plates on their laps, Ginny leaned back against a log near the bonfire. Brogan told her that when they came back from the military, Mitch and the rest of the Baytown boys had hauled the large logs from a neighbor's farm and cut them to place in a circle around the fire pit. It allowed visitors to either sit on the logs or sit in the sand and have something to lean back against, which was what they were doing now.

The area was big enough to hold most of their group sitting on the sand with a few others in beach chairs to the side. Callan and some of his Coast Guard buddies were on one side, entertaining Jade and Belle. Jason and Gareth were in a discussion about the businesses in town. Jillian and Tori were bringing out trays with graham crackers, chocolate bars, and marshmallows for the group to make s'mores.

Ginny sat next to Brogan, their legs, hips, and shoulders touching. Occasionally she glanced up and noticed the shared smiles of the others as their gazes landed on her, and instead of filling her with anxiety, she felt a warm peace slide through her.

"What's got you grinning at your hamburger?" Brogan asked softly, his eyes focused on her.

She twisted her head around and for a moment was lost in his eyes once more, before leaning in to say, "Nothing much. Just happy, I guess." She glanced at his empty paper plate and, before she could offer to get him more food, he tossed it into the fire and curled his arm around her.

"Babe."

With that one word, she knew he wanted her to share. She glanced back up, twisting slightly so she could see him better. Leaning forward, not wanting anyone else to hear her confession, she said, "I've never had this before." Seeing his brows lower in question, she added, "This kind of relationship. You...but not just you. All of this."

"All of this?" he asked, concern filling his face as she struggled to find the right word.

"My family was never like this. Other than when I was first in the Army and thought I had good people to work with, I've never had this kind of camaraderie. And when that all went to shit, I felt like I had no friends. No one I could trust. It stole my peace. And I was just sitting here thinking, I have my peace."

"Baby, special is all that you are," Brogan said, softly. "Before you, this was just me with a bunch of friends, but I was angry...tied up in knots...pissed at myself and the world." His chuckle rumbled deep in his chest before he added, "But you've given me a new life...a chance at finding my own peace as well."

Her lips curved up as she settled into his embrace, her plate still on her lap.

"Better eat up, honey," he encouraged. "A strong wind could blow you over."

"Then I guess it's a good thing I've got you as my anchor."

The cool blue of his eyes flared hot as he whispered in her ear, "Always, babe. Always."

The clanging of a utensil on glass brought their attention to Mitch, who was standing with Tori at his side, both smiling as they gained all eyes on them. Pulling Tori in close, Mitch grinned at the crowd of friends and said, "Got an announcement to make, and figured this was as good a time as any to make it."

The large group quieted, and Ginny noted the air of expectation hovering over the area. Sucking in her breath, she wondered if the news was what they all hoped for.

"Tori and I are expecting a baby," Mitch announced, the words barely leaving his mouth before the whooping and shouting began.

Cries of congratulations rang out as toast after toast was made. Ginny watched as Tori grinned, her hand resting on her still flat stomach. Jillian and Katelyn rushed to hug her as the men circled Mitch with hugs as well.

Hanging behind, to allow the closest friends in first, Ginny watched as Brogan approached Mitch and her breath caught in her throat as she saw him blink back tears. Her man…her large, muscular, tatted, ex-Marine, bar owner man had tears in his eyes. She swallowed several times, breathing through her nose to battle back the sting of tears herself, before moving in to offer her own congratulations to her friends.

28

She is beautiful in the morning. Brogan walked out of his bathroom, staring at Ginny as she lay in his bed, the sheet barely covering her breasts, her sleepy smile greeting him.

"Hate that I have to go in early," he said. "This would've been the perfect morning to make love again, the sun coming up."

She stretched her arms toward the ceiling, the sheet slipping to her waist. "Well," she tempted seductively, "are you sure you have to be at the pub so early?"

"We've got a delivery and it's on the schedule for seven this morning," he said, then shook his head, "but this does suck. You've got a late evening shift, don't you?"

Ginny rolled to her side, propping her head on her hand as she stared at him, standing in the doorway, his jeans tight in all the right places, worn at the knees and crotch, his tight, Finn's T-shirt molded to his muscular chest, and the tats down his arms—which she still needed to find time to ask him about. "Ugh, yes," she confirmed, "and you're right, it does suck when you're standing there looking all lickable and I just want to lay in bed with you."

He planted a knee in the bed, leaning down to capture her lips. "Lickable?" he muttered, as his mouth plundered hers.

For a few minutes, they forgot about work schedules, deliveries, and cases as their lips and tongues danced together. Pulling back regretfully, Brogan heard her little groan and grinned as he kissed her once more before standing.

"Be safe today, honey," he said, a strange sense of worry filling him.

"Always," she replied easily, throwing back the sheet, smiling as she watched his eyes drop from her face to her toes and back up her nude body.

"Damn, woman," he said, grabbing her by the shoulders and hauling her against his body, her front plastered to his as his lips latched on once more.

Laughing, she grabbed one of his t-shirts, jerking it over her head, and gave him a little push. "Off to work," she said, "or I'll never let you leave this room."

"You comin' here when your shift's over?"

Nodding, she said, "Yeah, I'm off tomorrow and, since you managed to get Aiden to open tomorrow, we'll have a nice morning at the beach."

A minute later, in his truck, Brogan looked back toward his bungalow, seeing her wave as she stood at the door, MB circling her legs, and his heart pounded heavy with an unknown dread.

Both of them missed observing the man, lying past

the dune, his binoculars now hanging about his neck as he slid down to the beach, completely out of sight.

With a final pat of MB, Ginny left Brogan's house about an hour after he did, deciding to run by her house to water her plants. Opening her front door, she stepped inside, smiling as she always did when looking at her little house. Throwing open the blinds, she let the sunshine pour in as she looked over at her plants on the table near one of her windows. Walking into her kitchen, she started the coffee and then filled a pitcher with water and walked to the living room to take care of them. Leaning her hip against the table, she thought about her little house. Sweet. Nice. Comfortable. Small. Sighing, her mind wandered to Brogan's bungalow. Definitely not as nice. And even smaller.

Wonder if cats eat houseplants? As soon as that thought ran through her mind she startled. Giving her head a little shake, she headed back to the kitchen and made a cup of coffee.

Her backyard neighbor was in his yard trimming a tree as she took her coffee out on her little patio and waved to him before sitting down and putting her feet up on the other chair. Sucking in a deep breath, she knew where the thought had come from. So far, she and Brogan had bounced between her house and his. Hers was larger, more of a home, and in town so it was closer to their work. His was small, somewhat run-down, but was right on the water. She had a nice master bedroom and bath, but her bed was much smaller than his and if she bought a bigger bed, it would significantly cut down on the space of the room. She loved the loft space in her house, but admittedly, seeing Brogan in it caused her to giggle—he nearly whacked his head on the sloped ceiling.

Closing her eyes, she allowed the sun to warm her as her thoughts about Brogan flowed through her mind. Jolting awake, she heard her neighbor call out to someone and she blinked several times as her eyes readjusted to the light. Holding her hand over her forehead to shade her eyes, she watched as Saul ambled from his truck to the back windows of her neighbor's house. He carried buckets and wipers, in preparation to begin cleaning, before climbing his short ladder.

She watched, her heart in her chest, as he wavered at the top. *How old is Saul anyway? Jesus, he needs to hire more help so he's not teetering at the top of ladders.* She noticed her neighbor had finished his tree trimming and was hanging around the bottom of Saul's ladder and she wondered where his new help was.

Twisting her neck back, she took an appraising look at her windows. *Ugh, they could use a good washing.* Wondering if Saul would be interested in the job, she rose from her chair and made her way over her small yard to the fence in the back. Waiting until he climbed down from his ladder, she called out, "Saul, where's your new help?"

He turned, smiling as he waved. "He's working another job. I trust him to work on his own now, since he's followed me over the past couple weeks."

"I was thinking about having you do my windows, but my house is small—"

Mitch's father, Ed, was the police chief. She liked working for him, but a year later a heart attack took him off the job and the town called to his son to take the reins. She was glad Mitch was ready to leave the FBI and return to his roots, even though the pay cut had been substantial. But before Ed, Mitch's grandfather had been the longtime police chief. For a few seconds, she allowed her mind to slide over the fact that Mitch's family had been glad to have him come home but they would have been just as proud if he continued to work for the FBI. He had that—family support and pride.

"You got something?"

Blinking out of her reverie, she said, "Still just checking something out. I'd like to clock on about twenty minutes early if you don't mind."

Nodding, he responded, "Got no problem with that. You wanna tell me what you're checking on?"

"I saw Saul Hudgins earlier, washing windows on a neighbor's house. I know he's got a new man helping him, been working with Saul for several weeks and now working on his own, not having to be right with Saul. Anyway, Saul mentioned they did the windows at the Masterson's house." Shrugging, she said, "It's a long shot, but I was just thinking that—"

"That it'd be a great way to check out houses, to see inside the different rooms, know where bedrooms might be," he interjected, his eyes pinning hers.

"Yeah. I've checked him out, but nothing turned up on a preliminary computer search, other than a charge when he was a minor."

"What's your plan?"

"I know where he's working today. It's here in town.

Thought I'd go by and talk a bit. See if I could find out more."

"Need assistance?"

Shaking her head, she said, "Nah. Just talking to him right now. Nothing official. I'll be fine."

"Stay in contact," he ordered.

His command was unnecessary, but she was not offended. Mitch took his duties seriously and, while she knew she had his complete confidence, he still wanted to make sure his officers were protected. With a nod, she left the office and headed out to the SUV.

29

Brogan came in from the back of the building, a crate of liquor in his arms, and moved to the bar, setting it down carefully. The lunch crowd had left and he used the time before things got busy again to re-stock. Aiden followed a minute later, his arms full as well. Katelyn stood behind the bar, a clipboard in her hand as she noted the stock.

Turning around, she nodded toward her brothers. "That should do it, guys. I'll add it my list and we'll be good to go. Then, I'm heading back to work."

Brogan walked past Katelyn, leaning over to kiss her head. "Thanks, sis," he said, "but you go on back to Gareth. You've got a job there and this is extra."

Katelyn reared back and narrowed her eyes at him. "Who are you and what did you do with my grumpy brother?"

Aiden burst out laughing, and said, "I was wondering the same thing."

Unable to contain his chuckle, Brogan grinned. "Just being a good big brother, for once."

Katelyn's face softened as she placed her hand on his arm. "Brogan, you have always been a wonderful brother. I think, though, I know what is the reason for your less grumpy self. Would I be right to say that you and Ginny have acknowledged your feelings for each other?"

Brogan glanced around, his natural shyness not wanting eavesdroppers, but other than two tables of customers that the server was taking care of, the pub was empty at the minute. He cut his eyes back to his siblings, both with smiling faces aimed toward him.

Leaning his hip against the back of the bar, he placed his hands on the edge behind him, crossing one booted leg in front of the other. Sucking in a deep breath, he let it out slowly.

"Brogan," Katelyn spoke, "you're not facing a firing squad. Honey, this is us. We've got your back. You can talk to us."

"I love her."

The air was still for a few seconds before Aiden laughed again as Katelyn snorted, before she said, "Duh."

Pinching his lips, he glared at both of them. "Do you want me to talk or do you want to piss me off?"

"Come on, Bro, loosen up," Aiden said. "You know we want to know, but if you think telling us you love Ginny Spencer is news, then you need to catch up with the times."

Brogan wanted to be irritated but knew he needed their input, so he sucked in another breath before continuing. "Like I said, I love her. And she loves me. Don't know why but not going to question it. She does and I plan on holding on to that."

He looked up and both siblings were smiling in agreement. "Not sure how to do that."

Katelyn jerked as she carefully stared at her brother, before saying, "I don't know what you mean, Brogan."

"We've been spending the nights at one of our places, running back and forth between the two. I thought about putting a few things at her place and telling her to bring some of her stuff to my place. But that still feels transient."

"You want to move in together," Aiden said, nodding his head, not waiting for confirmation. "Sounds good."

"Doesn't seem too soon?" Brogan asked.

"Not when you feel the way you do about each other. I know you two haven't been together that long, but I know. When it's right, it's right," Katelyn said, her enthusiasm overflowing.

"It's not just the emotional aspect of moving in together, but the logistics," Brogan continued. "My place is small…really small. But it's got privacy and beach access. Her place is in town and convenient to our work. It's homier…but not much bigger. She's got two bedrooms but one is small. Got a loft for extra space, but swear to God, I feel like I'll hit my head on the ceiling when I'm there."

Katelyn let loose another giggle at the thought of huge Brogan hitting his head, then immediately mumbled, "Sorry," as he glared once more.

"So, essentially," Aiden said, "you want to ask her to

move in together, but neither of you have a great place for a couple."

Brogan nodded, pleased that Aiden understood. "Yes, exactly."

Rubbing his chin, Aiden said, "I don't know that you have an instant right or wrong decision here. I mean, it's not like either of you are going to be buying a bigger house right now. Maybe you should just keep sharing places."

Seeing Brogan's thoughtful look, Katelyn added, "Take some clothes to her place and she can leave some at yours. Make the most of the best of both places. Your beach access and privacy and her proximity to town."

Hanging his head, he said, "Maybe this is all premature. I mean, I'm talking to y'all but haven't talked to her yet. I guess I was just working on my courage."

"Brogan, you've got more courage than most men," Katelyn said, "but I think you're trying to figure out the best situation and maybe you need to talk to Ginny to get her input. Work on it together."

"You know," Aiden said, moving next to Katelyn as he leaned against the stock bar, "you could think about keeping your property and doing more with it." Seeing he had Brogan's attention, he said, "You bought that piece of property for a song when you got back and it's not the house you got that's worth anything, but that beach front land is a gold mine. You got room to build a house there...one that's big enough for family."

Brogan's gaze landed on Aiden, hard and fast, as his breath caught in his throat. Family. Wife. Kids. *Ginny and their kids.* Things he always wanted but never thought would happen filled him with the thought that maybe, with her, he would not only get peace, but a forever.

Aiden and Katelyn stayed quiet, both seeing emotions cross the face of their normally stoic brother.

Finally, Katelyn whispered, "What are you thinking, Brogan?"

Sucking in another breath through his nose before letting it out slowly, he said, "Never thought this would happen. Find a woman that could see through my shit. Make me face it, get it out, and get help for it. Make me feel like I got something to look forward to each day other than just coming to work or coaching the kids. Make me think about having a future."

Aiden lifted his chin while saying, "Glad for you, man. No one deserves that kind of happiness more than you." Katelyn nodded, as Aiden continued, "Keep going with Ginny. Talk to her and find out what her thoughts are. If she's agreeable to keeping your beach property, and she'd be crazy not to be, then see where everything goes and you can plan on building on your property some time to make a bigger place."

Chuckling, Brogan nodded. "Never thought of that, but gotta say, it makes a helluva lot of sense."

Katelyn lifted her eyebrow and said, "This is a red-letter day. Brogan's in love and not grumpy. Aiden's giving good advice. I don't know if I should go play the lottery, figuring the jack-pot's just around the corner, or get the hell out of here 'cause the world's coming to an end."

Both brothers moved quickly to her sides, immediately creating a Katelyn sandwich with their large bodies on either side, throwing their arms around her, squishing her until she screamed with laughter.

Ginny drove along Main Street, but did not see Ralph or the Hudgins Window Washing truck. Making another pass along the businesses in town, she still did not view him. A glance at the clock told her it was time for her to begin her patrol, so she had no choice but to abandon her attempts to talk to him today and start her circular drives around the town's streets.

Passing by Tori's Sea Glass Inn, she parked along Beach Road and walked over the slight dune to the town beach. Many families were enjoying picnics on the beach and she was pleased to not find anyone openly defying the rule of no glass on the beach. With only one dog owner having to be warned that their beach privileges would be revoked if their dog was not contained on a leash, she weaved around the beach-goers and over the dune. Climbing in the SUV, she made her way to the harbor, checking out the activity there.

Stopping to chat with a few of the fishermen coming in from their day's run and to wave at Callan and some of the Coast Guard as they went out for a routine exercise, as well as check in the with the owners of the kayak and ski boat rentals, carved out part of her afternoon patrols.

She eventually made a circle back to Main Street, her eyes still looking for Ralph, but having no luck. Seeing Jason standing outside his garage, she pulled up.

Hopping out, she walked toward him, noting his wide smile. "Hey, Jason," she greeted. "You look happy."

"Just got the go-ahead to open my tattoo shop right next to the garage," he said, his satisfaction evident as he swept his arm in the direction of the storefront next to the garage.

"Silas and the town board agreed?" she asked incredulously.

Nodding, he said, "Seems that the town's so glad to finally have a reputable garage in town that not only repairs cars, but also tows, that they're ready to bring in more business. And my business plans include motorcycle repairs and to bring in more mechanics, plus at least one or two tattoo artists." He ran his hand over his head and added, "I kinda feel bad 'cause I know that woman was trying to get this storefront for her ice cream business, but I haven't seen her around here lately."

"Rose Parker," she said, nodding her head in agreement. "I heard someone say she had to put a halt on her plans to take care of a relative back home. But don't worry, she'll find another place if she comes back. But, for your business, I'm really happy for you," she enthused.

The tall, tatted man smiled down at her and said, "Same for you." She did not respond, but her silent question must have reached him, because he continued, "You and Brogan. Been waiting for the two of you to hook up for two years. Glad to see he pulled his head outta his ass and did something about it."

Blushing, she grinned. "Thanks. 'Preciate it." Looking down the street, she said, "By the way, have you seen one of Saul's window cleaning trucks around? Maybe with his new guy doing the work?"

"Yeah, saw him up the street about two hours ago. Haven't seen him since."

Nodding, she threw her hand up toward him while calling out, "Thanks. See you around."

She stopped at the station to check in an hour later, but Mitch had already gone home. Mildred and Mable were getting ready to leave, but stopped to ask if she needed anything.

Smiling at the two women, she said, "No, thanks. Just taking a break and then I'll be back out until the end of my shift. She watched as they left the station, locking up behind them. Taking a quick bathroom break, she headed back to the SUV and began her drive through the town's residential streets, occasionally sweeping by the business areas again.

The evening settled over the town and her mind wandered to Brogan, wondering if he was still at the pub or had gone on home. *Home*. She liked the sound of that. Not her home. Or his home. But *home*.

Sighing, she turned a corner and tried to focus on her task at hand, but as she passed house after house, many with lit windows, some where she could see the families watching TV in their living rooms, or eating a late dinner at their dining room tables, she felt longing. Longing for what she had not had with her parents. Oh, they had sat down at the table together, her father had demanded that. But there had been no laughter and certainly no fun. Her mind rolled back to dinner with the MacFarlanes. Laughing. Talking. Gentle teasing.

Parents who obviously loved their children and had no problem showing it. *And they would adore grandchildren.*

At that thought, she slammed on the brakes, her mind suddenly thinking of a real future with Brogan. A home with him. Children with him. A future with him.

Seeing no one on the road, she parked next to the curb and pulled out her phone. Dialing him, she closed her eyes in pleasure as she heard his warm voice answer.

"Babe?"

"Hey, honey" she said, not having any other words to say.

"You okay?"

"Yeah. I just…uh…I…"

Chuckling, Brogan said, "You want to spit it out or did you just call for no reason?"

"Actually, I just called for no reason," she admitted. "Other than I wanted to hear your voice."

"Seriously?" his deep voice rumbled straight into her.

"Yeah. I'm on patrol and had you on my mind. Then I just wanted to tell you that." There was a hesitation on the other end and, for a second, she wondered if he was still on the line.

Then, he spoke and his words curled around her heart. "Babe, I love you. I want you here and not on the other end of this phone, so you'd be in my arms as I tell you that."

Sitting alone in the dark, on the side of the road, she smiled. "Love you too, Brogan."

"As soon as you get off, I want you here, but drive

safe and let me know you're on your way," he ordered gently.

"Okay."

"I've got something I want to talk to you about," he continued.

Interest piqued, she asked, "What is it?"

"Tell you when you get here."

"Okay," she readily agreed again. "I gotta finish patrol, but I'll call as I'm heading your way." She almost said goodbye, but hurriedly said, "Brogan?"

"Yeah?"

"Thanks…for…well, just thanks for loving me."

Once more there was a pause before he growled, "Ginny, you've got no reason to thank me. Loving you is easy." Then he chuckled as he added, "But, I've got no objection to you showing your gratitude once we're in bed together tonight."

"That I can easily do," she laughed in agreement.

Disconnecting, she laid her head back against the headrest for a moment, the knowledge that at the end of her shift she did not have to go home alone but had a good man—a man she loved—waiting for her, made the night easier. Starting the SUV once more, she glanced at the house nearby, the family gathered in the living room together and, instead of envy, she felt peace.

30

Shift almost over, Ginny took one last pass by the gazebo side of the park, her headlights joining the park's illumination in cutting through the darkness. No movements caught her eye and, as she rounded the last corner, she looked at her clock. Shift over. Grinning, she headed back to the station. Parking the SUV, she jumped in her car and backed out of the lot.

She knew Brogan had wanted to go running on the beach the next morning and she had planned on joining him, but her running shoes were at her house. Knowing it would only take five minutes, she decided to make the detour to pick them up.

Parking on the street in front of her house, she hurried up the walk to her front door, thinking maybe Brogan would not mind if she started keeping a few things at his place...*and he can keep some of his things here.*

Brogan leaned deep into his sofa, the game just going off. Thinking of Ginny coming over soon, nerves hit his gut. Tonight, he would ask about her moving in...or at least agreeing to share houses until they could figure something out. All he knew was, he wanted to fall asleep with her by his side every night, regardless which bed it was in.

Suddenly looking around at how dark it was, he realized the game had gone longer than intended and she would be there soon. His dinner dishes were washed, but still in the sink. His beer bottle sat on the coffee table, a condensation ring at its base. Snagging the bottle, he stalked into the kitchen, tossing it into the recycle bin before placing the dishes back into the cupboard. Grabbing a paper towel, he wiped the counter and then the coffee table. Walking into the bathroom, he pulled clean towels from the small closet in the corner and hung them on the towel bar. Moving to his bedroom, he checked to make sure his work clothes had been tossed into the hamper.

Nodding, he was satisfied it was as good as it would get, but kicked himself that he had not thought to buy flowers. Rubbing his hand over his face, he walked back into the living room, his nerves still working their way through his stomach. Glancing at the clock once more, he knew she would walk through the door any moment. *Please let her say yes.*

Smiling at the thought of seeing Brogan soon, Ginny entered the living room, flipping on the light switch, surprised she had not left it on when she went to work. Hurrying to the bathroom, she quickly used the facilities and decided, since she was home, she might as well change out of her police uniform and into something more comfortable.

Standing at the bathroom vanity, she pulled out her phone. Hearing Brogan's deep voice again, she smiled. "Hey, honey. Sorry I'm late, but I'm at my house to grab some things. I wanted my running shoes for tomorrow and, since I'm here, I'm going to get out of my uniform and put on something comfortable."

"I'm sitting on the porch waiting to see your headlights, babe. Make it soon," Brogan said. "We've both got tomorrow off and I'm itching to get our time together started."

"Couldn't agree more," she said, moving into her bedroom, her hands at her belt buckle as she held the phone between her ear and shoulder. Flipping on the light, she jerked as she saw her bed linens mussed just before seeing someone crawling out her open window.

Screaming into the phone, "Intruder! I've got an intruder!" she disconnected with Brogan, immediately drawing her weapon and pressing the radio at her shoulder, calling it in to the emergency dispatch.

"Officer Spencer reporting an intruder in her home. Just left premises. In pursuit."

Running to her window, she looked out, seeing the fleeing subject, and crawled out the same window, dropping lightly to the ground. Shouting, "Halt. Police!" had no effect, so she began running after the intruder, continuing to shout her progress into her radio.

Brogan's heart stopped at her words, his feet rooted to the wooden porch. *Intruder? At her house?* Two seconds later it hit him and he bolted back inside, grabbing his keys from the counter before racing toward his truck. Hitting redial, her phone went to voice message.

"Fuck!" he yelled, climbing inside his cab and starting the engine. Gunning out of his sandy drive, the back fishtailed as he dialed Mitch.

Mitch answered with, "I know. I got the call. I'm on my way."

"I'm heading there too."

"Bro, don't get in the way of police business."

"You've got to be fuckin' kidding me," he growled. "I'll be there." Disconnecting, he called Aiden, not giving his brother a chance to speak before yelling, "Get to Ginny's house. She had an intruder." Disconnecting again, his heart pounded as he stomped on the accelerator, churning up the road to town. Only a ten-minute drive, he nonetheless hated every second while shaving the time in half, wondering what he would find when he got there. *Please, God, let her be all right.*

Pulling up in front of her house, he saw Sam, wearing jeans with a BPD t-shirt, talking to Aiden. Knowing Sam and his wife lived down the street from Ginny, he was not surprised to see him there. Jumping out of the truck, he ran to them. "Where is she?"

Sam looked at him, listening to his radio, then said, "Mitch is in pursuit. Grant and Burt are on their way. I'm here at her house to keep anyone from entering if we need to collect evidence."

"Bro," Aiden said, his hands up toward his brother, but got no further.

"Where is she?" Brogan roared.

Just then, the trio heard Sam's radio squawk Ginny's voice. "Mitch, I've pursued the suspect to the corner of Fig and Washington. Request backup immediately."

Mitch was heard responding, "On my way." He also radioed Grant and Burt, both responding they were heading in that direction.

Without a word, Brogan took off running, recognizing the address as only being two blocks away. He knew these streets and every piece of property, even in the dark night, having run them with the other Baytown Boys as a child. Hearing footsteps running behind him, he did not have to turn to know Aiden was right with him.

Ginny pinned her eyes on the figure she was chasing. Male. Good runner. Dark clothing with a dark hat. Calling these descriptors in as she ran, she hoped the North Hampton County dispatcher was able to understand her.

Her intruder led her on a chase through several streets, weaving in and out of yards and alleys. She pressed on, determined not to lose him. *Where are the others?* Just as she was wondering if she were all alone, she heard Mitch's voice come over her radio, announcing his location. Radioing her location back, she calculated he was close by.

Just then, she rounded the corner of a house still in

close pursuit of the intruder, only to see him easily scale a wooden, privacy fence. Smiling, she knew she could do the same after years of military training. She ran full force, giving a hop at the bottom to gain height, then grabbed the top with her hands as one foot hit the fence to propel herself upward. Swinging her leg over, she pulled her body over the top and landed softly on both feet on the other side.

She stilled momentarily, listening, not hearing footsteps. Slowing her breathing, she walked slowly forward, her eyes discerning shapes in the backyard of the residence, the dim porch light offering little illumination.

With a quick glance toward the house, she noted all the lights were out, but did not know if the owners were home sleeping, or gone. A creak from squeaky hinges sounded out and she slipped around the back corner, giving her eyes a chance to adjust to the space. The yard was not large, but held a shed in the back corner, the type usually for holding tools and, perhaps, a lawn mower.

Calling out, "Baytown Police. Come out with your hands where I can see them," she waited. "Backup is on its way. Come out with your hands in the air."

The door to the shed slowly opened outward, the inside dark, shielding whoever was inside. Hearing Mitch on the other side of the fence, Ginny was about to call out again, when the lights to the house came on, temporarily blinding her.

"What's going on?" a male voice boomed out as a man threw open his back door, stepping out onto his porch, tying his robe around his waist. "Who's out here?"

"Sir, Baytown Police. Get back inside!" she shouted, just as she saw the dark figure dart out of the shed and around to the back corner of the yard.

"What the hell? I'm calling the police!" the homeowner continued to yell.

"Sir, I am the police. Get back inside!" she screamed again, racing through the backyard toward the corner, seeing the intruder jumping to scale the fence.

Mitch jumped the fence and rounded the back in time to see the homeowner pull out a shotgun as he continued to yell for the police. Rushing to the porch, he subdued the elderly man, pushing him back inside with orders to stay.

Brogan, right on Mitch's heels, jumped the fence as well, taking a few steps before hearing Aiden land heavily behind him.

Grant and Burt rounded the alley that ran behind the yard, pushing trash cans out of the way as they neared the property, calling out their location as well.

Ginny made it to the man, his feet scrambling for purchase as his hands pulled from the top of the fence, in an effort to make his way over. She tugged on his ankle and, as his body came down, he managed to backhand her, causing her grip to slip and she stumbled backward.

"You can't get away!" she shouted, righting her body before rigidly locking as she saw a gun in his hand.

"Keep 'em back," he ordered.

She was unable to see his face in the dark, with both of them behind the shed where no illumination pierced his features other than the slight glistening on the barrel of the weapon in his hand.

"He's armed," Ginny announced loudly, hearing the footsteps around her come to a halt.

Mitch cursed softly, turning back to warn the homeowner to move deep inside his house, thankful when the older man followed his instructions. Weapon drawn, Mitch stealthily walked down the deck stairs to the back yard, joined by Brogan and Aiden. He stared at them for a moment, his gaze hard, but knew they would not be persuaded to leave. His eyes dropped to the Brogan's hands clinched into fists.

Brogan looked at his friend, not caring that he was now the Police Chief, seeing him ready to take out Ginny's threat.

"Ginny," Mitch called out.

Ginny looked into the darkness, ready to speak into her radio, when the gun came slightly closer to her, and this was because the intruder stepped forward just enough for her to see his face.

Ben. *Ben? Oh, my God, Ben Hudgins. Saul's grandson.*

31

Ben's face twisted, as though tortured, his mouth turning down. His heavy breathing filled the void of sound, as his hand shook holding the gun.

"Ben," she said gently, her eyes staying on his as she forced herself to not look down at the weapon.

"I…I…" he haltingly spoke, his words as shaky as his hand.

"Ben, give me the gun and we'll talk."

Mitch came into sight, his weapon raised, sliding his eyes to the side as Brogan came into view as well.

Ben's gaze jumped to the added people, his hand shaking more, before settling on Brogan's furious expression. Swallowing deeply, he said, "Get back. You gotta get back."

Mitch calmly said, "Not going to do that, Ben. We're not going to leave you here with Officer Spencer. You need to lower your weapon and come with us."

"No!" he shouted, his voice hoarse with emotion as

he cut his eyes back to Ginny. "I didn't mean to scare you. I just like to look, that's all. Just look."

"But Ben, looking isn't all you've been doing," Ginny said gently, her hands clearly in sight, not wanting to startle him. "You went beyond looking."

His face contorted as he bit out, "Not if they're good. But that woman in the park…I'd watched her before. But then she was with a man…and drinking. I wanted her but she was with someone else. And then that bitch at the bar. She flirted with me to keep me buying drinks but then acted like I was nobody when some other guys came into the bar."

Brogan growled low in his chest at the thought that Ben had been in Ginny's house. She was so close to being violated like the others. He slipped backward, into the shadows, and moved stealthily to the left, glad the dim light from the back porch shone onto the path around the shed.

Grant and Burt were on the other side of the fence corner listening, unable to see what was happening. Grant looked at a tree nearby and, with a nod toward Burt, he jogged over, holstering his gun so that he could climb onto a lower limb for a better vantage point.

"What about your grandfather?" Ginny asked, her voice still soft as she kept an eye on the weapon pointed at her.

Snorting, Ben said, "Granddad? I was eleven years old when I first worked summers for him. He told me to keep a close eye on what was going on inside the houses in case I needed to back away. Hell, the first time I saw a woman taking off her bathing suit in her bedroom and she never noticed me standing on the ground peering in. All I knew, was that I couldn't back away." He looked at Ginny, his eyes pleading for understanding, "It was like a drug. I had to have more."

She quickly calculated and realized he had been peering inside windows for over fifteen years and no one knew. "Ben, I want to get some help for you. You need to be able to—"

"You think I don't know that?" he yelled. "I tried…I tried to fight it. Granddad wanted me to join the business, but I knew if I did, I'd never be able to stop." His face fell as his eyes pleaded for understanding. "I went away. Went to college, came back to teach, thinking it would all stop. But the urges were still there. They were still there."

"Ben, without counseling, it's too hard to stop. I can get help for you—"

"You? Oh, that's rich. You, who fucks your boyfriend with the windows open. I had a straight view right over the dunes, into the bedroom, and you never realized. How the hell can you help me?"

Ginny heard a growl before realizing it was from her, but forced her fury down. "You need to put the gun down, Ben. You need help and you don't need to make it worse."

"I need you, 'cause you're gonna get me out of here," Ben said, stepping closer, the barrel of the gun now only a few feet from her.

Brogan moved noiselessly around the shed, his eyes landing on the back of the man holding a gun to his Ginny. First fear, and then anger, coursed through his blood. Ben. Who the hell would have thought it was Ben? Thinking of the times he had served him in his bar as he probably scoped out women, including Ginny, brought his rage boiling. *And now he has a fucking gun on her and I'm powerless.*

His vision narrowed, darkness filling in around the edges as he was taken to a different place...a different time. The Afghan husband dragging his wife into the street, tossing her down into the dirt before using his foot to keep her down as he took a stone and threw it.

In years to come, Ginny would remember what happened next, but at the time, her mind was only filled with Brogan's anguished face as he moved toward Ben, his hands raised in an attempt to hit his gun hand. Several shots were fired, but her mind would only remember them as one loud noise reverberating throughout the space. There was the firing of a weapon from behind Ben, coming from somewhere over the fence, causing his right leg to buckle underneath him. Then his scream piercing the night as another shot was fired, this time aimed at her, while another shot caught him in the arm.

He fell to the ground at her feet, as pain seared her side. Knocked backwards, she fell against the shed, slumping to the ground. Unconsciousness descended as she heard multiple voices, all shouting and demanding, indistinguishable to her ringing ears, except for one. One lone voice pierced the others as blackness overtook her. One voice...low and deep...full of anguish... howling like a wounded animal. Brogan. She wanted to tell him she was fine. But no words joined his cries.

Ginny opened her eyes, Brogan filling her gaze. His face, ravaged, stared back at hers. She offered a slight smile before the reality of her surroundings slipped in. She was lying on a stretcher in the back of the ambulance, Zac nudging Brogan out of the way as he checked her out.

Lifting her hand toward him, Brogan leaned back in, her hand cupping his face. "Hey," she breathed, trying to rub away the deep creases in his brow. "I'm okay."

Gasping, his face closed the slight distance, his lips a breath away from hers, as he blinked back tears. "Fucking hell, babe. Thought...I thought..." Unable to put words to the memory of tackling Ben while watching Ben's gun fire, he closed his eyes, a tear falling down his beard-stubbled jaw.

"Body armor works," she said, although she did not mention the ache she felt in her side. Her thumb swiped his cheek, wiping away the moisture.

"Only if he hit you there," Brogan rasped. "If he'd gotten you somewhere else—"

She remembered the reverberations of gunshots, but could not remember being hit. "Babe, you knocked his arm downward and saved my life. Grant got him in the leg, but it didn't stop him. You, Brogan, you saved my life."

He dropped his forehead to hers, his breath still ragged. Ginny tried to reach up with her other hand, but Zac had hold of it as he checked her blood pressure. Glaring, she said, "Zac, I'm fine. The force pushed me back against the shed and knocked the wind out of me, that's all."

"Ginny, if you think for one second that I'm going to

shirk my examination of a police officer shot, much less one of my friends, you're crazy. Hell, I'm letting Brogan get in my way as it is. Now, lay there and let me do my job."

At that, she relaxed slightly, knowing as soon as Zac could finish, she would be able to get up. "Where's Ben?"

"Another ambulance took him to the ER. He'll be fine. Sam went with him and a North Heron deputy will be with them at the hospital as well."

Shifting her eyes back to Brogan, she held his cheek closely, pulling slightly until his lips landed on hers. Soft and sweet, but she could tell he was holding back.

"Honey," she said, gaining his attention. "Kiss me."

"I don't want to hurt you—"

"Brogan, kiss me like you're glad I'm alive," she ordered, a ghost of a smile playing on her lips.

His eyes widened, then narrowed slightly, as he fussed, "Oh, babe, you'll remember that remark when I get you home, pamper you, and then get you in my bed."

Grinning widely now, she said, "I'll hold you to that."

Closing the distance, he claimed her mouth, licking, sucking, delving, as he relished knowing she was alive and she was his.

"I hate being treated like an invalid," Ginny grumbled, two days later, sitting on Brogan's comfortable sofa.

"Shut it, beautiful," Brogan ordered, standing in the kitchen deciding what to heat up for lunch. The community and their friends had descended the previous day, bearing casseroles, pies, cakes, platters of cut fruit, cold-cuts, homemade jams and jellies, and more things that Brogan had no idea what they were as Katelyn packed his freezer. His counter resembled a table at the county fair. Brogan had been happy for the support, but irritated that Ginny had not gotten as much rest as she needed. By the time Zac released her, she had had to fill out report after report in the police station. Mitch and Grant had taken Ben's statement and gone back to examine Ginny's house, which became a crime scene when they discovered Ben had ejaculated on her bed linens, and the night was gone and the morning had arrived.

He managed to get her to sleep, drawing the curtains in his room, wanting to shut out the world, as well as any peering eyes after hearing Ben's confession of spying on them. Then he kicked out the well-wishers, telling them to come back later. He meant days later, not the next day, but hearing a knock on the door, he dropped his head to his chin.

Hearing a giggle from the sofa, he pretended to glare as Ginny smiled at him. Walking to the door, he swung it open, seeing Katelyn and his mom. Glancing behind them, he was pleased there was no one else.

Corrine stood on her toes to kiss Brogan's cheek, saying, "Your dad and Pops went into the pub today to work with Aiden, so you have nothing to worry about there. Just concentrate on your girl." Back down on her heels, she rushed over to Ginny, scooping her into her arms.

"Corrine, I'm fine, I'm fine," Ginny assured, seeing tears forming in the older woman's eyes.

"My boy would not make it without you," Corrine whispered into Ginny's ear.

Humbled, Ginny patted her back, and reminded, "I'm here and I'm fine.

Corrine stood and wiped her eyes. Pulling herself up to her full height, which was not very tall, she announced, "Katelyn and I are here to work."

Brogan's eyebrows lifted as he repeated, "Work?"

"Ginny can't go home right now—" A slight gasp from Ginny halted Corrine, who immediately turned and apologized. "Sweetie, I'm sorry."

"No, no, it's fine. You're right." A shiver slid over her, noticed by Brogan who stalked to her, shifted her over, planted himself in the sofa and pulled her into his lap. Wrapping his arms around her, he said, "We're gonna take care of it, babe."

She looked into his eyes, both worry and anger filling them. "When I saw him leaving through the window, I noticed my bedspread was messy, but I was focused on the intruder. I'm so glad I didn't really see what he had done."

"That bed's gone," Brogan announced. "Grant and Mitch took what they needed for evidence, and then Aiden and Lance came and hauled the mattress to the dump."

Her mind whirling with all that she was hearing, she focused on the one thing that did not fit. "Lance? Lance came to help?"

"He's not much into socializing," Brogan agreed, "but he hated what had been done to you. He called Mitch and wanted to know if he could help. Mitch sent him my way and I told him to get with Aiden and get that mattress out of your house."

Corrine said, "That's why Katelyn and I are here. I know you got a lot of food yesterday, and we're going to sort that out for you. We'll label some of it, wrap some more, freeze what we can, and set out some for later."

"Later, Ma?" Brogan asked, his attention pulled back to the dynamo already in the kitchen working.

"Brogan, friends are going to come by. You kicked everyone out yesterday so they'll come by today to check on Ginny."

"She was shot. Doesn't matter if it didn't penetrate, she was still shot," Brogan argued. "She needs rest and not a bunch of our friends coming—"

"Honey," Ginny's soft voice broke through his rant as her hand grasped his arm. Holding his gaze, she said, "I want to see our friends. This should be a celebration... I'm fine, we're all fine."

Ginny's phone rang and Katelyn picked it up from the counter, looking at the caller ID as she walked toward Ginny. Eyes wide, she stopped in her tracks, her mouth open but no words coming forth.

Ginny's hand reached out, but before she closed her fingers on it, Katelyn turned her stare toward Brogan. "It says *Dad* on the ID."

Brogan's longer arm snatched the phone from his sister's hand and hit answer. "Yeah?"

Pause. "Brogan MacFarlane. Ginny's boyfriend. And I already know who this is since the word *Dad* came up on the caller ID."

Pause. "That depends on why you're calling. If you are

calling to apologize to Ginny, then I'll have no problem handing the phone to her. If you're just calling to check on her since she was in the news for getting shot at, then I'll tell you that she's fine, surrounded by good friends and my family, who adore her. If you're calling for any other reason, then the answer is no. At least not now. She can call you when she feels like it, if she feels like it."

Pause. "Those are the only options."

Pause. "Right, then she can call you when she's ready." Disconnecting, Brogan tossed the phone to the coffee table and announced, "Sweetheart, your dad's a dick."

Ginny burst out laughing, her head leaning back, full belly laughing that made everyone in the room smile. Wiping tears from her eyes, she held her side, saying, "You could not be more right." After a moment, as her mirth slowed, she sighed heavily. "You know, honey, I could have handled him."

"Your parents haven't come to see you in the two years you've been here. You told me they also haven't called to see how you are doing. I know you worked the past two Thanksgiving and Christmas holidays because you've had no family to spend it with. Something that ends now. And I also know you are more than competent to handle them. But right now, with the reminder that just two days ago I might not be sitting here with you in my arms, is too damn fresh for me to let one more thing steal your peace."

Ginny's eyes filled with tears as she swallowed deeply. "You've got my back," she whispered, clutching his face with her hands, the feel of his steel arms around her. Embracing. Protecting.

"Always got your back, baby," he agreed.

Brogan took her lips again, his arms wrapped tightly around her body, making sure to avoid her bruised side. As Corrine and Katelyn worked in the kitchen, Brogan leaned back, tucking Ginny's head against his heartbeat.

32

Ben's arrest shocked the community. A hometown boy, Saul's grandson. Saul immediately announced his retirement, shaken to the core about his grandson's confessions.

Ginny sat in June's office, heaving a sigh as she talked through her feelings. "I feel sorry for him, in a way. He knew what he was doing was wrong, but couldn't seem to stop. And then his behaviors became more and more overt."

Looking at June, she said, "I know this is part of his police report but, with our confidentiality, can I talk in here with you about it?"

"Absolutely," June assured. "What is said in here, stays in here."

"It seemed he was only a pre-teen when washing the windows of a woman who realized he was there. She must have been an exhibitionist. She would strip while staring at him outside. He started going more and more to see her and, each time, she would increase her activity. Stripping, touching herself, and according to him, she even had a male guest when she knew he was there. The desire to watch women became everything to him. He couldn't achieve sexual satisfaction unless there was an element of voyeurism."

Nodding, June said, "That is so often how it starts."

"So, I do feel sorry for him, and yet, as a woman, I'm so creeped out by it."

"And as a woman, you've had to deal with these issues before," June prompted.

"I know, as a police officer, I will always have to deal with assaults against women. I can handle it, but I admit it trips some triggers."

June smiled. "Yes, it will. But you recognize those, get help for them, and then you can still do your job." Leaning back in her chair, she asked, "What about your house?"

"God, I hate even going into it. My bed is gone… Brogan got rid of it. And just knowing Ben was in there has made it difficult for me to return."

"Where are you staying?"

With a smile, she replied, "With Brogan. He told me that the night of the attack, he was going to talk to me about us moving in together, but deciding which place would be difficult. So, for right now, we're staying at his bungalow. It's small, but we're talking about enlarging it."

As the two women stood, Ginny's session over, they embraced. June said, "It's so good to see you moving forward." She smiled, knowing she had…with Brogan.

Several days later, Ginny sat in the back of Finn's Pub, surrounded by friends. Brogan worked behind the bar, his eyes continually straying to where she sat.

"She's good," Aiden said, coming up behind him, pulling a beer for another customer.

Brogan dropped his chin to his chest for a moment, keeping his eyes open because closing them meant he saw her fall backwards again in his mind.

"You been back to see your counselor?" Aiden asked.

Clearing his throat, Brogan shook his head. "Not yet, but I go tomorrow. I wanted to make sure Ginny got in as soon as possible."

"Has she?"

Brogan nodded, "Yeah. She went yesterday. She seems okay. I mean, look at her...smiling, happy."

"She's found peace with it all, Bro. You need to make sure you do too."

Turning to look at his brother, Brogan said, "I never thanked you for having my back that night, but you know you've got my gratitude."

Laughing, Aiden flashed his famous smile and said, "Always got your back, Bro. But just remember that when you make up the next work rotation." Clapping Brogan on the back, Aiden headed off to deliver the beers.

Shaking his head, Brogan could not keep the grin from sliding over his lips. Looking over, he saw Ginny walking toward him. Moving behind the bar, she stepped right into his embrace and, leaning her head back, she held his gaze.

"You okay, honey?"

"I am now," he admitted, his blue eyes twinkling as his arms held her tight.

One Year Later

"Hi. My name is Ginny MacFarlane. I'm a police officer. Former soldier with the Army Military Police. And I'm a victim of sexual harassment and sexual assault."

Ginny saw the eyes of the women in the assembly widen, but held their gazes as she finished her introduction. Working with June had given her the courage to now talk with women's groups, providing education on personal safety, as well as with other victims.

At the end of the group session, Ginny drove from the northern end of the Eastern Shore down to Baytown. Pulling onto the road leading toward Brogan's house…their house, she slowed down as the structure came into view.

Ginny had not slept in her house since the night of Ben's arrest, preferring to stay in Brogan's bungalow. One night, as the group of friends had sat around Mitch's bonfire, they began to toss around ideas for Brogan's property and Aiden suggested they turn the bungalow into a garage when they built another house.

"You could keep living in the bungalow while you have a house built next to it…a real house. Then, when the house is finished, turn the bungalow into the garage.

You've got a place to live and keep the essence of what you originally had."

The group had fallen silent for a few seconds before cries of *"brilliant"* and *"good idea"* sounded in the night. Ginny's eyes had grown large as she turned to Brogan, who was sitting behind her, his long legs bent at the knees on either side of her.

"Honey, that's perfect! I love that idea," she gushed.

Brogan looked over at Aiden, chuckling, "Looks like you might have something there."

"Hey, I'm not just another pretty face," Aiden joked, his smile wide.

Ginny had watched as Brogan looked across the fire pit at Aiden, the two brothers sharing a chin lift, her heart full.

A few months later, she and Brogan married in a small ceremony at the spot where the house was being built. Neither wanted a large wedding, the ceremony only attended by close friends and his family. For the reception, they invited the members of the American Legion, Auxiliary, more friends, and held it at Finn's. Informal. Fun. Not complicated. Completely Brogan and Ginny. Jillian's mom made the cake. Tori provided flowers from her garden. Katelyn and Aiden ordered the alcohol and sodas. Not wanting presents, the couple asked for donations for the American Legion, but many people brought gifts as well as donations. With only a weekend off, they drove to the Blue Ridge Mountains to have a two-night honeymoon in a place Mitch had recommended—Mountville Cabins. Mitch knew the owner, Bethany Bryant, and had worked with her husband at one time.

The private, A-frame cabin near a lake had been the perfect honeymoon. They barely left the cabin with only a few walks around the lake and through the beautiful woods. Other than that, they stayed in bed for most of the weekend. Ginny smiled at the memory...perfect.

Now, parked at the end of her driveway, she continued to smile at the thought of her future here with Brogan. Professional builders had built most of the home, with Brogan and their friends providing a lot of inside labor. The roof was on, the cedar siding planks were stained, and the windows and doors stood solid.

Her phone rang and as she pulled it from her purse, she saw **Brogan** on the caller ID. Confused, she answered, "Honey—"

"You gonna just sit there or come inside?"

Lifting her gaze, she saw him standing on the front porch, one hand holding his phone and the other on his hip. His legs were slightly apart, his jeans fitting just right. His t-shirt was old, worn, and tight across his muscular chest. His tats were visible, each memorized by her—she finally got to have that conversation. His handsome face framed by his dark hair, still cut short, and his dark, scruffy beard. And even from the distance, she felt his blue eyes pinned on her.

"Baby?"

Jolting, she replied, "Coming!" Dropping the phone onto the seat, she drove the rest of the way to the house, parking out front.

Brogan opened her door, offering his hand to assist her down. His eyes searched hers, checking her emotional pulse. "You okay?"

Standing on the ground, she looked up, her palms

flat on his chest as his hands rested on her waist. "Yeah. I'm good."

"I was worried—"

"Honey, I wouldn't do it if I thought I couldn't handle it. But talking to women's groups is good for me as well as them."

His smile melted her heart, then he melted it further, when he said, "You're better than good. You're perfect...for me."

Brogan's lips met hers, slow and soft, pulling back only when he knew he needed to or he would carry her to their bedroom in the bungalow and make love to her and, right now, he wanted to show her what had been accomplished while she had been gone.

He touched his lips to her forehead and grinned, turning as he tucked her close to his side, walking her to the door. Bending, he scooped her up, one arm under her knees and the other supporting her back, stepping through the front door, over the threshold of their house.

Throwing her head back in laughter, she clung to his neck. As he settled her feet carefully on the floor, he said, "Been waiting to do that for a long time."

Grinning, Ginny took his hand as her gaze moved from his to around the inside of the house. The drywall was now up in most of the rooms, giving her a chance to really see what it would look like. The entry foyer was not large, but held a coat closet to the left and directly in front was the staircase leading to the second-floor bedrooms, as well as a hall leading to the kitchen and family room in the back, facing the bay.

Holding her hand, Brogan led her through the

rooms, the living and dining rooms first, facing the front. Then, down the hall to the kitchen, where he motioned where the appliances would go, just as she had planned. Turning to the den, she smiled as he said, "And this is where we'll hang with the kids...have Christmases, lazy Saturday mornings, friends over."

She looked at the newly hung windows facing the bay, the sun already beginning to set, creating the pastel sky that they had viewed so often together. Heart light, she felt a tug on her hand and, turning back to him, she followed him to the stairs.

The banister had not been installed yet, so he made her walk close to the wall, holding her tightly. At the top, she looked around at the four bedrooms. The house was larger than they initially planned, but Corrine and Eric had convinced them it would be more economical to build it completely now than to keep adding on later. So, they agreed.

Entering what would be the master, she smiled at the large space.

"Got more than enough room for my king-sized bed, sweetheart."

Laughing, she admired what would be the master bathroom before they stepped back into the hall.

"And we've got three rooms for guests and kids," he added.

Ginny moved into the smaller bedroom, directly across the hall from the master. Her mind already painting it in greens, yellows, and blues. Maybe a rainbow mural on one wall.

"What are you thinking, babe?" Brogan asked, seeing her gaze moving studiously around the room.

Her lips curved slightly as she looked up into his face, turning her body toward his, taking both hands in hers. "I was thinking this would be a perfect nursery, honey."

Brogan let out a huge breath, his smile settling on his face. "Me too. That was exactly what I thought earlier."

Biting her lip, she said, "So when will the house be finished enough for us to move in?"

"Should be ready in about two more months."

"Good, that'll be plenty of time."

Tilting his head, he asked, "Time for what?"

"Time for us to decorate it as a nursery since it'll be occupied in about seven months."

Brogan said nothing. He just stared. His eyes narrowed for a few seconds before flying open. "What? A baby? Oh, Jesus, Ginny…a baby?" He picked her up and twirled her around and around, their laughter filling the air.

Two souls…once filled with pain…finding peace…together.

Don't miss any news about new releases! Sign up for my Newsletter

For the next Baytown, click below!
Picking Up the Pieces

Lance Greene. Former military. Current artist. Recluse.

Moving to Baytown was a chance to get away and

forget the friends he lost on his last mission and the nightmares that followed. Staying away from people worked, until he met her.

Jade Lyons. Elementary teacher. Sea glass collector. Eternal optimist.

She embraced all that Baytown had to offer, especially her early morning walks on the beach to find sea glass. Until she met him… the overbearing, rude man with secrets.

But sea glass works magic and when she discovers a body washed up on the shore, Lance vows to protect the woman who had wormed her way into his heart.

Can picking up the pieces bring two souls together?

Please take the time to leave a review of this book. Feel free to contact me, especially if you enjoyed my book. I love to hear from readers!
Facebook
Email
Website

ALSO BY MARYANN JORDAN

Don't miss other Maryann Jordan books!
Lots more Baytown stories to enjoy and more to come!
Baytown Boys (small town, military romantic suspense)

Coming Home

Just One More Chance

Clues of the Heart

Finding Peace

Picking Up the Pieces

Sunset Flames

Waiting for Sunrise

Hear My Heart

Guarding Your Heart

Sweet Rose

Our Time

Count On Me

Shielding You

To Love Someone

For all of Miss Ethel's boys:
Heroes at Heart (Military Romance)

Zander

Rafe

Cael

Jaxon

Jayden

Asher

Zeke

Cas

Lighthouse Security Investigations

Mace

Rank

Walker

Drew

Blake

Tate

Hope City (romantic suspense series co-developed with Kris Michaels

Brock book 1

Sean book 2

Carter book 3

Brody book 4

Kyle book 5

Ryker book 6

Rory book 7

Killian book 8

Saints Protection & Investigations

(an elite group, assigned to the cases no one else wants…or can solve)

Serial Love

Healing Love

Revealing Love

Seeing Love

Honor Love

Sacrifice Love

Protecting Love

Remember Love

Discover Love

Surviving Love

Celebrating Love

Follow the exciting spin-off series:

Alvarez Security (military romantic suspense)

Gabe

Tony

Vinny

Jobe

SEALs

Thin Ice (Sleeper SEAL)

SEAL Together (Silver SEAL)

Letters From Home (military romance)

Class of Love

Freedom of Love

Bond of Love

The Love's Series (detectives)

Love's Taming

Love's Tempting

Love's Trusting

The Fairfield Series (small town detectives)

Emma's Home

Laurie's Time

Carol's Image

Fireworks Over Fairfield

Please take the time to leave a review of this book. Feel free to contact me, especially if you enjoyed my book. I love to hear from readers!

Facebook

Email

Website

AUTHOR INFORMATION

I am an avid reader of romance novels, often joking that I cut my teeth on the historical romances. I have been reading and reviewing for years. In 2013, I finally gave into the characters in my head, screaming for their story to be told. From these musings, my first novel, Emma's Home, The Fairfield Series was born.

I was a high school counselor having worked in education for thirty years. I live in Virginia, having also lived in four states and two foreign countries. I have been married to a wonderfully patient man for thirty-six years. When writing, my dog or one of my four cats can generally be found in the same room if not on my lap.

Feel free to contact me, especially if you enjoyed my book. I love to hear from readers!

Facebook
Email
Website

Made in United States
Troutdale, OR
09/05/2023

12653942R00222